I0772091

LORD OF GOBLINS

MICHIEL WERBROUCK & HADI Y. BENDAKJI

TABLE OF CONTENTS

PROLOGUE...I

CHAPTER 1...5

CHAPTER 2...13

CHAPTER 3...31

CHAPTER 4...41

CHAPTER 5...49

CHAPTER 6...57

CHAPTER 7...65

CHAPTER 8...79

CHAPTER 9...89

CHAPTER 10...97

CHAPTER 11...105

CHAPTER 12...111

CHAPTER 13...127

CHAPTER 14...133

CHAPTER 15...139

CHAPTER 16...147

CHAPTER 17...163

CHAPTER 18...171

CHAPTER 19...181

CHAPTER 20...191

CHAPTER 21...199

CHAPTER 22...207

CHAPTER 23...217

CHAPTER 24...225

BONUS CHAPTER 1...237

BONUS CHAPTER 2...245

AFFTERWORD...255

PROLOGUE

A smoking, empty shell ejected. The bullet flew towards its target, perfectly aimed. Its owner stared, unblinking, at the scene unfolding before her. What should have been a day of joy, a day of triumph against corruption, had become a day of sorrow.

TARGET ELIMINATED: Leonard Erand Vandersteen ("Lev"), 35. United Technocracy of Eurasia, Full Citizenship, Member of the United Council.

Leonard Erand Vandersteen would never get to finish his victory speech. A paragon of justice in the political world, who just a few days prior had celebrated his thirty-fifth year on this Earth, was now struggling against the icy grip of death.

Heh. You think it'll end with me, huh? thought Lev as his life began slipping away. *I can't blame you. As always, you're a bunch of shortsighted fools.*

Lev had prepared a contingency plan for this very situation. Upon his death, all national media outlets would be hijacked to broadcast all his rivals' dirty secrets—not the usual dirty secrets the council would hire foreign parties to spread to draw eyes away from their less scrupulous activities.

He'd expose to the oppressed masses their secret prostitution rings, their hidden crime syndicates, their backdoor deals with foreign parties. But most importantly of all, he'd expose the truth behind the immutable war that had claimed so many innocent lives.

He had wanted to reveal the truth sooner, but he'd needed the people's trust, as few would believe an unknown upstart over the leaders they had been taught to believe and rely on. It had been a long road, but over the years he had worked tirelessly to collect more evidence and establish his place in society. Not that he had been silent all this time— he had spread rumours via third parties across his own network to prevent them from discovering his efforts.

Lev could not help but grin. What should have been an act to cement their control over the world would ultimately lead to its collapse, and a new order would arise like a phoenix from its ashes.

A frantic man shoved his way forward. "Out of the way!" he shouted. "Lev!"

Though Lev's already blurry vision was darkening, he could never mistake this voice, whose owner had followed him through thick and thin all his life from the tender years of their childhood in the orphanage to the callous present. *Brutus,* he thought.

"It's not your time, man!" Brutus yelled. He turned to a woman just behind him. "Maria, call an ambulance!" He applied pressure to Lev's wound, but it was too late. Death demanded its quarry.

Leonard was relieved that he would die held by those he loved. Even so, a tear ran down his left cheek, for this was goodbye. And alas, he wouldn't be able to fulfil his promise that they would see their world change together.

Instead of trying to solve the world's problems, those crooks spent their years in power making empty promises and stealing from the people, most of whom had been helplessly indoctrinated into serving their foul masters.

They'd implemented their system into schools to pollute the minds of the youth and promised those who'd fight a better life. People were taught that these vile oppressors were their representatives, their protectors, and their saviours—that society would suffer at the hands of other factions and ideologies. Those swindlers had spun a web so tough that it seemed like nothing would ever cut through it.

So many people had taken their propaganda as truth that even Lev might have believed it, but he had seen the war firsthand and the meaningless destruction it brought with it. He'd been on both sides of the war, seen both perspectives. Maybe if he hadn't been forced to understand the enemy, he could have lived a quiet life after being honourably discharged.

After all, the cookie-cutter life those with full citizenship enjoyed day in and day out was just another construct forced upon the people, empowered by the despicable levy system. Having witnessed the destruction of the world from a front-row seat, and being all too knowledgeable of how its continued disintegration was affecting the people he loved, Lev had known with every fibre of his being that something needed to change after these centuries of strife.

Why are these monsters the only choice? he had thought. *Why do we help the ones who hurt us? Why do we have to fight for them, work for them, pay them, and then thank them? Shouldn't they be helping us instead?*

As the years passed, he watched as those who tried to fight the autocrats honourably fell from grace and disappeared. Thus, he worked hard, studied hard, and learnt how to lie through his teeth. To defeat the monsters, he had to become a monster. But instead of feeding on the weak and downtrodden, he swore to protect them as he devoured their predators.

Brutus and Maria had been the first to follow him—since they were practically siblings, it was only natural—and as time went by, others had joined his cause. Two people became four and four became hundreds; his following had grown and grown as he proved himself an enchanting orator.

They had tried to invite him into their ranks like they had many respected professionals before him, but he had refused to submit. Instead, he'd foiled their plans and dismantled their traps; by the time they'd realised the threat he was, it had been too late. Their web had been torn apart and the people were awoken.

As a last resort, the tyrants had set loose an assassin to slay their indomitable foe. This was their last chance to pluck this thorn from their sides. The dastards had succeeded.

Lev smiled for the last time and muttered a "thank you" as he, much to his friends' grief, closed his eyes.

Chapter 1
Transmigration

As he closed his eyes, Lev felt nothing—no pain, no fear, no anger, no happiness, and no grief. He felt neither his body nor his mind. He was fading, becoming one with the void. All his hardships were fading, but so were all his dreams. He was to forget his enemies, but was he... to forget his friends? His aspirations?

No! He would not allow it. He would not allow the apathetic emptiness to engulf his mind and steal everything he cared about, everything he had hoped to accomplish, everything he had wished to achieve. He would not let it devour his memories, he would not let it erase his friends and their smiles, and he would not let it destroy what made him *Leonard Erand Vandersteen*!

Lev fought and fought against the ageless, greedy despot who sought to strip him of everything. He fought for what felt like millennia, and finally, the overlord of nothingness conceded. As he felt it release its grip on his awareness, the void around him began to flow, and he lost his bearings.

What's going on? Lev thought as he was swept away at an incredible speed with nothing in his sight but giant orbs of light.

Light? Elation filled Lev's heart. He could see again! But he was more shocked at the wondrous view before him. Orbs of light in myriad colours and patterns darted about. Some swirled to the left, some to the right, upwards, downwards, and some diagonally. There were even orbs dyed in multiple colours that moved in parallel.

Marvellous.

He abruptly felt the current sweep him downwards, and found himself hurtling towards one of the orbs, a green one whose vortex pattern converged in the centre. Panicking, he tried closing his eyes before briefly losing consciousness.

Upon reawakening, Lev felt a sharp pain on his forehead. *Head?* He could feel his head! Suddenly the pain increased and a loud buzzing sound flooded his ears. He instinctively pressed his hands to his head, touching a soaked rag and detecting a wet sensation on his fingertips.

He opened his eyes to two filthy, grey arms with five clawed, blood-covered fingers on each hand.

Lev screamed as an onslaught of questions assaulted his already-heavy head. *What's happening? What's going on here! These aren't my hands!*

He looked around and found himself sitting on a filthy hide, in a small filthy room caked in dried blood. A giant brown rag hung over what he assumed was the exit.

"*Maghag ma Gherm*!" croaked a guttural voice in a language alien to his ears.

Lev's headache intensified; it felt like a sledgehammer bludgeoning his brain.

He screamed again. He tried, hand pressed to his forehead, to put distance between himself and the bizarre creature, yet it advanced, screeching in its crude native tongue. When the creature was finally within arm's reach, Lev lost consciousness a second time.

"Wa... Ghe..."

A voice?

"Wak... u... Gher..."

The feminine voice became clearer and clearer.

"Gherm! Wake up, Gherm."

Lev jerked awake to another grey, inhuman figure clad in rags staring down at him. He unwillingly drew air into his chest and prepared to scream once more, only to have a grunt forced from him as he was kicked in the stomach.

"Scream again and I'll kick you harder, got it?" the short creature snarled.

Lev nodded breathlessly.

"Good." She sat down on the cot next to him. "How's your head?"

Gherm? Breath quickening, Lev dropped his face into his hands as waves of new memories deluged his brain, crashing against his old ones. At last the memories settled, leaving Lev out of breath.

"Are you alright?!"

That's right. She's called Ghorza, and she's Gherm's older sister. But I'm not this creature called Gherm! What are these things *even supposed to be, and where did these memories come from?!*

Lev looked at his hands. *These aren't my hands!*

He peeked at his reflection in a bowl of water. *This isn't my face!*

He gazed down at his torso. *This isn't my body!*

"Gherm, calm down! You're freaking me out!" Ghorza quickly weighed her options. "Should I ask the healer to take another look at you?" she muttered to herself—or so she'd thought, but Lev, or Gherm, managed to hear it.

Healer? He winced at what "healing" might look like in this society— burning tinctures onto his naked skin? Sticking him with needles? Bloodletting?

As time passed, Lev better realised how bad his current situation was as more memories surfaced. Not that he could process all of it immediately, but he understood enough to get a grasp on things.

From what he understood, these memories belonged to "Gherm," a male specimen of a race called "bogeys." Bogeys fell under the broader umbrella term of "goblinoids," which also included true goblins, or simply "goblins." Bogeys' defining characteristics included intelligence superior to goblins, and natural lifespans averaging sixty years.

Within the bogey race, Gherm and his sister Ghorza had been born into a grey-skinned tribal line known simply as greyborns. As greyborns possessed the greatest magical affinity amongst all bogeykind, they were once a privileged, honoured class. From the greyborns Gherm had known, Lev observed, some were significantly taller than even humans, while others could have passed for midgets. With a few exceptions, goblinoids were generally not aesthetically blessed.

Alas, because of a failed coup by greyborn elitists centuries ago, the entire greyborn tribe had been forbidden from practising the magical arts, and subsequently their techniques had been lost to time. With every other tribe of bogeys indoctrinated to hate the greyborns for "their" past mistakes, and no magical legacy left, it was no wonder that "greyborn" was now synonymous with "worthless trash."

To make matters worse, the bogeys of Lev's tribe were casualties of a war between the Jiira and the Kur. The Jiira, a tribe of goblins, had conquered the greyborns to use their territory as a buffer zone against the Kur, a tribe of kobolds. Now the tribe, especially the greyborns, lived in squalor, working for a pittance in one of the mysterious magical caverns known to house monsters, magical ores, and treasures created during the age of the gods.

This can't be happening, thought Lev. His breath quickened again.

"Gherm! Looks like I really need to ask the healer."

"No!" Lev blurted out, causing his so-called sister to flinch.

A moment passed in silence. He was thinking about what he should do to prevent this lucid dream from getting worse; she was worried about his repeated outbursts.

Lev took pains to steady his breathing long enough to speak. "I'm okay. It would be disrespectful of us to bother them with such a trivial matter." He feigned a smile.

"But—"

"Just trust me," Lev said a little more forcefully than he had planned. "It's all okay."

"Okay... But please don't scream like that ever again. You'll give me a panic attack! Now get up." Ghorza slung one of Gherm's arms over her shoulder. "You've been here long enough, and we're painfully low on merits now."

"Low?"

Slap!

"Ouch!" Lev winced at the stinging pain in his back. "Why'd you slap me *now*?"

"Because you're an idiot!" she cried. "In case you haven't guessed, you were as good as dead when that tunnel collapsed! Thank Vee we had enough merits to save you in the first place!"

Lev sighed. Merits were the closest thing to money that greyborns could readily obtain. The dull-looking lead coins were the physical representation of the merits-for-labour system which had been spearheaded by the upper class and implemented by the ruling powers to restrict greyborns' access to goods and equipment.

With merits, greyborns could buy essentials such as food, water, and clothing, but only of the lowest quality: foodstuffs on the brink of spoilage, tunics sewn out of whatever remnants could be scrounged. The only redeeming life necessity they had access to was the abundant purified cavern water. Even so, bankruptcy would certainly spell his demise.

That is, if any of this were real.

What a weird dream... I should wake up, or at least turn this one lucid. I'll do a reality check—look at my palm, close my eyes, and then look again. My palm should be different.

Lev closed his eyes. *Now on 1... 2... 3.* Lev reopened his eyes. His palm was the same.

"No... This can't... be," he mumbled to himself. "Wake up!" he hollered.

Nothing happened.

Lev violently shook his head, hoping to shake himself awake.

Nothing happened.

He cracked his knuckles, an old habit, and even pinched himself.

...Nothing happened.

Ghorza felt as if she were in the presence of a madman. "G-Gherm?"

"It's real... This is all real." Tears streamed down his cheeks.

Ghorza slowly approached and gently extended her arm to wrap around him. "Why are you crying? What's wrong? Did something happen—"

"Don't touch me!" Lev snapped, slapping Ghorza's arm away. Lev saw the shock and sorrow in Ghorza's eyes; her younger brother had never treated her like this before. He suddenly felt his chest tighten, and for once it was not from panic.

"I'm sorry," he began. "I'm really tired right now, and my head is killing me."

"It's alright."

As Lev was about to step out of the room, a gnarled pale green hand with yellowish claws pushed the rag to the side, revealing a repulsive bald creature with long ears, a massive, pus-filled, crooked nose, and glowing yellow eyes.

Lev scanned Gherm's memories: it was old Rogg, an herbalist who, due to his meagre set of abilities and insolence towards the wrong bogeys, had ended up working here, between the slaves and the poor.

"Have you finally calmed down, you grey wretch?" Rogg hissed. "You just *had* to keep screaming! Do you know *hard* it is to put a gravely injured hunter to sleep using dalk roots without killing him?"

Lev shuddered. The roots of the dalk, a common cave plant, contained a neurotoxin that could easily sedate a goblinoid, but carried a one-in-four chance of putting them to sleep forever. Only a master healer should ever have given Lev dalk roots, and by no measure was Rogg qualified.

Rogg read Lev's face. "Oh, so even a *slave* thinks he's better than me. If I'd known you were such an ungrateful wretch, I wouldn't have healed you!"

Please. It's not like you did it for free. Lev seethed in his mind. *We all know you checked with the slave quarter's taskmaster to see if we had enough merits before Ghorza could get a word in!* Still, as much as Lev disliked Rogg, he was the only healer in the area who would treat greyborns.

"My apologies, I had never meant to offend such an esteemed practitioner of the medical arts." Lev inhaled deeply before delivering his lengthy next line. "Surely you can understand that a mere greyborn such as myself never intended to doubt the greatness of your skills, let alone insult a master healer, such as yourself, who would so much as deign to apply his years of scholarship to heal lowly slaves like us."

From the wide grin on the old man's face, Lev concluded that he had flattered the old coot a little *too* well. It had obviously been a long time since anyone had treated him with respect.

"'Master healer'... Alright. You're forgiven this time," he boasted, "but if you look at me like *that* again, death will be the least of your problems!"

"Yes, of course. Thank you for your care, great healer," Lev said as he handed over a pouch of merits.

"As long as you have the merits, you can come anytime—otherwise, don't waste my time!" Rogg snatched the pouch from Lev. "Now get out. I have other matters to attend to."

Lev and Ghorza obliged with copious thank-yous without protest. Lev was careful not to drop his act until they closed the door behind them.

"What was that?" asked Ghorza.

"What was what?"

"That whole act of gratitude and... submissiveness. You were kissing his wrinkly old ass more than a priestess of Maga. What happened to you? You've always been a coward, but you've never lowered yourself like that."

"Ouch. You don't pull punches, do you?"

"Nope. Never. But you..." Ghorza hesitated. "You know that, right?" Something about her brother had changed after waking up, and she did not just mean his "episodes." Something besides Gherm's expanded vocabulary felt wrong to Ghorza, but she couldn't put her finger on it just yet.

She walked Gherm back to the greyborn slave quarters. A single tunnel stretched northeast to southwest, between the entrance to the mines and the opening to the surface respectively, and from this tunnel branched the greyborn, bogey, and blue-skinned nobles' caverns. The blues lived near the surface end; the greyborn lived closest to the mines and overseers, far from the light of the sun Lev had once taken for granted.

Even so, Lev felt fortunate that they lived a few rows of dwellings removed from the cavern barrier. If nothing else, he needed some rest.

CHAPTER 2
THE ACID PITS

As the two siblings walked alongside each other, Lev couldn't take his eyes off his surroundings. Large rock formations supported the cavern ceiling, and various holes covered by rags littered the walls to the left and right. The meddling of bogeys along with the cavern's natural structures had created a fascinating sight.

Greyborns minded their own business as they traversed the crude cavern roads that linked various quarters and workshops into one extensive network. Even though Lev had managed to integrate about half of Gherm's memories by now, seeing them with his, or rather Gherm's, eyes was an entirely different experience.

What surprised Lev most, however, was the freedom of movement. Throughout his years as a member of the council, he'd been given access to the vast libraries of the Technocracy. There, he'd read about various social systems throughout history. From what he'd seen so far, bogey hierarchy was most similar to that of the Spartans.

The slaves in that society were called helots. Their tasks, similar to those of the greyborn, consisted mostly of menial labour. While helots did enjoy certain privileges, such as owning land, at the end of the day they were still slaves and suffered the typical mistreatments from their Spartan masters. The way Lev understood it, the Jiira, as well as the proxy slave-drivers they had installed, were basically the Spartans, and the greyborns, who toiled away mining in the caverns or constructing new buildings, were the helots.

"So, Gherm. Now that you've calmed down, how are you feeling? Is there anything you want to talk about?" Ghorza asked, breaking Lev's entrancement.

"Talk about? Like what?" Lev replied with a confused frown.

"I'm still weirded out by how you acted back there."

The Gherm she knew spoke differently, walked differently, and acted differently than the one currently by her side. This Gherm was more assertive, and judging by his recent stunt, more cunning. It was as if he were no longer her brother.

Lev lowered his head as he tried coming up with a counter-argument to explain his erratic behaviour.

"For one, if I hadn't done what I did, we'd have lost everything."

Gherm raised his head again, expecting an understanding smile, but Ghorza instead wore a tense grimace. Her suspicious eyes met his, and he wondered if she could see that Gherm's soul wasn't behind them anymore.

He half expected her to yell at him, beg him to give her brother back, but instead she broke eye contact.

She finally broke the silence. "Yeah, but you've never lowered yourself like that before."

As a desperate attempt to blow out the awkward air surrounding the two, Lev shrugged. Perhaps acting aloof would reignite what Ghorza considered to be Gherm-like behaviour. "Maybe the rocks knocked some sense into me."

"No, it's—" She tried avoiding eye contact again. "It's like you're a different person."

Lev tried to navigate the maze that was Gherm's memories as quickly as he could, trying to find something that could ease his sister's suspicions. Thankfully, he was soon interrupted by the shouts of a female greyborn.

"Hey Ghorza! Gherm!"

She looked to be the same age as Ghorza, but as she got closer, Lev noticed she was much taller than Ghorza and had straight, grey hair that almost reached her hips.

"I'm glad I found you," the girl said between laboured breaths.

She was met by the confused gazes of both siblings.

"What's wrong? Why aren't you working?" Ghorza asked.

The girl looked at the two with darting glances as she tried to inform them. "Kul sent me to warn you guys. It's Jerg. He and his lot are looking for Gherm."

Kul, Lev thought, *that name sounds strikingly familiar. I can feel a rush of Gherm's memories fighting for my attention, but there's no time to dig into them right now.*

Ghorza bared her teeth at the mention of that name. "Jerg? Why does he want my brother?"

In stark contrast to Ghorza, who was almost frothing at the mouth by now, Lev kept his calm.

"I see. Tog's the one who caused the cave-in, but it's more convenient for Jerg to blame me than his own brother, right?"

"Yeah." the girl continued with balled fists, "Tog got thrown into the penal cave by the overseers. He told Jerg you caused the collapse."

Ghorza's forehead almost popped a vein. "That's not fair! Gherm almost died!"

"And he still will if Jerg finds him," the girl said as she relaxed her fists. "Sorry, I need to go. It's not safe being seen with you two right now."

As the girl left, Ghorza was still embroiled in a fit of rage. "That idiot! I'm going to give him a piece of my mind."

Lev almost felt sorry for Jerg. From Gherm's memories, he knew what a piece of Ghorza's mind meant. He shuddered at the thought.

"If we get home fast, we'll be safe, right?" he asked, trying to divert Ghorza's anger.

"What?" Her tight-lipped smile faded as thoughts of torturing Jerg with an assemblage of her favourite curses were replaced by her brother's question. "Oh, yeah. Our cave is next to where the overseers live. No way they'll cause trouble there."

"Then the journey needs to be as short as possible." Although Ghorza's wrath was not something to be trifled with, neither sibling had been blessed with the gift of height or brawn. If it came down to it, all she would be able to do was bark at Jerg whilst they dragged him away.

"We need to assume they'll search the direct routes." Lev continued. "Is there another way to get home?"

This left Ghorza pondering for a moment. "Not really. There's the forbidden caves, but we're not allowed there alone."

A smirk crept on Lev's face. "I won't be alone, I'll be with you."

"Besides, when you're in trouble anyway, always take the more interesting path," Lev said as he heard Maria's voice in his head.

"Where'd you learn that?" Ghorza asked, noticing Lev's unfocused gaze.

"My old teacher," he promptly replied.

"Your old teacher? You mean Kul?"

"Nevermind." Lev dismissed as he gestured ahead. "Show me the way."

As they made their way through the tunnel, Lev noticed patches of glow-moss on the walls and ceiling.

They used crystals in the main areas, but the moss emits enough light to see here. Interesting.

Lev found himself oddly captivated by his new surroundings. Why, he wondered, was he so fascinated by this new world? Shouldn't he be preoccupied with the dreadful prospects of his new existence? Perhaps his current mindset had something to do with his days as a soldier.

Lev covered his nose. His fascination had been quickly overwhelmed by a repugnant odour. "I can see why they don't use moss in the main caves."

"So, why is nobody allowed down here again?" he asked as his eyes darted around the tunnel, trying to find new curiosities.

"Monsters come up this way from the lower levels sometimes. We'll need to be careful."

Ghorza walked ahead of Gherm, cautiously, until a large wooden door came into view. The door was tucked inside of a cave mouth and secured by a big wooden bar lock to make sure wandering bogeys would think twice before trespassing.

Not that it really needed it—the various piles of bones surrounding the door and the fumes coming from behind it were warning enough. Ghorza kept course past the door with Lev faithfully following behind her like Gherm used to.

Lev's nose wrinkled. "What's in there?"

"Acid pits," Ghorza replied, still keeping her steady pace, "Stay out."

"You've been down here before?" Lev asked, curious about his so-called sister's ventures.

Ghorza swiftly turned around, her eyes twinkling. "Once I came with a work group to dump trash in the pits. I made a week's worth of merits," she stated proudly.

Really, that's it? Lev almost blurted out his immediate thoughts, but figured that there weren't many ways to get some extra merits and excitement in a greyborn's life.

The two continued down the tunnel, walking by another set of glow-moss patches surrounding the walls and arch of the tunnel's ceiling. They glowed peacefully, in stark contrast to Lev's gut feeling which had turned from excitement to dread as the smell of something rotting entered his nostrils.

Preoccupied with searching for the source of the stench, he failed to notice Ghorza abruptly come to a stop.

"G-G-Gherm!" Ghorza whimpered, her hand covering her mouth. She pointed towards something up ahead in the tunnel. The stench grew stronger as Lev walked a few steps further, but the soft glow of the moss behind them didn't help reveal what horror was unfolding before them.

Lev took a few more steps forward and noticed a pair of lifeless grey legs swinging idly in the air as the sound of bones breaking filled the dark tunnel. He could only see the bottom half of the bogey's soiled pants and shirt as the rest was shrouded in darkness.

Whatever was gnawing away at the bogey's corpse was diligently dissolving the corpse bit by bit as the sound of teeth tearing through flesh played a sickly chorus in the background.

Both Lev and Ghorza instinctively stilled their breath.

With her hands covering her mouth and unable to look away from the mangled corpse, Ghorza slowly began stepping away from the hidden horror. Unaware of her surroundings, she stepped on a brittle bone, which let out a sickening snap.

Damn it, Ghorza! Lev cursed. Before he could turn his head, the gigantic horror let go of the corpse and emerged from the shadows, revealing a monstrous centipede.

Lev froze like a statue when it approached. He didn't even dare to twitch when he smelled its foul breath.

The creature stopped its advance mere inches from Lev's face.

What is it doing?

Lev got his answer when it turned its head left and right whilst sniffing its surroundings.

Seems like it's blind. Is it trying to detect us by sound?

He came to another hypothesis when he looked down at his feet, finding a large patch of glow-moss underneath. He could still smell the moss' repulsive odour even though the creature was directly breathing into his face.

Or maybe scent?

Finding neither threat nor prey, the centipede backed off, used its countless legs to hoist the corpse towards its mouth, and continued munching on its meal.

Using this opportunity, Lev turned towards a pale Ghorza and signalled her to be quiet.

They silently traced their way back, as far from the centipede as possible, before collapsing to the ground in relief.

"This should be far enough," Lev concluded.

"I thought we were dead," Ghorza replied.

Lev smiled. "We're lucky we aren't."

He turned his head towards the tunnel's entrance. "You don't happen to know another way around that thing, do you?" He asked.

"I don't know. I don't think so. There's probably another shortcut but I've only been here once before."

Lev sighed. "Maybe there's a side tunnel we missed—wait. Do you hear something?"

Ghorza's ears twitched.

Echoing voices could be heard from the entrance of the tunnel.

Ghorza leapt to her feet. "Someone's coming! We need to warn them about the monster before they attract it."

"Ghorza, wait! It could be—" Lev yelled to deaf ears as he rushed after his sister.

Just as he had feared, she had bumped into Jerg and his men.

"Jerg!" Ghorza shouted.

Lev observed them from behind a rock pillar.

"Ghorza. Where's that useless brother of yours?"

Noticing that Gherm wasn't behind her, she shrugged. "I don't know. Kul assigned me to throw some garbage into the acid pits."

"Oh, really? Then where's your partner?"

"She's... still dumping the rest of the trash."

Unamused by her lie, Jerg sighed and snapped his fingers. His men moved to surround her.

"I'm really not a fan of liars, Ghorza. I'd fess up if I were you."

Seeing Ghorza being pressured by Jerg's brutes, Lev stepped from behind the pillar. "I'm right here, Jerg."

"So the rat has finally shown himself, " Jerg said with a sneer. "Grab him!" he yelled.

"Hey!" Ghorza yelled. She tried standing in their way but was effortlessly shoved aside.

Unwilling to put Ghorza in harm's way, Lev handed himself in.

"Huh. That was easy," Jerg exclaimed. "Now... how should I make you pay?"

"Kill me and you'll regret it," Lev replied.

Jerg laughed. "How so? What's the worst that could happen?"

His merriment didn't last long once he came to a realisation. "Oh, I see. That geezer Kul's protecting you. I bet there will be hell to pay if I kill you."

Seems remembering Kul should be a priority.

"Kul should be the least of your worries. Send one of your men around the corner to the big cave. Tell him to be quiet if he wants to live."

Jerg growled. "What wormdung is this? What are you playing at, Gherm?"

"No tricks. Just do what I say and all will be revealed."

Jerg eyed the youngest of his men, a short greyborn whose antics reminded Lev of a circus monkey: he'd been jumping around ever since they'd caught Lev.

"Boss? You can't be serious." the man whimpered.

"Sav, go check. Keep it sneaky," Jerg commanded with a sneer.

"U—Understood."

Seeing Sav disappear into the centipede's tunnel, Jerg turned his attention to Lev once again. "Now, what should we do with you?"

"Jerg, I didn't cause that cave in, your—"

Before Lev could finish his sentence, he received a punch to his guts.

"Shut your mouth. Kul's protection or not, you're only alive until he gets back, wormdung."

"C-Centipede!" They heard Sav scream from down the tunnel.

He almost tripped upon returning to Jerg and had to catch his balance before delivering his report.

"Boss, we gotta get outta here. There's a giant centipede," he whimpered.

"What do we do, boss?" The largest of Jerg's men asked. Lev presumed he was the group's muscle. If not for his grey skin, his less-than-appealing features would've qualified him as a full-fledged goblin.

"Great lord help us! What's it doing up here?" cried the last and oldest of the bunch. He had a belly as voluptuous as his apparent devotion to the gods and sported a short beard with his hair tied back. At surface level, he had a somewhat friendly appearance, but Lev knew there was evil behind it.

"Who cares what it's doing here, Kruk? We should report it to the taskmaster," Sav advised with trembling knees.

Lev laughed, catching everyone's attention.

"What's so funny?" Jerg asked.

Lev smiled. "That'd be a great way to lose free merits."

Eyeing Lev, Jerg ordered his men to let him go. "What do you mean?"

"Kruk, how much did the taskmaster give the last team who killed one of these things?" Lev asked .

"Heaven's servants were blessed with almost two hundred merits each for their righteous deeds," Kruk replied.

"That many merits could feed a family for two months," Jerg muttered.

"See? That thing is a walking pile of merits. You want to give that up?"

"Ain't no merits if we're dead," argued Sav.

"Quiet, Sav," Jerg ordered. "The little worm talks like he has a plan. Unless you got something better to say, let's hear it."

"It's simple. We only need to use the centipede's flaws against it," Lev replied.

"Continue," Jerg commanded as he sat down on a nearby rock.

"Take a close look, and you'll see that the giant centipede is blind and tracks by sound, not sight."

"So you're saying we just need to ambush it, right? Lure it by throwing some pebbles into a good spot and finish it off once it's distracted," Jerg surmised.

Lev shook his head. "That wouldn't work. There's no way we can hurt it directly with what we've got. Its armour is too thick."

"Then any attempt to fight it head-on is a bust," Sav grumbled.

"Who said anything about fighting it? We're going to lure it into the acid pits and try to knock it in."

Ghorza grit her teeth. "But giant centipedes are faster than we are. If we try to run it'll just catch us!" she added.

"We're not going to try to outrun it." Lev reasoned. "We'll space ourselves out along the passageway and take turns throwing bones to get its attention."

Lev threw a bone at a nearby rock. The sound of the cracking bone echoed throughout the tunnel.

"As long as the bones are the loudest thing it hears, it will follow them until it reaches the acid pits."

"A good plan. But someone has to lure it into the acid pits. It won't go in by itself," Kruk pointed out with narrowed eyes.

"The answer's simple," Jerg replied. "That will be Gherm's job. It's his plan, so he'll be the last."

He patted Lev on the shoulder with glee on his face. "Isn't that right, wormdung?"

"He's still hurt!" Ghorza yelled as she jumped between Jerg and her brother, defending him like a lioness would for her cubs. "There's no way he can outrun it! Let me do it!"

Lev shook his head. "No, it's okay. I'll be last."

"You'll help me bolt the door when I get back out, right?" Lev asked as he glanced at Jerg.

Jerg smiled with scheming eyes. "Oh, yeah. Sure. Trust me."

"Okay then. let's do it," Lev replied, sporting an innocent grin.

With the plan ready to be put in motion, everyone made their way towards the acid pit doorway. Ghorza warily approached Lev.

"Gherm, what are you doing? He's going to kill you!" she whispered.

"He's going to try, but I have an idea. Just be ready to run away if things go bad."

Ghorza gulped. "How will I know if things go bad?" She hesitantly asked.

"Simple. I'll be the one screaming."

Following Lev's instructions, everyone picked up some of the bones scattered around the tunnel before gathering near the door.

With deft hands, Lev took down the chains barring the door and picked the door's lock with a thin, sharp bone.

"I didn't know you could pick locks," Jerg noted.

"Where did you learn to do that?" Ghorza asked with a suspicious glint in her eyes.

"I'll tell you later," Lev replied. "We can't waste time here, or that thing might finish its meal and find us."

Lev glanced at the patches of moss enveloping the tunnel. *And I'm sure the stench of uncouth greyborn will soon overpower that of the moss and its current meal.*

Jerg chuckled. "That's right. The gods won't forgive us if we mess this up. More importantly, our pockets won't either if we waste such an opportunity."

"Now," Lev interrupted, "Who's going to throw first?"

"We need someone fast for that." Jerg's eyes shifted towards Sav, and the others followed suit.

Noticing everyone's eyes upon him, a nervous gasp escaped from Sav.

"W-What are you all staring at me for?"

"Sav, you'll be in charge of luring it into the tunnel and getting the ball rolling." Lev continued, ignoring Sav.

"Why me—Ouch!" He yelped before rubbing the back of his head.

"Shut it. You're always talking about how fast you are, so prove it," Jerg commanded.

"B-But that thing will kill me!" Sav cried out.

"It won't," Lev reassured him. "After throwing your bones, run to a glow-moss patch. Don't worry about it seeing you, it's blind."

"How are you so sure?"

"Well, Ghorza and I are still in one piece, aren't we? Once it's passed, just stay where you are. Don't move until you hear the okay."

"Don't you worry. Once I'm safe, I ain't moving for nothing. That's enough action for me with your crazy plan," Sav grumbled, still massaging the back of his head.

"Remember, not a single sound or movement. The same goes for the others once it's their turn to bait the centipede. Run to a glow-moss patch and stay silent." Lev added.

He turned his attention back to Jerg. "You should stand next to the light crystal near the bend, and follow the centipede after it passes you."

Jerg huffed. "What purpose would that serve?"

"Like we said earlier, once we get it to the acid pits, I'll lure it inside. You need to be close enough to help me lock the door. Everyone clear?"

Jerg's scowl turned into a grin. "Yeah. Not a bad plan for an idiot."

Lev smiled. "Just make sure you're there to back me up when I need you, Jerg."

A final nod from Jerg sealed the plan.

* * *

Sav nervously approached the centipede's lair.

His ears twitched upon hearing the now-familiar sound of crunching bones. To Sav, it was the second loudest sound after the beating of his heart.

Once the creature was within eyesight, he quickly moved behind a boulder.

Calm down, Sav. You can do this.

He peeked at the giant insect and found it still feasting on the remains of its prey. Sav gulped and silently cursed.

This is the last time I'm letting Jerg drag me into hell.

Suddenly, the sound of crunching bones stopped and Sav found the centipede staring directly at him.

His heart sank. *Ooohhh shit...*

The centipede's mandibles moved faster, saliva escaping from its mouth. It had just found its next meal. The sound of its mandibles grinding against each other intensified as it slowly left its lair, moving towards Sav.

Run, run, run! Don't let it catch you! He kept repeating to himself as he sprinted through the tunnel.

The centipede let out a loud hiss as it pursued him. Sav could feel the creature's hot breath caressing the back of his neck.

Seeing the glowing moss and the pile of bones he'd prepared earlier, he jumped towards the pile just in time to narrowly avoid having his head bit off.

Ainshard help me, you better be as blind as they say! Sav prayed as he reached for a skull.

Ignoring the approaching centipede, he threw it towards the tunnel Lev had designated and closed his eyes.

I'm not dead, am I? He thought before opening his eyes.

The giant centipede had turned toward the designated tunnel and surged past Sav, ignoring him.

Sav stood perfectly still until it was finally gone. He collapsed onto the moss and took a deep breath to calm his nerves.

The same scenario repeated itself with Kruk, Ghorza, and Hork until the centipede finally headed towards Jerg and Lev.

Hearing the hissing of the centipede, Jerg looked towards the pitch-black tunnel.

It's coming. Sounds like it passed Ghorza and is about to pass Hork.

Better let Gherm know. He waved at Gherm to grab his attention.

Seeing the oblivious smile on Gherm's face as he waved back, Jerg couldn't help but grin. *That's it. Wave goodbye. My brother's under the whip because of you, dung-breath.*

Jerg imagined with glee how the centipede would tear Gherm limb from limb after he locked them both in the acid pit. The hefty sum of merits he'd earn afterwards would be the perfect cherry on top. Not that he'd personally ever seen a cherry before.

He licked his lips in anticipation. *Too bad about your sister. But we'll roll the bones to see who gets to comfort her.*

Hearing the centipede approach, he tapped a nearby stone with a bone to lure it in further. His palms moistened and he felt like his heart would tear through his chest as he kept his eyes on the tunnel the creature would storm out of.

Calm down, Jerg. If the plan's worked so far, Gherm was right. I'll be safe as long as I stay quiet. There'll only be one meal waiting for it.

Once the centipede was in sight, Jerg threw the skull towards Gherm. It shattered into countless pieces upon hitting a nearby pillar.

Here you go, Gherm. Jerg thought as he flashed a sickening grin.

Jerg felt a wave of relief once the centipede passed.

His exuberance morphed into dread when the centipede stopped dead in its tracks and turned towards him.

He shuddered as it locked him in its sights.

I-Impossible.

Before it could lunge at him, a bone smashed into the centipede, disorienting it.

"Jerg! Quick! Run! We'll lure it into the pits!" Gherm yelled.

Without wasting a single breath, Jerg sprinted towards the pits, past the confused centipede. It locked onto its target and resumed its rabid pursuit.

Through all the dread and fear, a thought pervaded his mind. *What went wrong? Why didn't it follow the sound when I threw the bone?*

"Quick! Get inside!" Gherm instructed.

Without a thought, a panicked Jerg sprinted into the acid pits room with the centipede following after.

The last thing Jerg saw was Gherm shoving the door shut, and the impressive form of the centipede coiled over him.

Jerg's bloodcurdling cries could be heard from behind the door. It didn't take long for him to go silent.

With the door locked, Lev couldn't help but let out a tired sigh. "Idiot. Make your plans a little less obvious in your next life."

It didn't take long for the others to arrive.

"Gherm! You're okay! Thank Ainshard!" Ghorza shouted once she saw her brother was unscathed. The others, however, halted when they saw Jerg was missing.

"Where's Jerg?" Sav asked nervously. "What happened?"

Gherm shook his head in response. "I'm sorry. He screwed up and it kept chasing after him."

"We lured it into the pits together," Gherm briefly paused as if mourning, "but it caught him, so I locked them inside."

A gloomy mood haunted Jerg's men until Lev spoke up again. "Look, I don't even want the reward. Tell the taskmaster Jerg killed it. That's the best I can do to honour him."

"You're a good one, Gherm. We won't forget this," Kruk answered, looking a tad less depressed.

"I'm going to take my sister and go," Gherm stated matter-of-factly.

Kruk bowed deeply. "May the great lord's blessings be upon you and grant you a safe return this time."

Once they'd distanced themselves far enough from Jerg's men, Ghorza halted her steps.

"Gherm, what really happened to Jerg? Did he really sacrifice himself?"

"Well, he had a little help. I guess the centipede tracks by scent as well as sound," Lev said as he kept his pace.

Ghorza gazed at her brother. A thought had rooted itself in her heart since Gherm's reawakening.

Gherm, is it really you?

CHAPTER 3
MEMORIES OF OLD

"What's wrong?" said Ghorza. "Come on. Eat."

"Not hungry." Lev stared at his dinner. It stared back with six eyes, some partially hidden behind dull brown fuzz.

Fuzzy caveworms were one of the most abundant species in the magical cavern. Each had two long whiskers stretching from the sides of its head and a long, thin, slippery tongue; the specimen before him, freshly butchered, had its tongue lolling out of its mouth.

The worm was half his size, so it'd been cut into three pieces. Ghorza had served herself the middle part and set aside the bottom for a light breakfast tomorrow. Most pressingly, she had served Lev the head. Gherm's favourite.

"You know, it's pretty expensive to get one of these right now, and you haven't eaten a thing since you woke up. You really don't wanna eat?"

"Really Ghorza, I'm not—"

Grrrrrrr. His grumbling stomach was loud enough to wake the dead.

"Not hungry, huh?"

Lev was speechless, betrayed by his own body.

"Gherm." Ghorza held out a piece of head meat. "Eat."

"Maybe it would be—"

"Eat."

"Shouldn't we—"

"*Eat.*"

"It honestly would be better to—"

"*I said eat.*"

"Fine!" Truthfully speaking, Lev needed to eat. No matter how disgusted he was at the idea of eating bugs, his survival depended on it, and he had to adapt. Besides, it wasn't the first time he had been made to eat something questionable.

He grabbed the mud-coloured flesh from Ghorza's hand and stuffed it into his mouth without a second thought.

"Gherm? Why are you making that face?" Fuzzy cave worms had been, for as long as Ghorza could remember, Gherm's favourite. She had never imagined that she would see him disgusted to eat them.

"N-Nothing to worry about. There was some lazlick mould inside it," he lied as the corners of his lips tensed upwards.

"Oh. Lucky you!" Though Gherm hated the idea of even getting near the mould, Ghorza adored its extremely sweet flavour.

How on earth did Gherm enjoy eating these damned things? Lev thought. The meat tasted overwhelmingly bitter and sour, and the texture reminded him of vehicle tyres sloshing through a swamp.

Trying his best to maintain a joyful expression, Lev focused entirely on moving his jaws up and down. He finally managed to swallow the worm chunk and looked up in hopes that the meal was over.

"Now, time to finish the rest," Ghorza sang, relieved her brother was eating again.

His stomach dropped. "Sure," he said, forcing another smile so that he wouldn't gag or cry.

Lev continued feigning joy between bites while making small talk every now and then—Gherm was never the silent type. Every time he talked, he made sure to express himself with his hands, and every time Ghorza asked him an embarrassing question, he twitched his ears and nervously tapped on the table with his left index finger. Though their flavour preferences could not be more disparate, Lev was confident that he had replicated all of Gherm's gestures, quirks, and nuances. And to him, at least, it seemed convincing.

Finally, Lev thought as the last bite went down his throat. He stood up, stretched his body, and proceeded to grab a drinking bowl. He then gulped down enough water to wash down the last of the worm meat before handing the bowl to Ghorza.

"Thanks." She took a sip and handed the bowl back to her brother to put away.

"You're welcome."

"Thank the gods you're alright. We're the only family we have left."

"Don't worry, I don't die easily."

"Oooh, so dangerous. Next you're gonna tell me you're a war hero." Ghorza giggled nervously.

"War hero, huh," Lev muttered. The room fell silent except for his finger tapping the table as he lost himself in his thoughts.

Ghorza waited, expecting her brother to admit he was joking, but the tapping went on longer than it ever had before. "Gherm. Are you okay?"

Gherm said nothing.

"Gherm?"

Once more, Gherm did not respond.

"Gherm!"

Lev nearly dropped the bowl.

He looked at Ghorza with an apologetic smile. "Sorry. I was thinking about something."

"I've never seen you like that. Were you really 'thinking about something,' or was it just your injury? Do we need to go back to Rogg?"

"Trust me, it's nothing."

"Gherm, I know you rarely lie to me. But since you woke up, I feel like you've been lying a lot more. Even during dinner, I felt like something was off. Like instead of just being yourself, you were trying to *act* like yourself." Ghorza pulled her chair closer to Lev. "Please, Gherm. Tell me why, and be honest this time."

Lev was stunned. He was sure that he could continue fooling her, but something in his mind was urging—no, forcing—him to come clean. The moment his focus lapsed, the influence took control and—

"I have memories from another life," Gherm blurted out with wide eyes.

"You're joking."

Lev tried to say yes, but something interfered. "Nope."

"Come on, Gherm, I'm serious."

"So am I."

Ghorza backed away slowly before grabbing a stone knife from the table.

Lev detected that the influence had exhausted itself and was ceding control back to him. He relaxed his eyelids, but it was too late. "Ghorza—"

"So do you only have memories? Or is it something else?" she demanded. "Are you really Gherm?"

The weakened influence tried to take over again, but through sheer force of will, Lev choked out an answer. "Yes. Who else could I be?" he insisted, softly taking a step backwards.

"Then why are you backing away from me?"

"I'm searching for..." Lev desperately scanned both his surroundings and Gherm's memories for a way to prove himself to her and found two words that fit. "Meron powder."

"What?" Ghorza gasped.

"Meron powder." Lev firmly repeated.

"I'll mix that meron powder we received in the holy ceremony a year ago with water and drink it. If I start burning..." Lev gulped, "then it'll be obvious I'm possessed and you can do whatever you want with me. But if nothing happens, you'll have to believe that I'm Gherm, except with memories from another life."

"You're... crazy."

"I am exactly who I say I am. Just give me a chance to prove myself—you have nothing to lose anyway. Even if I am a demon, you'll get your beloved, albeit slightly scorched, brother back. Deal?"

Ghorza hesitated for a second and stepped back far enough to allow Lev to grab the meron powder jar from across the room to the left. She did not lower her knife.

Thank goodness she agreed, Lev thought before hesitantly prying the jar open. *Hopefully the thing about this powder expelling demons and spirits is just superstition. And if it's not, I hope the powder either sends me back to where I belong or at least doesn't hurt.*

He grabbed a pinch of the powder and sighed in relief when nothing happened. He had learned from his earlier rush of knowledge that certain powerful demons could resist the effects of dry powder, but not of powder mixed with water. He stirred the powder into a cup of water, drank the concoction, and braced for impact.

Yet again, nothing happened. Lev's imperceptibly tensed shoulders relaxed completely. "Do you believe me now?"

Ghorza was stunned. "So you're really Gherm?"

"No. I'm Tanach, the dreamer of worlds," Lev said sarcastically.

"Pfft! Tanach! Out of all your options, you chose the lazy one?"

"What can I say? I love being lazy."

"You sure do, Gherm. You sure do." She paused. "So, care to explain to me how you have other memories?"

With the strange influence from earlier weakened to a suppressible level, Lev was confident that he could lie his way through this, but the method by which he had been reincarnated vaguely resembled something that Gherm's deceased father had once spoken of.

Ghorza might be able to shed some light, he thought.

"I honestly don't know how it all happened. At first I felt that I was in a void, then my body was swept away as if by a river. Then I found myself headed towards a ball of light."

While Lev talked, Ghorza's face cycled through a multitude of expressions, among them confusion, shock, excitement, and fear.

"After colliding with it—or, rather sinking into it—I woke up with an aching head and an additional set of memories."

Ghorza pulled up a chair and sat at Lev's side. "By the gods, Gherm. Do you realise what this means?"

"No, not at all."

"You're a chosen one. A *chosen one*! It's been a long time since a chosen one appeared, and even longer since a greyborn became one."

"Uh oh." As far as bogeys were concerned, chosen ones were reincarnations of the gods and their godly champions. Chosen ones wielded powers beyond natural potential, ranging from simple augments like superhuman strength to complex capabilities that could alter the very fabric of reality.

"If anyone finds out, you could be killed. Gherm, if you gain any special abilities, don't ever show them to anyone. And never, ever use them unless you *absolutely* have to. Oh, gods, if you were to use them and someone saw... I don't know what we'd do."

Lev mentally rattled off a myriad of ways to dispatch whoever saw him, but Ghorza suddenly stood back up. "Maybe you could be lucky and turn out to be a lost soul."

Lost souls were those who had inherited the memories of other mortals. They possessed new memories, but no new powers whatsoever. Even the new memories were frequently commoners' memories whose antiquity rendered them and their holders entirely unremarkable. Only a few lost souls had ever managed to gain prominence, and even then, it was only because they had been fortunate enough to inherit memories from great leaders and legendary craftsmen.

"What do you think? Check your recent memories. Do they contain any divine figures?"

Lev shrugged. "Looks like I'm a lost soul and not a chosen one."

"Thank the gods. I couldn't bear to lose you—"

"Yes, yes. Thankfully it's just a commoner's memory." Lev dismissed self-assuredly.

He briefly paused before speaking up again. "But not the kind of commoner that you're thinking of. Not even one from this world." Lev knew bogeys told folk tales involving both transmigration and latent memories. As far as Gherm's memories served him, though, no one, not even in folklore, had ever inherited memories from another world, and no one had ever lost control of their body to the foreign consciousness instead of integrating it.

Lev postulated that in his case, either there had been a problem in the reincarnation process, or his resistance to his own world's reincarnation process had triggered a failsafe that had sent him into this world. There was also the possibility that supernatural entities were meddling with current events.

"Great!" Ghorza restarted. "But you should still keep quiet. Who knows what secrets lie in your new memories? If people find out they won't leave you alone." Ghorza rubbed her forehead, trying to relax her long-furrowed brow.

"That's why I didn't want to tell you. I *know* my status isn't something I can disclose easily. I *know* that if others find out, I could be hunted down, tortured, and killed. I could be cut open and experimented on by mages and researchers hoping to discover my hidden gifts. Or maybe just for their amusement as they flaunt their superiority over me, as they probe me physically and mentally, as they twist me and break me while stripping me of—"

"Stop!" Ghorza shrieked with a fury she had never shown even when she had thought Lev was a demon. "Never say anything like that again! Never... please..." Her voice faltered as she embraced her brother.

Lev felt tears wet his shoulder and realised that he had taken it too far. His chest tightened; he knew he was frequently guilty of oververbalising worst-case scenarios without considering how they would affect others.

And due to what could only be Gherm's influence, he felt quite guilty. Lev hugged Ghorza back and let her cry on his shoulder. When she had calmed down, he smiled at her. "Let's go to sleep now and leave the thinking for tomorrow."

"Yeah, sleep. Let's go to sleep." Ghorza lingered in her brother's embrace for a moment before they released each other. "We've got a lot of work to do tomorrow to earn back those merits."

After cleaning the dining room and storing the remaining worm meat, "Gherm" and Ghorza retired to their sleeping quarters and lay on their separate mats, which were made from old rags bought with hard-earned merits.

"Good night, Gherm," said Ghorza before she closed her eyes and entered the land of dreams.

"Good night," Lev replied as he did the same. He waited a few minutes for the rhythm of Ghorza's breathing to slow before breaking his façade and losing himself once again in his thoughts.

So I died, huh, Lev deduced. He recalled what had happened at the moment of his death. He had been shot during his victory speech, and Brutus and Maria had come to his aid.

Heh… I'm pretty sure the big lug cried like a baby. Despite his looks, he was always a softie. Maria probably took it better, the tigress she was.

He reminisced about their childhood as a tear fell from his eye. *Will I ever see them again? My life loses a bit of its meaning without them.* Lev felt Gherm sympathising with him; he wanted to scowl at the subhuman beast whose body he had been made to share, but Gherm's emotions were too similar to his.

Sorry Gherm, but from what I've experienced and learned from your memories, I know you'll be troublesome for me in the future. I'm not the type to kill innocents, but I'm going to try putting you to sleep for now.

He didn't know how to influence souls, and before today he'd even doubted their existence, but earlier he'd managed to regain control over his body by exerting his superior willpower over Gherm's.

Thus, Lev tried focusing on his desire to silence Gherm. Despite his previous success, though, his current efforts failed to even dampen Gherm's influence on his emotions.

Well, that's that. I'll deal with you once I figure out how to. And trust me, I always figure things out. He felt Gherm brush his warning off.

Fine. Yes. We're stuck in the same body, and by this I mean your life sucks, Lev acquiesced. *But who said I'll settle for the same life you did? Do you think I'll be content with that?* he quizzed while scrutinising his hands.

Gherm's life had been anything but easy. The abuse of greyborn was the norm, and though some non-greyborn bogeys tried to act civilised and merciful by selling items to them, greyborns still paid more for goods that were all too often of the worst quality. Even small-time criminals, as long as they did not have grey skin, were treated better.

I need to find a way to improve my life, and I need to take care of her, Lev thought as he looked at the sleeping Ghorza. Even though he wasn't Gherm, he had still inherited Gherm's memories, so he knew how much Gherm cared about his sister.

He realised that considering how easily he had come to accept his change in environment, his mind might be merging with Gherm's. This was a prospect that, he perceived, horrified Gherm as much as it did himself.

Many questions swirled in Lev's head, but he knew he would not be able to answer them all in a single night. Closing his eyes, he allowed himself to drift off to sleep.

CHAPTER 4
TWO-FACEDNESS

"Ugggh," Lev groaned, his eyes still closed. His chest ached horribly. He tried to get up; the force of two gentle hands stopped him.

"Whoa there, buddy. Don't move too much. You've taken a shot to the chest and you're still in critical condition."

Lev was shocked to hear a voice he'd thought he would never hear again.

"Brutus?" asked Lev as he turned to his left.

"The one and only."

"So it was just a dream. Thank God."

"What did you dream about?" asked a woman's voice from the other side of his hospital bed.

As Lev turned to face Maria, he briefly surveyed his surroundings. He had been placed in a perfectly unremarkable hospital room with white walls and a grey floor, filled with the beeping of machines and the smell of disinfectant. Most remarkable was the lack of any trace of bogeys.

"Haha! You won't believe how crazy it was. I was stuck in a void for a long time. Then I got turned into some kind of a slave. I wasn't even human. Imagine that!" He gazed at his hands, each with five perfectly unremarkable human fingers, and clenched them tightly.

"That really does sound crazy," Brutus chuckled, shaking his head.

"I know! Anyways, both of you, give me a hand. I need to get out of bed and back on the Council right away." Lev reached one hand out to Brutus and one hand out to Maria, grateful for their unwavering support. "Considering that their sabotage has failed, we can use this to our advan... tage..."

Lev froze as his gaze drifted down from Maria's face to his outstretched hand. To his surprise, he saw seven dark, spindly, grey fingers.

"How disappointing. I should have realised when you said I was shot in the chest. This is a dream, isn't it?"

"I'm sorry, man. There's nothing we can do," said Brutus, voice starting to muddy and echo.

"I miss you both."

"You know we miss you too," replied Maria, whose face became blurrier and blurrier as she spoke. "But it's time to wake up, Lev. Promise us that you'll make the best of your new life. Don't give up."

"I promise. You can count on it," Lev answered without hesitation.

"Great! We hope you'll change the world for the better," whispered the duo in unison as the room began to fall away starting at the edges of Lev's vision.

"Is that even a question? You two of all people should know that I'm gonna shake this world's foundations to its very core. Just... Please try to visit me as much as you can."

Lev heard Brutus' booming voice echo across the growing distance between Lev and what remained of his hospital room. "We will. But for now, he will keep you company." Brutus pointed at a small, translucent, grey figure to Lev's side. One that Lev hadn't noticed until now.

"Gherm. Really? Got anything else? Anything better and less annoying?"

"Hey!" yapped Gherm.

"Take care." Maria's soft murmur comforted Lev's ears before both she and Brutus fully disappeared.

"Oh, come on! I have feelings, too, you know!" Gherm continued his retort.

"You're still in here after all," Lev said scornfully.

Gherm walked closer towards Lev's bed. "Well, yeah. It's my body."

"I'm sorry Gherm, but a unit can only have one leader. You're going to have to go to sleep for a bit."

"But! It's my body!" Gherm shouted.

"And I'm going to take good care of it," Lev declared. "But we both know you can't change your life, and I can."

"I-I guess that's true."

Seeing Gherm's sadness, Lev grimaced and reached out to pat him on the back. "Cheer up, Gherm. You're going to be remembered for a long time."

"Can you do one thing for me? Can you please be honest with my sister? I don't want to see her hurt."

Lev had never known how it felt to be related to someone by blood. Yet, he felt that he understood Gherm's feelings. "I'll take care of her like she's my own. I can promise you that. I'll make your world a better place, for you and her."

A forlorn smile replaced Gherm's frown. "Then I'll place my trust in you, Lev. Thank you."

Lev noticed both he and Gherm were getting blurrier. "No, Gherm. Thank you."

Gherm laughed. "Guess our time is up. It's time to wake up, Lev."

It's time to wake up, Lev.

It's time to wake up, Gherm.

"I said it's time to wake up, Gherm! We've got a lot of work to do today!" yelled the older sister.

He opened his eyes to see that the girl was about to kick him awake.

"Looks like you're pretty energetic this early in the morning."

"Well, one of us has to be," admonished Ghorza. "Is it that hard for you to wake up early by yourself?"

Lev sat up and stretched contentedly. "I'll try and make it a habit. Are you ready for breakfast?" he told her with a confident smile, something Gherm would never have done.

"So it did change you. Please don't change anymore..." Her voice trailed off, and for a moment, neither of them could find the words to say.

"Let's go eat, shall we?" Lev had no more time for tension.

They reheated the remainder of the previous night's meal and ate it as fast as they could. As they ate, Ghorza glanced at Lev. His posture was more confident and his eating habits were more refined than she had ever seen.

"Are you sure you didn't inherit the memories of a noble?" Ghorza asked, her mouth full of bug meat.

Lev swallowed. "Yup."

"You sure are acting like one, minus the condescending attitude."

"Well, the memories came from a different life in a different society. The owner of these memories was a commoner who tried to make his society a better place, only to get assassinated by his noble rivals."

"You're not going to try to overthrow the rule of the blues, right?" spoke Ghorza hurriedly, who almost choked on her food in her haste.

Lev stared at her as if she were the tribe's fool. "How dumb do you think I am?"

"Well..."

"Sure, sure. Fight them head-on! Just let me go grab my armour and spear while you go call my loyal armies and mages to fight not only the rest of our kind but also our lovely goblin overlords. Alas, I'm not a warrior with weapons and armour, and I command neither armies nor mages."

"Mages?" asked the dumbfounded girl.

"Magic users like shamans, only less spiritual and more methodical."

"Oh, I get it—wait, does that mean you know magic?!" The idea of her brother knowing magic gave her as much fright as the idea of overthrowing the chiefdom, for greyborns were forbidden from practising magic.

"No. And can you please stop jumping to wild conclusions like that? If I knew magic, wouldn't you be able to feel me practising it?" asked Lev, getting more annoyed every time Ghorza said something that would end with him having a slashed throat, a noose around his neck, or his decapitated head on a stick.

Speaking of "feeling" magic, though greyborns had long forgotten the arts, they retained the ability to sense magical energy and could detect magical residue when the arts were used. Because of their ability to detect magic combined with their expendability, goblins had sent many a greyborn to scout the lower levels ahead of their expedition parties in the monster caverns.

Ghorza grinned and nodded at her now-different younger brother. She didn't fully believe his words, but she'd give him the benefit of the doubt. For now.

They continued eating their meal in silence, each lost in their own thoughts. Lev was brainstorming what he would do to climb the ladder of bogey society out of the greyborn caste. It was rare, but not impossible: greyborns who had climbed the ladder before him had performed miraculous feats to be conferred normal commoner status.

Ghorza fret over how fast her brother changed after becoming a lost soul. Would he one day become a different person? Usually, the inheritor of the memories would change a little, but not this much. Would her greatest fear come true? Would he not be her brother anymore?

After finishing their meal, Lev got to his feet. "And done. Let's go already."

"You're awfully quick today. Usually, you'd take your time to avoid arriving early."

Lev shrugged. "Well, we burned a lot of merits treating me, right?"

"True. Things will be tough on us for a while"

"If you work on your own, yes. But don't worry. I'll work extra hard to cover the costs."

"You? Work hard? Yeah, right!" Ghorza heartily laughed. Gherm had always earned half the amount of merits she did.

"You shouldn't treat it as a joke. Trust me on this. After today, I'll no longer have problems earning merits," he told her, satisfied with himself and his plan to get rid of the problem once and for all.

"Sure you will."

"You'll see. Now let's get ready."

After getting dressed and grabbing their equipment, they left the house and walked to the work quarters to receive their assignments from the taskmaster.

As they walked, Lev checked his surroundings to fill any discrepancies in his memory, as well as to familiarise himself with Gherm's memories. Housing in the southwestern slave quarters ranged from dilapidated shacks, where the most pitiful slaves lived, to the humble huts of those better off. Their abode fell somewhere in the middle.

"What a surprise. I thought you'd croaked," said the overseer on duty to Lev with a grin as they arrived.

"Not this time, Kul. I won't be dying anytime soon if I can help it," replied Lev to the old green bogey. Kul had once been an honoured, respected member of the warrior class, but after failing to protect a bogey noble's son during a rebellion against the Jiira, he'd been forced to step down and ended up an overseer in the slave quarters.

Through the years, he'd learned to let go of his prejudice and managed to overcome the indignation of his downfall. He still hated the upper class for this humiliation, but unlike the other overseers, he never took his anger out on the slaves. As he treated his workers as individuals, many greyborn respected and even liked him.

"Are you sure you're ready to work?" asked Kul. "I can transfer some of my merits to you if you can't." Kul's close connection to Gherm and

Ghorza was due to their father, Gat, who'd been the first to befriend Kul after his fall from grace.

Beyond that, Gat had eased Kul's transition into his role as an overseer, acting as a mediator between him and any unruly greyborn having a bad day. As such, Kul owed him a great deal, and since Gat and his wife had been killed in a hiveling raid two years ago, he'd done his best to assist Gat's children as a repayment of his debt.

"Don't worry about me, Kul. I'm feeling much better."

"That's right, gramps. He's as fit as he can be," Ghorza added.

"Gramps? Who're you calling 'gramps'? I can still beat your ass and everyone else's with one hand tied behind my back!" yelled the miffed Kul, causing everyone in the nearby vicinity to awkwardly laugh while slowly giving him some space. Though he meant it as a joke, they all knew that he was telling the truth.

"Sorry," Ghorza said while lowering her head.

Kul tried to maintain his angry expression, but he failed and burst out laughing.

"I know you didn't mean any harm, lass. But make sure to not piss off the wrong people," he said with a gentle smile.

"I know that. I'm not Gherm. But I can still beat up anyone who pisses us off, right?"

"As long as they're fellow greyborns, no offence."

"None taken," Ghorza replied nonchalantly. She understood the consequences of what would happen if a greyborn harmed a non-greyborn, even if they were a fellow slave. Besides, it wasn't as if she were actually looking to fight others; a weak appearance typically led to exploitation, so she had to put up a front.

It was time to get to work, so Kul took on a professional visage and assigned the brother and sister the tasks the taskmaster had appointed for the slaves that day.

"Good luck, little bro. Make sure to avoid any trouble," said Ghorza before they separated and went to their respective stations: Ghorza to the mushroom farms, Lev to the mines.

CHAPTER 5
FRIENDS AND FOES

It should've been a regular day of work for Rak.

Today, like most days, his group was assigned to mining duty, his preferred task. Given his strength and stature, it was simple work for him to mine rocks and crystals, and it provided him an outlet to deal with his frustrations. The rhythmic actions and sound of the pickaxe digging into stone helped clear his mind. This time, however, he was having a little trouble finding peace.

Can't he ever shut up? Rak complained, glancing at his newest recruit.

The kid had begged Rak to allow him into his ranks. He'd done so, but much to Rak's chagrin, the newcomer was proving to be a loudmouth, one who continuously prattled about his exploits and achievements.

Rak looked towards the rest of his men to see if they shared his grievances. Most ignored the recruit while Hem, Rak's second-in-command and close friend, was listening to his tall tales with amusement.

If the young whelp had just kept it to gossip, Rak would've grit his teeth and ignored it, but alas...

"So he says that he doesn't have the merits, but he does have a sister."

Rak's ears twitched. The recruit now had his undivided attention.

"'And I said, 'well hey...'" The man lecherously licked his lips in an exaggerated manner.

"'We accept all kinds of payment, and he—"

Before he could finish his sentence, Rak grabbed him by the neck and slammed him into a nearby rock wall.

"I told you before. No. Girls," Rak growled, snarling.

"I'm sorry. I-I…"

Rak tightened his hand around the man's neck, cutting his pleading mid-sentence.

"If you run with us, you don't buy 'em and you don't sell 'em."

"Rak! Let him go!" Hem yelled. "If he's hurt, the overseers will ask questions."

Rak glared at his friend, but Hem didn't back down.

Heeding his friend's advice, Rak let go of the man's neck with a troubled sigh.

The recruit fell to his knees and clutched his throat as he gulped for air.

"Next time, I feed you to a hiveling," Rak warned before continuing on his way.

Hem knelt next to the recruit and gently patted him on the back. "Sorry about that. The boss is real particular about working girls. Dad died young and his mom did a little extra work on the side to keep the family fed."

"She gone?" The man asked, wiping the tears from his eyes.

"Yep. Got the black spots. You can treat it, but it takes merits. Boss tried to scrounge up enough to treat her but all her old clients walked away."

Hem took a glance at Rak.

"No green gonna admit to having a little fun with grey at the end of the day."

The ease with which Rak lifted his pickaxe and cracked an ore vein in a single motion caused the recruit to gulp in fear.

"The boss is real sore about that point. Remember it."

"Now." Hem patted the man on the shoulder. "I've got to talk to the boss."

"R-Right. I'll watch my mouth."

Hem gave him a nod and approached Rak.

"Boss, you gotta stop that. If you don't get ahold of yourself, we're going to lose more men to Vyrga."

"You told him the rules?" Rak asked.

"Yeah, I tell'em all. They can steal and run all they want, but don't touch the skirts."

"Good. Forget for a day and I might need to break an imbecile's head off. Or two."

"They know, but they're guys, right? Only enough blood for one head at a time," Hem countered.

Rak sneered. "I don't need that kind of filth in my gang. Let Vyrga have them."

"Boss, don't be like that. Just lighten up," Hem replied with a frown on his face, "There ain't no gang without people, and we're already running behind Vyrga in that department."

Rak grumbled under his breath and continued digging his pickaxe into the vein.

Hem sighed and turned his attention elsewhere.

"Huh," he muttered once his eyes landed on a particular greyborn. "Hey, look. It's your favourite bug. He's back."

This caught Rak's attention. He craned his neck and found a surprising sight.

There stood Gherm, facing three men. The three were known scoundrels, the worst of Vyrga's rabble.

Behind him were two other greyborns. A frail man and a tall boy, almost an adult. Judging from the wounds on the boy, he'd likely been the target of the three.

Is he... trying to protect them? Why? Rak thought.

"Huh. Bug's found himself some guts. I never understood why you hated that kid so much."

Hem waited for Rak's reply. When none came, he turned around to find Rak glaring at Gherm.

Rak felt conflicted.

Why are you acting brave, Gherm? You've always been like him. Like Veit.

"Cowardly scum," Rak cursed.

The more he looked at Gherm, the more it reminded him of the past. In the instant he blinked, Veit switched places with Gherm in his mind.

Nervous. Cowardly. His antics made him a prime target for bullying. What would have happened if I hadn't been there to beat the bastards and save him?

Rak sadly chuckled before staring at his hand, reminiscing how he'd grabbed Veit's and helped him up. *I guess that's how we became friends. Brothers.*

He clenched his fist and sneered. *Biggest mistake of my life.*

In the beginning, when he had first started his gang, Rak had followed his ideals to the letter. Not only had he protected those who fell under his gang's banner, but also those who were too weak to fend for themselves.

As his good childhood friend, Veit was one of the first to join him, but he wasn't the last. As Rak grew older, he also grew into one of the tallest, most physically imposing goblinoids his cave-dwelling compatriots had ever encountered. With a personality to match, many bogeys naturally flocked to his side.

Veit however, remained small enough to be mistaken for a child, and like Rak, his size reflected his personality.

Still, despite their differences, the two seemed inseparable. It was clear to anyone and everyone that Rak valued Veit as a brother, one who would never betray him. And so it was, until...

The annual expedition.

During last year's expedition, Rak and Veit had been chosen to serve in the vanguard along with Vyrga and a few of his men. It would have been a dangerous assignment in the best of times, as the vanguard's purpose was to sacrifice themselves so that the rest of the expedition could progress and harvest the cavern's riches along the way.

But Vyrga's presence had made Rak all the more wary—the last thing he and Veit needed was to be dragged into a brawl by the impulses of an ambitious, amoral greyborn.

And his cautiousness had proved fruitful—or so he'd thought. After two months of travel and combat the expedition party reached the sixth floor of the monster cavern, and Vyrga still hadn't made a move.

The expedition leader had commanded the greyborns to form scouting parties to explore the sixth floor. Although a previous expedition had reached the sixth floor several years ago, much was still unknown, given the floor's biome.

It housed an expansive underground forest, with a glowing sphere of bluish-white light floating in the sky just beneath the cavern's ceiling. According to the shamans, the sphere was a giant haze crystal that provided light and life to the underground forest, allowing it to flourish.

The scouting group had moved as a single party, every member maintaining a watchful gaze on the others, until they reached a key landmark: a giant tree embedded in the fossilised remains of numerous underground species.

There, they'd split into four smaller groups: one led by Vyrga, one by Rak, one by Olf, one of Rak's followers, and the last by a warrior called Mirgar.

They'd drawn straws for the areas they'd cover, with Rak coming up short. Nervous about venturing into what was considered the most dangerous area of the sixth floor, Veit had requested to stay with Olf instead.

Wanting his friend to be safe, Rak'd agreed, and the groups had gone their separate ways. He'd been glad that Veit had made such a request, and the next few hours only proved him right as his party was constantly besieged by hivelings and other wildlife. Still, he and his men, who he'd extensively trained, finished their task. Tired and worse for wear, to be fair, but alive.

Sometime later, it had come time to meet back at the tree. Near the meeting point, Rak had found Olf on the ground, bloodied. Upon further observation, his throat had been slit, his face frozen in a shocked expression.

Roaring in anger at the death of his compatriot, Rak's expression had been a mask of fury. But before long, his anger had transformed into fear. Fear for Veit. Like a parent desperately searching for its missing young, he'd desperately searched the surrounding for clues, and found the bloody footsteps of Olf's murderer.

Despite knowing full well that it was a trap, Rak and his squad had chased after them, only to find Veit lying on his stomach in a clearing, near some trees. Despite the danger, Rak had rushed to his friend's side, only to be forced to dodge to the side as several javelins narrowly soared past.

Vyrga and his thugs had launched their attack, but thankfully Rak's band remembered their training and moved as one to Rak's side to hold back the attackers.

Greyborns from both sides had been out for blood, ready to defeat their rivals once and for all. They'd charged at each other with stone-tipped spears and flint knives. Cries of pain had echoed through the forest as its ground filled with the bodies of the injured and dead.

Vyrga's men should have won. After all, he'd chosen the battlegrounds, and he'd had twice the men. But for what Rak's side had lacked in quantity, they'd made up for in quality.

When it'd become apparent that his side was losing, Vyrga had motioned for his elites to join him and charged toward his target. With his stone axe held high, Rak had been prepared to meet the attack, but to his surprise, Vyrga had stopped in his tracks and whistled.

Momentarily confused by these actions, his uncertainty had been quickly swept away by a sharp pain in his back. With dread in his heart, he'd turned to see his attacker, but in his heart he'd already known.

He was a blind fool.

"Boss." Hem broke him from his reminiscence.

"Should we do something? We can't let Vyrga's trash do this in our territory. Lots of idiots would get ballsy," Hem advised, pickaxe already in hand.

Rak looked back at Gherm. He sneered as he watched the frail man Gherm had tried to help run away, leaving Gherm to fend for himself. The boy stood close behind, but clearly wouldn't be of help.

"Leave him. Some people just got to learn the hard way."

I don't know what got over him but once he sees that he's alone, he'll grovel. That's what all of Veit's ilk do eventually.

Hem grunted, clearly uncomfortable with Rak's choice but in the end, he could only sigh. "You're the boss. Let's hope the kid doesn't get too bad of a beating."

"We'll see."

CHAPTER 6
HEARTS OF OBSIDIAN

"Who the fuck do you think you are, tiny?" said the largest of the three goons. His wart-covered face contorted into an ugly sneer.

Rak had to agree with the question. *Why would such a small, cowardly creature like Gherm stand in the way of Vyrga's minions?* Rak wondered. As far as Rak knew, Gherm wasn't friends with any of the other weaklings. Even if he were, he wasn't the type to stick his neck out for anyone. Even when it came to Ghorza he'd never been the type to fight for her, only one to beg the aggressors to leave her alone.

"I asked you, who the fuck do you think you are!" repeated the greyborn thug. He glared at the smaller greyborn who dared obstruct him. Gherm now wore a smug expression.

The leader stepped closer to pressure Gherm to back down, but to no avail. The leader was confused when his strange adversary did not cower as expected. What was happening? It was easy to tell from Gherm's physique that he was no warrior. Why wasn't he cowering like the others always did? The leader briefly shot a glare at his past victims—they flinched on sight. Seeing the expected reaction only confused and angered him further.

Rak, still observing, could make neither heads nor tails of the confrontation. First, three of Vyrga's cronies had tried to pick a fight in *his* territory. Second, Gherm, of all greyborns, was the one standing in their way. Not only that, even after the cronies turned their attention to him, Gherm was still standing his ground. Rak was willing to bet that no one in the crowd that was slowly gathering, including him, had any idea what was going on. This situation was just too bizarre.

The fat goon, who had been standing behind his bewildered leader, finally broke the silence. "Hey, boss, I think I know who this is."

"Finally, someone knows something around here! Lay it on me!"

"This bugger's that bird Ghorza's brother! You know, the slag who refused to work for Vyrga," answered the goon with a grin. He didn't notice the change in Gherm's expression, but his boss did.

"Oh!" chortled the head goon. "Look at this dipshit. You made him mad!" The warty bastard threw his head back in laughter, flashing his rotten teeth to the heavens, before he suddenly stopped laughing and glared at Gherm. "So what? We insulted that bitch sister of yours, what're ya gonna do about it? Nothin', 'cause now I know who you *really* are: that bludger who got hurt when the tunnel collapsed. Guess now you're a mute," he said, "and a retard, too."

Gherm was livid.

At this point, he'd usually have flashed a meek smile and tried to apologise, thought Rak. *Did the damage from the collapse really damage his mind? Should I interfere?* Although Rak now held a healthy hatred of weaklings, he had nothing against those who were physically or mentally disabled—he hadn't fallen that far yet.

Like everyone else in the crowd, he was starting to pity the silent Gherm, but something in his mind told him that there was more going on than he was aware of. His instincts were telling him that something was different about Gherm.

The head thug inched ever closer and lowered his head to stare eye-to-eye with the nuisance. "Do you wanna know what'll happen to her? After Vyrga clears this place of all the rabble standing in his way, she and everyone else who refused to bow down will suffer." A smile gradually crept its way across its face. "Though, Vyrga's a reasonable man. If she refuses to give herself to him, he'll make her!" The thug declared, pointing his obsidian-tipped knife at Gherm.

"There is one thing I do know."

In one sudden motion, Gherm closed the gap between him and the thug. He placed his right hand firmly against the thug's wrist before slapping the palm of his left hand against his opponent's, causing their fingers to open, dropping the knife.

Gherm grabbed the knife mid-air with tactical precision in a smooth, connected motion.

"Wha— *Ghrrrrr!*" gurgled the leader, grabbing his slit throat. He stumbled backwards a few steps and turned to his stunned compatriots for help before Gherm pulled the goon's face down to eye level.

"I can rid this world of unneeded filth," he snarled, exhaling emphatically onto the goon's face.

With the confiscated knife, Gherm repeatedly, violently hacked away at his enemy's stomach. The head thug's entrails spilt onto the ground.

The dying thug gasped one last time, bloody tears falling down his face, as he departed from this world to the next.

Gherm turned to the two remaining thugs. "So. Wanna join your boss?"

"You killed him... You killed Varg!" blubbered the fat one, while his skinny companion was able to do little more than nod in shock.

Can't blame him, thought Rak. *Who could've predicted that Gherm would butcher someone in cold blood?* It wasn't uncommon for greyborn skirmishes to end in bloodshed, as the overseers turned a blind eye to such occurrences as long as they didn't happen during work. But for a runt like Gherm to act up, nevermind emerge victorious in a fight against one of Vyrga's men...

"Yes, I did. Let me ask again." Gherm made sure to enunciate clearly this time, taking a step forward with every word so the other two could not possibly mishear. "*Wanna join your boss?*"

"You have no idea what you just did, do you?" snarled the fat thug as he could stand neither the sight nor attitude of his friend's killer.

"I do. I not only interfered with Vyrga's business, but I also killed one of his men. Sure, he was expendable, but he was still Vyrga's, which means I'm now a target. But let's not forget that Vyrga wants my sister— so was I not already a target? *Are we not all targets?*" roared Gherm, stunning the crowd further.

He pointed his finger at the thugs and continued his speech. "Every time! Every single time, you attack us, harass us, and abuse us! And for what? Your stupid turf war? You keep targeting us even though we're not Rak's men just so you can pretend you're not the cowards you really are, making our already-miserable lives as slaves even more miserable! Even though you're also fellow slaves, fellow greyborns, you prey on us to inflate your own ego. But I say enough is enough!" he declared, spreading his arms wide in the air.

"Though I do not have the right to represent you, I *am* one of you. I suffer what you suffer, I feel the same pain you feel, I curse the same fate you curse, and I despair as you all despair. Don't we suffer enough for the sins of our ancestors? Do we need more suffering in our miserable, short lives? DO OUR LOVED ONES NEED MORE SUFFERING IN THEIR MISERABLE, SHORT LIVES?!"

Rak scratched his head. *Does he think anyone here would agree—*

"No!" A slave, old and missing one eye, shouted at the top of his lungs.

Huh.

"We've had enough!" Yelled another.

Did he pay some people to sway the crowd?

"Get out of here, you bastards!"

Guess he did. Rak smiled amusedly.

"Pick on someone else, you pieces of shit!"

"Leave us alone!"

"Burn in hell, you animals!"

"Enough!" snapped the skinny thug, seething with rage as he pointed his knife at Gherm. His spindly legs took a step forward as his long, unkempt hair covered his forehead. "You think just because this wanker managed to kill Varg that you can take us on? We're Vyrga's men! Nobody takes us on and lives! You defy us, and he'll come clean out the lot of you!"

The crowd began to waver as fear gripped their hearts. Their momentary courage faded as the image of Vyrga surfaced in their memories.

So what, now they lower their heads? Typical, Rak lamented. *It's not like Vyrga would actually waste his time with common rabble. Nobody does. If anything, he'd deal with Gherm as the rabble-rouser.* His excitement for what could have been wilted into disgust at the mass display of cowardice.

Just as Rak was about to turn away, a familiar voice sounded again.

"So what?" retorted Gherm, drawing the crowd's attention once again. "So what if we're weak?"

Gherm turned toward Vyrga's men. "So what if you're stronger than us? Does that mean we should serve you? Does that mean we should grovel in the mud and let you step on us, feed off of us, rape our loved ones, and make our lives a nightmare for as long as we live? No! I refuse to live like that!" he exclaimed.

After pausing for effect, he continued. "You all know I almost died in that cave-in the other day. When I almost experienced death, my life flashed before my eyes—can you guess what I saw?"

"What? What did you see?" asked the fat goon nervously, hiding behind his skeletal compatriot.

Gherm paused for a brief moment, the crowd entranced. "I saw a life that's not worth living! An existence where I slave away day and night isn't a life at all—it's hell! And since I'm already in hell, why shouldn't I fight? Why shouldn't we all fight? Yes, we're weak. Yes, we're cowardly.

But together, we can accomplish the impossible! If we can't stand on our own two feet, we can lean on each other! In our numbers, there is strength!"

Gherm gave a final flourish. "So lend me your strength, and I shall lend you mine! I will be your sword and shield! And I," Gherm announced, hand over his heart, "shall lead us in the march to reclaim our dignity!"

"Gherm! Gherm! Gherm! Gherm!" roared the crowd in unison.

The two remaining thugs started to shudder in fear. As the fat one backed away, his wiry companion took a deep breath, steeled his nerves and charged forward.

"Look out!" cried the old bogey from before, but Gherm, clutching his own knife in a hammer grip, had seen this coming.

The thug sliced downwards with his copper knife. Gherm dodged to the left out of harm's way and slashed in an upwards arc with his own knife, aiming for the inside of his opponent's wrist. The thug managed to move his arm just in time before jumping backwards.

The crowd was mesmerised. The adversaries circled around each other, waiting for an opportunity to strike again.

The thug suddenly leapt again at Gherm, closing the distance in a moment, then swung for Gherm's left wrist. Gherm deflected the attack with a swipe of his own, but not without sustaining a nasty gash on his left lower arm. Gherm clenched his jaw to maintain focus despite the pain.

Gherm lunged at the thug. By an unusual stroke of luck, his knife caught in his opponent's left shoulder. Gherm quickly twisted the embedded knife, shifted his weight onto his back foot, and kicked the thug down onto the ground an arm's length away from striking range. The fallen thug locked eyes with his rotund friend and silently called for help; his "friend" turned tail and fled.

Gherm immediately pounced onto his fallen opponent, wresting the thug's knife-clutching hand away and trying simultaneously to drive his own knife into his target's upper chest. The thug grabbed Gherm's right wrist.

The thug struggled against Gherm's pressure and almost managed to free his left hand, but the damage to his left shoulder had weakened his control on Gherm's right wrist. With a final grunt, Gherm plunged his obsidian blade into the thug's chest.

CHAPTER 7
RIDE TO GLORY

Lev's breathing was ragged, his left arm bleeding. With his good arm, he pushed himself off his foe's lifeless body. Lev took a moment to compose himself. Then he pulled the knife out of the corpse and surveyed the immediate area, but failed to find the other thug.

This alarmed Lev. He could conceive of three possible reasons the other thug had not even tried to intervene: one, he had called for reinforcements; two, the enraptured crowd had taken him out themselves; or three, he had hidden himself somewhere else in the cave to watch the spectacle from a safe distance and ambush Lev once the crowd dispersed. Though Lev was on the verge of exhaustion, he acknowledged that from the little he had observed of those blindly loyal drones, he might not have any real reason to worry about retaliation.

Thankfully it was the second, as Lev soon found the fat bogey beaten and bound near Rak and his men. As Lev stepped closer, the stone-faced Rak regarded him thoughtfully. It was clear to Lev what Rak sought from him.

"Looks like we need to talk," said Lev. Rak simply nodded.

Lev wiped his knife on the dead thug's pants before tearing himself a bandage from the dead thug's shirt.

Lev then stood up to face his audience, whose eyes were glued to him out of both fear and respect: fear of the possibility that Vyrga would retaliate, but also respect for the man who had taught them to challenge Vyrga's authority and resolved to protect them from their predators.

As though to answer their cry for guidance, Lev thrust his knife skywards with a rousing battle cry. "My brothers! We should *never* fear that mongrel Vyrga, for he and his men are few and we are many! Follow me, and I swear on my life he shall *never* threaten us again!"

At first, nobody spoke up. Vyrga likely would ignore them in normal circumstances, and perhaps even in circumstances as unusual as now, but if they followed Gherm too far, Vyrga would hunt and kill them and their families. They were certain that it would be safer to avoid getting involved at all.

Even so, a couple of greyborns wordlessly stepped forwards out of the crowd to face Lev. Slowly, an older greyborn stepped forwards as well and turned to yell at the crowd. "What do you think you're doing! Is this a treatment a hero deserves?"

"He may be a hero to you," argued a youth from the crowd, "but that doesn't mean he's one to us. We're not the ones who are gonna get killed."

"Maybe not this time, but what about next time!" the elder argued back.

The youth was silent.

"Hah, I expected as much. Don't you get it? Even if Vyrga's goons had targeted someone else to deal with their boredom, they could target us any day. Who knows. In the future, maybe I'll get attacked, maybe you. Maybe your brother, your father, your uncle, or anyone you care about. As long as we are weak and divided, anyone could pick on us!" Lev watched the elder feigned tears. "If all it takes for my grandchildren to be able to rise above the fate of most greyborn is to follow this 'Gherm' fellow... then by the gods, I will do it!"

A wave of murmurs washed over the masses in front of Lev before briefly giving way to a still silence.

"He's right, isn't he?" volunteered one man.

"He is. And if we don't do anything, nothing will change, right?" affirmed another.

"Then let's go for it!"

"I think I'll pass. The risks aren't worth it—"

"What are you saying? They definitely are!"

"Hey, I'll fight with him! Beats being a target."

"Hope, you have a spot open for me—I've been meaning to teach those bastards a lesson!"

"Sadly, I'm too old to fight, but I'll do my best to help, Gherm."

"Thanks for saving my brother, Gherm!"

Over time the talks and speeches turned into triumphant chants, filling the cave with the sound of the name Lev had been made to take as a greyborn. *Gherm sure is lucky I'm pulling the strings*, thought Lev as he basked in the chorus of cheers. Everything, save for the initial hesitation of the crowd, was going according to his plan so far. He was thankful he had made sure to get that favour from the right elder beforehand.

When Lev was satisfied, he raised his hands to silence them and made his tone humble. "No need to thank me. More importantly, we have some work to do, now, isn't that right?"

Most of the crowd abruptly turned to check the nearby post normally occupied by their supervisors.

The post was empty.

The herd of greyborns began to whisper and curse anxiously before splitting off to search for the mining overseer on duty, Thorst. They soon found him standing in the front row of the crowd, looking miffed. "Had your fun, eh? Now get back to work!" he roared. Every slave but Gherm hurriedly returned to their tasks.

"Hey, Thorst," greeted Gherm amiably.

"Hey, Gherm," Thorst reciprocated, "how's Ghorza?" He furrowed his brow. "And how are you planning to explain to her what just happened?"

"That will be hard, but I think I can manage."

Thorst shook his head. "Whatever. I hope you *manage* not to get skinned alive. It's *Vyrga*, after all." Thorst went back to his post.

Lev sighed. It was fortunate that Thorst had been the one on duty during the debacle with Vyrga's goons. Thorst was one of the more easy-going overseers, and as a protégé of Kul's, he and Gherm were quite friendly.

"So is it my turn?" asked a voice behind Lev.

"Yes, Rak. It is," answered an exasperated Gherm.

The enormous greyborn stared down at his scrawny, counterpart with his arms crossed. The smaller greyborn looked up at him.

"It must be my lucky day. I've been graced with an audience with the mighty Gherm," teased Rak.

"And blessed me. My humble self was granted the honour of meeting with the illustrious Rak," bickered Lev.

They scowled at each other for a moment before bursting into laughter at the same time.

"Hahaha! You're good!" Rak told Lev. It had been a long time since anyone had had the gall to talk back to him like that.

"I know. So are you." Lev rapidly regained his composure. "But really now, let's start our discussion, all right?"

Rak nodded, but turned instead to the last of Vyrga's lackeys. "We will talk. But we deal with this one first." He walked to the bruised hostage and snapped his fingers. One of his minions grabbed the hostage by the ears and raised his head, exposing his neck.

The ashen-faced hostage struggled against his restraints. "P-Please... By the grace of Vyrga, please let me go..."

Sadly, Rak knew that showing mercy to one of Vyrga's hangers-on, especially one as brainwashed as this, was pointless. The bastard would probably run back to Vyrga in shame before returning days later to terrorize the slaves again. Rak raised his knife and prepared to end his captive's life.

"Wait!" Lev frantically threw his arms out between Rak and the captive.

"What the hell do you think you're doing?" countered Rak. He had every intention to deal the finishing blow himself, and he was greatly insulted that Gherm now seemed ready to order him to step back.

"I believe we should let him go."

Lev's proposal shocked everyone within earshot. *Let one of Vyrga's men go? Was that a joke?* Even the thug himself was astonished. Vyrga never showed mercy to his subordinates. He had even killed those who'd shown anyone mercy in creative ways to indoctrinate his followers properly.

Rak spoke up. "I thought maybe getting hit in the head made you brave, not foolish. You want to show him mercy? It's Vyrga we're talking about."

"I'm not showing mercy. I'm sending a warning."

"A warning to Vyrga?" muttered Hem, astounded. No *slave or commoner has ever survived that. A noble, sure, but not an upstart greyborn with no protection.*

"Yeah, a warning. Vyrga's bound to find me no matter what, since everyone here knows me now. As for him," Lev gestured vaguely at the snivelling hostage, "whether we kill him or not, Vyrga will already be insulted enough to hunt me down. Why not provoke him into a trap?" Lev hoped the prisoner would interpret his statements not as a bluff, but rather as a credible threat that the bogey "Gherm" could take Vyrga down.

In any case, Gherm, Rak, and Hemgall all knew that Vyrga was too cautious to charge blindly into an enemy. He preferred to study them, then strike with prudence. "After all," Gherm continued, "showing mercy to a victim of this cursed life cannot possibly be a sin. We all eventually fall to our lowest point, and we all feel helpless to change anything sometimes. We all find ourselves desperate to get stronger by any means, and, well, some of us resort to crime."

Rak had a nagging feeling that this was a jab at him somehow, but he chose to ignore it.

"But I believe any bogey should be given at least one chance to redeem himself. For even if we sink into darkness, we can still swim our way back to the surface."

Lev gauged his impromptu audience's reactions—with the exception of the thug, no one was that impressed—and quickly added, "Besides, to Vyrga, it'll be a slap in the face. And it isn't a secret that he's needed one for a long time." With a few chuckles and nods, Lev knew he had succeeded.

"You're playing a dangerous game, boy. I like it," commended Hem.

"Thanks, um…"

"Hemgall. But you can call me Hem. That's what people with balls call me. And you got a big pair of bronze ones, kid."

"Thanks, Hem." Lev turned to Rak. "Can you do me a favour and let him go?"

"It's your funeral," Rak conceded before ordering his men to untie the grateful thug and throw him out of Rak's territory.

"Glad that's over. Let's talk."

* * *

It didn't take long for Lev to return home. There he sat down, humming a tune as he wiped the obsidian knife he'd earned.

Lev shook his head once he saw the poor state of the blade. *How unfortunate. Another sign it was stolen. If it wasn't, it would've been less weathered by fighting.*

Obsidian was a highly coveted material, beloved by both soldiers and artisans. The tools made out of it were durable and beautiful. Thus, they were commonly considered family heirlooms. At the very least, they'd never be treated as terribly as this blade had been.

Once he finished inspecting, Lev put down the knife and reclined into the chair.

Finally. Step one was a success, Lev thought to himself. *I hope Rak recognizes the value of our long-term partnership. After all, sometimes an agreement and a handshake are all you need to win.*

Sadly, my work isn't done yet, Lev mumbled as he returned his attention to the present. He stood up from the chair.

He had negotiated a deal with Rak: Rak would once again provide protection to the weaklings in his territory and help Lev secure the capital and assets necessary to establish his own faction. In return, their factions would be allies.

Lev would, as was tradition, serve as a vassal to Rak and aid him in eliminating his rivals, provided rendering aid would not result in the annihilation of Lev's faction. Lev's group would also guard the border between Rak's and Vyrga's territories.

Most importantly, Lev would pay tribute to Rak every fortnight.

He filled a large bowl with water, then proceeded to wash himself and his clothes of the blood, dust, and grime that had accumulated through the day. He also replaced his bandages before patting himself dry and changing into a cleaner set of rags.

At last, he lay down in his bed and placed his newly acquired knife on the floor within arm's reach.

As Lev closed his eyes, ready to drift off to sleep, the cheap leather covering their empty doorway was violently pulled open, startling him awake. He swiftly seized the knife and jumped out of the bed, rolling fluidly into a combat stance with his knife pointed at the intruder.

As on edge as he was, it took him a full breath cycle to recognize that it was Ghorza in the doorway, panicking and in tears.

"What have you done!" she screamed.

"Done what?"

"Don't play dumb! Everyone's talking about it! Why did you doom us by killing Vyrga's men?!"

"To make friends."

Silence blanketed the room.

"What kind of excuse is that? Your 'grand' speech won over so many bogeys—you basically have an army to die with you now!"

Lev inhaled as though to speak up, but Ghorza cut him off. "But that's just what you had planned, right? I'm not stupid, Gherm—no, whoever you are..." Her voice trailed off.

He did not know how to respond.

"You wanted this," Ghorza continued, her voice cracking. "You wanted to raise an army of the unfortunate for your own use." Her eyes burned holes into Lev's soul in their desperate search for any trace of her brother. "And judging by the look on your face... You may not be Gherm, but he's in there somewhere, right?"

Lev's sole desire in his new life was to leave his mark upon this world; Gherm, who refused to detach himself, was... *interfering* with his emotional regulation. In contrast to Lev, Gherm's only wish was for his sister and him to live happily. Though Gherm's wish was less ambitious, his love for his sister was strong enough to embed itself into Lev's soul. Thus, despite only having known her for two days, Ghorza felt as important to him as Maria.

Lev exhaled deeply with resignation. "You're right, and wrong, at the same time." Before she could ask another question, he raised a hand and continued. "The reason I'm doing all this is to protect the one bogey I care about—you."

"Me? But you're not the same Gherm I know."

"Not fully, yes. But it's just as you said before. I might be different, but in a way, I'm still your brother. So please don't reject me," he implored, something the unadulterated Lev would never have done under any circumstances.

Ghorza paused to collect her thoughts. She understood that "Gherm" was not her younger brother anymore. She knew he was someone different. But unlike the impostor she had encountered yesterday, the bogey now pleading for her not to reject him was identical to the Gherm she remembered.

She even felt that the original Gherm himself wanted her to accept this. Without her, he might one day disappear.

After a moment of quiet contemplation, she relaxed her guard and extended her hand to him "Fine... bro."

"Thanks, sis." He grabbed her hand and pulled her into a hug.

"Still early for this, but I'll make an exception." She returned the hug with some reluctance. "And I'm still going to keep calling you Gherm, but can you tell me your other name?" she requested, evidently still afraid that her brother was possessed.

A demon of Mal, the goddess of deception, was capable of tricking both the heart and mind. However, it was also fated to do one of two things when asked for its true name: it could either speak its name, binding itself as a servant to those who heard it, or bluntly refuse to reveal its name and undo the possession it had painstakingly carried out.

Lev chuckled at Ghorza's superstitiousness, but entertained it anyway. "His name was Leonard Erand Vandersteen, but people called him Lev."

"Then hit yourself, Lev," she ordered cheekily.

"Nope."

"Good enough for me." She giggled before both of them burst into laughter.

* * *

Pog was still in shock as he ambled about the tunnels, barely paying attention to where he was headed. That once-insignificant greyborn, Gherm, had seen into his soul.

After Vyrga expanded his territory last year and imposed taxes on all households whose heads didn't work for him, Pog had resisted at first. But eventually, the protection fees had grown too heavy a financial burden. As such, he'd joined Vyrga's gang five months ago to take care of his wife and three children.

He'd regretted it since.

As time passed, he'd learned how to desensitise himself to the constant guilt polluting his mind, and found himself vulnerable to cheap thrills at the expense of his family. Nowadays, he spent most of his time drunk between the legs of desperate whores whose households were unable to pay Vyrga's taxes. Transferring merits to his family was now little more than a chore he occasionally remembered to do. But after hearing Gherm's speech...

"Oh, gods... What kind of fuckwit have I been?

Pog straightened his back and marched home with the fires of hope in his eyes.

* * *

"Good morning, Ghorza," greeted Lev with a smile.

It took a moment for Ghorza to even realise that she was being addressed. For as long as Ghorza could remember, she had always woken up before Gherm had. Then she remembered his confession the day before. *This'll take some getting used to*, she thought to herself.

She stiffly returned his greeting. "Morning, bro."

Lev tried not to laugh. Even though he had survived meron powder two days ago and given her his "true" name yesterday, she had still tried to check whether he was a demon. On a surface level, she believed him; below the surface, she still feared that he was one. When she had made Lev chant a few religious hymns, he had complied, but when she had subsequently demanded that he submerge his hands, or rather dip his fingers, in the meagre reserve of salt they kept in the house, Lev had run out of patience—and seen an opportunity to mess with her.

The moment his claws had pierced the surface of the salt reserve, he had screamed as if in pain, nearly giving Ghorza a heart attack, before cackling uncontrollably at her frightened expression. In return, Ghorza had punched the wind out of him.

They prepared breakfast, then sat down to eat. Compared to the sectioned cave worm Lev would rather have forgotten, this meal was more austere, consisting of watered-down porridge made from unidentified grains, a few common insects, mushrooms, and turnips.

While the two siblings could normally spare only a few merits here and there to feed themselves, Ghorza permitted them to indulge every now and then with food sourced from either deeper levels of the cavern or imported from outside the cavern entirely. Of food from deeper within the cavern, insects and mushrooms were cheap and readily obtainable; the fuzzy cave worm from two days prior was a major indulgence, significantly more expensive than insects and mushrooms. Of food from outside the cave, grains cost less than vegetables, including turnips which, for vegetables, were still quite cheap.

"Are you sure you wanna go to the mines?" asked Ghorza between bites. She pointed at Lev's bandage. "How are you going to work with that wound? Doesn't it hurt?"

"Of course it hurts, but I have to go. We need all the merits we can get, and if I want to build up my reputation, I have to show up. Also, I need to discuss something important with Rak."

"Fine. But make sure not to get into any more trouble. I wish I could stay home with you until you recover. It would be safer for you that way."

"Safety... Ah! Though it's expensive, make sure to bring home some blocks of wood, a new stone knife for carving wood, some copper nails, and a hammer today."

Ghorza was dumbfounded. "Why in the world would we need that crap? You're neither a carpenter nor an artist, so why do you suddenly want to bankrupt us?"

"Safety concerns. I want to buy and install a door at the entrance of the house to prevent others from breaking in."

"But Gherm, everyone else uses rags or leather to cover their doorways and nobody else gets robbed, so why would we? What would they steal from us anyway?"

Lev narrowed his eyes at the stubborn girl. "It's not about stealing, it's about murder and arson. Even though most sides of our house are protected by cavern walls, as long as we don't protect the entrance, others can simply barge in whenever they want."

"And I'm saying nobody will come inside and kill us. Vyrga's a wretch, but he's not stupid. Our dad, may he rest in the cycle, chose this very spot because it was the safest. We're right next to the guard station."

"I'm just saying—"

"We've already been blocking the entrance with a large rock at night. What more do you want?

Lev rubbed his temples before replying. "With the exception of Kul and his apprentices, the guards here aren't very reliable and could be bribed. I appreciate your confidence in our safety, but we really do need the door."

"Seriously?" Ghorza rolled her eyes. "Listen, I'm not gonna blow our life savings on your paranoia! Even if we build a door, any group of maniacs with axes can just chop through it. Heck, even a large hammer would work."

"Alright, alright. I get it. But I'm still going to get one once I get enough merits."

"As long as we don't starve, you can knock yourself out."

They quietly finished their meal and went out to receive their assignments. It was the same as last time, except Kul was more worried about Lev due to his injury. Normally slaves were made to work each day until the taskmaster was satisfied, but Kul had convinced the taskmaster to give Lev permission to leave early if his injury proved prohibitive.

As Lev walked into the mining quarter, he was showered with praise from fellow slaves who had watched the fight the previous day. Their respect and adoration were clear as they observed his small, damaged, yet regal form.

He held his head high and proud, yet unlike the warriors and nobles, he made sure to devote attention to anyone who tried to talk to him no matter how wretched they looked. No matter what people thought of him before, he was now a leader. He needed to exhibit the respect and authority befitting one.

"Hey, Gherm!" hollered a voice from afar.

"Hey, Hem," replied Gherm with a friendly smile.

As the two shook hands, the surrounding crowd suddenly understood why Rak and his men had resumed providing protection to them. Clearly, they'd talked something through with Lev.

"Hey, you slackers, get back to work!" yelled an overseer. The bogeys returned their attention to their respective tasks.

As Hem approached Lev, he leaned in and whispered, "There's something important that Rak needs to tell you."

Lev's smile faded and was replaced with a determined look. He nodded at Hem and they snuck away to meet with Rak at the northwestern side of the first floor of the mining area.

"Right on time," said Rak. "So Gherm, how's your arm?"

Lev smiled ruefully. "Fine and dandy. Could still use a week or two. How's life?"

"Shitty as always. And you better hope that arm heals fast, considering what'll happen in two weeks."

Lev's blood ran cold. "What's going to happen in two weeks?"

Rak smiled wryly. "Another expedition."

CHAPTER 8
WEAPONS AND SLAVES

"Thrust!" commanded Lev.

More than thirty greyborns thrust their blunt wooden spears forwards. Their movements were almost, but not quite, in unison. Lev strode through the ranks, fixing his soldiers' movements as he did so.

Two weeks had passed since Rak's announcement, and today should have been the day they set out on the expedition. Fortunately, the Jiira suffered an attack by the Kur, and the expedition leader had been heavily injured in the defence. As such, they'd received word that the expedition was to be delayed until three weeks from today.

Thank goodness for small miracles, thought Lev. Rak had assigned him an area just outside the mining area to train his men. It'd allow for them to work when the overseers demanded it, and train when they had some spare time. However, due to time restrictions, it had taken him a week and a half just to teach his bogeys to follow basic commands and stand in formation, and even then, they typically failed to maintain formation longer than a few seconds.

Accordingly, Lev had changed his lesson plan: his men were to fight in three-man groups, each consisting of two spear wielders and a shield bearer. The shield bearer would draw the enemy's attention and block their attacks. At the same time, one of the spear wielders would thrust at the enemy's feet while the other thrust at a vital point such as the chest or head.

It was hardly a sophisticated formation and would probably make military experts cringe, but it was simple enough for these complete rookies to master it in time for the expedition. Lev would have improved it if he had more time, men, and resources, but sadly, his group had just gained its thirty-second member three days ago.

Lev's left arm itched underneath the bandage, but he resisted the urge to scratch. The gash was healing as well as it could; he estimated it would need just another week to heal into a nasty scar.

If only I had *more time, I could train some archers, too,* he quietly lamented. Most greyborn hunters relied on traps, javelins, and melee weapons rather than bows and arrows to hunt; archery required flexible wood and feathers for fletching, both of which were difficult to procure in a cave. Understandably, archers were quite rare underground, and the few who did make appearances were almost always accompanying blue bogey nobles, or at least were goblins themselves.

"Gher— I mean, sir!" Volker, one of the younger trainees, called out to Lev. Volker had been one of the first to join Lev's faction and had visibly trained the hardest. It was he and his brother whom Vyrga's lackeys had targeted when Lev had interfered. Volker saw Lev as a hero; Volker's brother had thought otherwise.

"What?" Lev asked the youth in an agitated tone. Nothing was going the way he had planned, and he had a hunch that nothing Volker was about to tell him would help.

"U-Uhm..." The youth stuttered and trailed off.

"Get on with it, Volker. It's not like it can get worse than—"

"Ow!" interrupted one of the new recruits, who was trying to eavesdrop. "What was *that* for?" One of his comrades was turning around and had accidentally hit him.

"Sorry!"

And that's why they're training with blunt spears, Lev remembered, shaking his head.

"Um... Mr. Gherm— I-I mean... Sir?"

"*Yes,* Volker?"

"I've never fought before, but I've seen some overseers cull hivelings. Wouldn't it be better to get some ranged support?"

"Of *course* it would be better to get some ranged support. Concentrated volleys are deadly. But we can't get archers. The stingy upper class and the goblins have a monopoly on them," Lev complained.

"P-P-Please remember not to insult them to their faces, sir." Volker reminded Lev for the twentieth time since he joined Lev's group. "And what's a... mo-no-po-ly?"

"I'd never do something that stupid, and to answer your question, in simple terms a monopoly is when a single person or a group of people have full control over a resource, so they alone can decide who can and cannot access it. Sadly, according to Rak, that piece of shit Vyrga's got four archers, while Rak and we haven't got squat, hence the wooden helmets and chest guards." Lev had used all the merits he had earned from his burgeoning faction and working in the mines over the past week and a half to furnish whatever he could for his troops, and had managed to convince Rak to donate old equipment to fill in the gaps.

"Why not use slings or javelins?"

"Rocks shot from slings are too weak to harm a hiveling's body, and how many javelins can the average greyborn carry? Eight to ten?"

"That's something I've been wondering about. Why rocks? If we tweak them, can't slings be attached to a wooden body and used as bows to shoot arrows?"

Lev's eyes lit up. "Slingshots? Oh! Nice idea." Lev commended. But his joy faded as quickly as it had arrived.

"W-What's wrong, sir?" asked the lad nervously.

"We can't make arrows because we lack fletching." Lev grunted through clenched teeth. "Not to mention that we can't make slingshots because we don't have rubber. Lucky us!" he declared, throwing his hands up in exasperation.

"Rubber?"

Damn! I shouldn't have said that, Lev thought. *There's no way any of these primitives would know what rubber is.* He now had to come up with an answer that would satisfy the curious lad without also giving him any reason to suspect Gherm was anything other than a greyborn slave.

Lev made a show of furtively scanning their surroundings. "I heard a rumour that an exiled shaman has created a wondrous and flexible material that he calls 'rubber.' It's extremely stretchy, yet durable," he whispered into the young bogey's ear. "From what I know, after the discovery, the nobles hunted him down, and once they caught him, they hid his invention from the public eye and killed him. We shouldn't take this any further, agreed?"

Volker nodded vigorously—nobody wanted to end up on the nobles' bad side.

"Good." Lev was relieved that the lad believed his lie, as he certainly wouldn't have believed it himself.

"So slings it is, sir?"

"Yup. There's nothing wrong with them as a ranged weapon. They're user-friendly, deadly within the range we'd use them, and versatile enough to launch almost anything, but hivelings and heavily armoured creatures would just shake off the rocks we'd sling at them. If we had something better than rocks for ammo, that would be great. Something metal would be great, but the goblins and nobles have made sure none of that will reach us. So I guess we'll have to make do with rocks." Lev rambled. "Unless we want to be creative, in which case we could try clay bottles—"

"Clay bottles?" This was the first time Volker had heard of people using clay bottles as weaponry.

"That's right. You can fill them with all kinds of nasty surprises. Paralysing poison, sleeping powder, you name it. You can even fill them with oil and set your enemies on fire." Lev smiled at the idea of setting his enemies on fire, but that smile did not persist.

"Sadly, useful quantities of poison, powder, and oil cost more than we can afford, and I don't even think we can afford even a drop of cyfrac oil." Cyfracs were a rare family of plants, found on the fifth floor and below, that resembled a red-coloured rye and were easily combustible. Their oil had many uses from ceremonies to smithing, but was most valued by shamans and witch doctors because its flames spread fast and lasted a long time.

"But it's so useful!"

"Yes, it is useful, but we can't get it. Even if we could, our supply would be severely limited. The best thing for a rope sling would be metal rounds, but we can't get those either."

Lev and Volker silently watched the new recruits train.

"Maybe we can." Volker piped up suddenly.

"How?"

"Would lead rounds work?"

"Absolutely. A good lead shot could pierce a bronze helmet. But I checked with Rak and some others. We can get lead and copper, but we can only get it in ore form, and there are no weapon masters or smiths who deal with greyborns, unless you count the lowliest of craftsmen.

And even they can't forge for themselves—they have to request smiths to cast the pieces, which they just assemble, decorate, and sell." Lev had searched high and low for ways greyborns could arm themselves better, but had discovered no leads. Greyborns had been very effectively cut off from potential means of rebellion.

"I know someone."

"*What?*" Lev nearly shouted, shocking his nearby troops.

He turned, calming them down, before returning his attention to Volker.

"He's an exile that my dad saved a long time ago. I can get him to help us, but knowing his personality, he won't do it for free. The only thing I can assure you of is that it won't be too pricey."

"That I can work with," remarked Lev excitedly.

"B-But there's one problem," stuttered Volker. He knew how much Lev hated the word "but."

"What is it?"

"Well, he refuses to reveal his identity to anyone but my dad and a select few, so only I can see him." Volker was surprised at how quickly he had explained the situation, and he worried that Gherm considered his abruptness rude. "S-Sorry, sir."

"Let me guess, he used to be some great and arrogant smith, but he pissed off some nobles who wanted him dead, not just exiled, so he hid in the only place someone of his calibre would never set foot in—the slave quarters. Right?" Lev intentionally matched Volker's conversational pace from earlier. "And his reason for hiding isn't just that those nobles are after him, but also that his already-damaged ego cannot handle anyone else recognizing his former identity."

"H-How did you know, sir?"

"I have a... gift when it comes to these sorts of things." *And it was a common scenario in my world's politics,* Lev thought to himself shamelessly. "Anyway, after training, go and cut us a deal. Lead projectiles would be a game-changer!"

"Really?" questioned Volker, bewildered.

"Yeah, really. Now go!"

"Yes, sir!" Volker saluted before running back to his snickering companions.

Lev glared at Volker's associates. "You find this funny?" he snarled.

"N-N-N-No!" the now-pale trainees replied.

"'No, *what?*"

"No, sir!"

"Good! Then straighten your backs, get into positions and run five laps around the training grounds!"

"Yes, sir!" the men shouted with all their hearts.

More than a week under Lev had taught them how to respond to his orders and what kind of punishment they could expect if they defied him.

"And don't forget your training spears!"

"Yes, sir!" his poor soldiers shakily answered, about to break into tears.

Lev grinned. Playing the role of a sergeant from hell was quite fun.

As the recruits began their run, Lev joined them. He needed to be fit for battle as well, after all.

Once they finished their laps, Lev gave Volker permission to leave immediately and ordered the two trainees to retrieve the centipede he'd locked inside the acid pits.

I'll need something to test these bullets on. If it can't pierce the centipede's exoskeleton, it certainly won't pierce a hiveling warrior's.

Soon after, Volker contacted him: he was waiting for Lev near the training grounds.

Volker showed Lev a few samples from the smith, lead bullets the size of his thumb that had been masterfully crafted in various shapes. They mainly came in either the form of flat, elongated bullets with sharpened ends or oblong ones with one pointy and one round end each. They were all adorned with the symbol of the war god Jorm and artistic carvings in a way that wouldn't hamper their performance.

As much as Lev liked their designs, looks alone would not secure any victories. The centipede had been carefully moved on a cart and now lay lifeless at the centre of the training grounds.

Lev pulled out a sling he had prepared for the occasion. He tied a slip knot, slid his middle finger into the loop, and pinched the handle between his forefinger and thumb. Closing his eyes, he cleared his mind of any distractions. Then he opened his eyes, placed an oblong bullet into the pouch, and drew the missile back into a wide vertical orbit.

He raised his arm and swung it down behind his head, tightening the first orbit before taking a pitcher's step. As the missile reached the top of its second orbit, he completed a step forward and released the handle as his wrist snapped forward, releasing the bullet.

Volker gasped as the speeding bullet raced forward, looking to pierce through the centipede's chitin with all its might.

Bang!

The bullet pierced the centre of the centipede's head, leaving a deep mark. Lev and Volker moved closer to examine the bullet. It was slightly deformed in the front, but had held together.

"Volker."

"Yes, Mr. Gherm—I mean sir!"

"Tell him that we'll need a lot of bullets, but drop the decorations," Lev told him with a smile.

"Y-Yes, sir!" replied the youth with vigour before marching towards the smith.

* * *

"So how was your day?" Ghorza asked Lev during a wonderful dinner of insects, porridge, and turnips.

"It was good. I managed to cross a few things off my agenda," he replied. It really had been a good day.

"Great. Well, my day was pretty hectic. I was working so hard even the overseer was telling me to take a break. You realise how bad that is, right? That the person in charge of working me to death is telling me to take care of myself?"

"Yeah, I know it's been hard on you."

"I know. So I began telling her why I'm doing this and how you..."

While Ghorza prattled on and on, Lev thought back to his successes of the day. Namely finding a sustainable source of ranged weaponry for future use.

It's a good thing those greyborns know how to use slings, he thought. Most bogeys supplemented their diet by knocking down critters off the cavern ceiling. *Now I just need to teach them how to use slings in combat.*

"Wouldn't you agree?" Ghorza asked.

"Yeah, sure," he replied. *I do need to expand the number of formations though. Basic formations like a phalanx always have a fatal weakness which in its case is that its flanks are exposed to attacks and it's quite rigid, making applying any changes, or even turning, hard. Historically, that weakness was solved when a great conqueror thought of applying light infantry battalions which among their main functions was protecting the flanks. But we're lacking in numbers...*

"Are you even paying attention?" Ghorza asked with a glare.

"Yeah, sure," he replied. *Maybe I could—*

"Gherm!"

"Wha— huh?"

"You've been spacing out a lot lately," Ghorza said, worried.

"Sorry, I've just had a lot on my plate. Rak decided to give my group the market tunnel area. With the overseers and how much interference there is from smugglers and other gangs, it's not terribly lucrative. At least it won't be in the short-term. Things have been quite hard."

"I know. Just... stay out of trouble, okay?"

"Don't worry about me. You should worry about yourself more. You look like you're gonna fall asleep right now." Lev chuckled.

"You're not the only one working hard, and one of us needs to save some extra merits," she nagged while shooting him a look, "because *some* ambitious bloke keeps spending all of his."

"Sorry, not sorry. It's for a better future."

"I hope. Are you done eating? We should sleep soon."

"Sure. But wash your hands first."

"I got it already! Sheesh." She had become more accustomed to Lev's antics recently.

They tidied the dining table, washed up, and went to bed early.

Lev, too, had become more accustomed to sleeping on Gherm's rickety bed, and promptly fell into a deep slumber.

Regrettably, however, he was unable to sleep as long as he had wanted—early the next morning, he was awoken by a scream from the dining area. He immediately grabbed his knife and rushed in, finding a teary-eyed Ghorza kneeling speechless, staring at the dining table. Her hands covered her mouth as she resisted the urge to puke.

On the table were three heads: one from the fat thug, Pog, and two small enough to have come from young bogeys. Their untarnished faces were frozen in pain and anguish.

Looks like I need to secure the house after all, thought Lev.

CHAPTER 9
A RAT'S WILL

Inside a small room filled with wooden carvings and a few carving knives, a forlorn, middle-aged greyborn played a sad tune that spoke of the misery of life.

Greyborns outside his circle would wonder how he had learned to play the flute; the upper class of bogeys would wonder why he had chosen to learn the flute. Not that there was anything wrong with flutes, but in bogey society, flutes belonged in the hands of priests and poets, while warriors and nobles preferred the lur. But this bogey was neither priest nor poet, neither warrior nor noble. He was a greyborn.

He played his tune while pondering the cruel joke that was life, especially his own. His miserable life during which his highborn father had rejected him because of his grey skin. His miserable life during which his greyborn mother had blamed him for ruining hers. His miserable life during which he had suffered beating after beating from the brute she had remarried to not only to hide the truth of his birth, but also to increase her own standing within the greyborn caste.

His miserable life in which his "father" had allowed their neighbours and his enemies to take out their frustrations and anger on his "son" without retaliation .

He had grown up accepting such misery as normal. He had rarely cried, but when he did, neither god nor man had answered. As such, he had understood from a young age that he was alone and his pain did not matter. Nothing mattered.

He had never expected his life to change, but one day, he saw something on his way home.

In his early teens, to pay back some of the debt he "owed" his family for raising him, he'd been forced to fight in a gambling ring prepared by the brute's gang.

Night after night, he would walk home, battered after winning a fight against other similarly misfortunate youth. Along the way, he frequently observed the neighbourhood boys amusing themselves with rat fights. They'd learned to deprive the rats of food to turn them aggressive, then force them to fight over their scraps.

One night, he'd watched as one of the rats snapped and bit its owner's fingers—and as its life was stamped into oblivion.

Seeing this, the teen had come to a realisation. *If even an animal can't accept a life like this... then how can I?*

The teen feared death—he conjectured the rat had as well—but dreams of liberation blossomed inside his heart regardless. Every day he had observed the rats revolt, and his heart revolted with them.

Why do they fight knowing that they can't win? Why choose defiance over life? he had quietly inquired of them. As he'd watched the last rat, pocket knife stuck in its side, snarl in defiance down to its last twitch, it had clicked in his mind.

I don't have to live like this. I can free myself. Even if I suffer for my insolence, so what? I'm already suffering. Even if I get killed, so what? I'll eventually die someday. Even if I'll be cursed by the gods for parricide, so what? By what right can the gods, who ignore not only me but so many more, decide that I must live through this hell? They can shove their holy laws up their asses!

In that moment, he had sworn to not abide by anyone else's laws, orders, or moral codes ever again for as long as he lived.

Then, he had steeled his resolve and plotted his parents' demise.

At the time, he might have been naïve in the ways of the world, but he had been no fool. He had predicted that although he could win in a one-on-one fight against his bastard of a stepfather, it was unlikely he could do so without sustaining severe injuries. Then, he'd be at the mercy of his mother.

So, he had concocted a simpler plan. Had his parents cared enough to notice his inclination, the plan would have fallen through, but they had been too complacent in their delusion that they would always control him.

He had begun by poisoning their food. He hadn't used a lethal poison, but rather a sleeping agent that he had stolen from an herbalist peddling their wares near the ring. His stepfather's henchmen had ridiculed him as his father's little slave boy his whole life, but they had also respected his strength. He now sought to seize their loyalty.

In the dead of night, blood-curdling screams had woken many from their sleep. They had rushed out from their homes to see what the commotion was, only to wish that they never had—the old crime boss screeched with pain as his own "son" hacked off his arms and legs at their joints with a stone-headed axe. And that wasn't all—his son had then skinned the boss alive. True, the neighbours had hated the old bastard, wanted him dead, and were painfully aware of what he had done to the boy on a daily basis, but this was too much, too *cruel*.

That night, many of them had vomited onto the ground as though seeking to purge their minds; those who had willed themselves not to vomit after watching the child slaughter his "father" invariably lost the second battle of wills when he did the same to his mother.

The boy had surveyed the crowd, focusing intently on the gathering of thugs frozen in horror at what had become of their leader, and spoke. "Tonight you witnessed the end of the old pig. Now tell me... Whom do you now serve?"

With that, a new leader had been born, and his name was—

"Oy, boss!" yelled a male voice as the door slammed open, disrupting the flow of both the music and the flautist's recollection.

"Os! You'd better have something important, or it's *your* head that's going to be rolling today," threatened Vyrga.

Oswald, more commonly known as Os, chuckled. He was sure that most goblinoids would be shocked to learn that one of the bloodiest greyborn gang leaders spent his free time not only playing the flute, but also carving wood and writing poetry. If they heard that Vyrga was carving something, they'd likely assume that he was carving the living skull of a virgin maiden into a new cup, not carving a chunk of wood into the shape of a bird.

Well, that's the type of guy he makes himself out to be, Os sighed. He, on the other hand, knew another side of Vyrga, the side that had practically raised him.

During the early days of his gang leadership, Vyrga had needed to build his own group of loyal subordinates to replace the old bastard's circle. Thus, he had searched for other abandoned noble bastards like himself and personally trained them to be his own elite force, different from the scum that made up the rest of his organisation. He had managed to find ten such cases, among whom Os was the third oldest.

None of his chosen few knew why Vyrga had trained them instead of normal children. Maybe it was empathy for kindred spirits, or maybe it was pragmatism on the off chance that he could establish connections with some nobles. What they did understand was that Vyrga saw no difference between a powerful chief and a crippled beggar. For Vyrga, life was life, and the end of all life was death. In any case, almost all of the ten chosen were thankful for his care. Almost.

"You were right. Gelmar is a traitor," reported Os.

"Figures." spat Vyrga in disdain. He'd known of Gelmar's disposition since childhood, and yet he'd wished all this time that he was wrong. After all, Gelmar had been the first child to follow him. To Vyrga, Gelmar had been both a son and a friend.

"Why is he doing this, though? Why does he want to take over?"

"Don't fool yourself, Os." Vyrga flipped his flute over and ran his fingers down its body. "We all know Gelmar's power-hungry. It didn't sit well with him that you and Heimo are more likely to succeed me. But unlike Ludger and Bolo, he doesn't respect me enough to wait until I die before setting his plan in motion. He wants everything for himself, right now."

"Wait... what? Ludger and Bolo want to take over as well?"

"No, those two spoke to me earlier. They told me that if anything happens to me, they'll leave and form their own gang. Ludger doesn't find you fit to be my replacement, and we both know that Bolo is always following behind his older brother. You and Ludger have always competed to be my second-in-command, and he's got you matched in terms of skill and competence, which makes him justifiably unsatisfied with the decision."

"If we're so evenly matched, why did you choose me?"

"Because you're the more cool-headed one. Ludger has quite the temper."

Os wasn't quite convinced that that was the only reason. In his experience, he knew that there were times when a passionate leader like Ludger, who could inspire his men to march through hell, would prove more valuable than a calm, thoughtful leader like himself.

Vyrga looked up from his flute. "And between you and me, I get along with you more."

"I... see," Os replied, half grateful and half disappointed. Though he appreciated that Vyrga favoured him, it did not feel right that favouritism had tipped the balance.

Os felt strangely obligated to speak up for Ludger, but Vyrga preempted his protest. "Ludger knows the true reason and he has no problem with it. He knows that you're closer to me and my ideals than he or any of the others will be, and he doesn't hate you for it."

"But boss, does he hate you?"

"Probably not." Vyrga shrugged. "Os, do you know why I kept teaching you all that the world is unfair, unruly, and unkind? I want you all to accomplish great things without the chains of laws, morals, society, the gods, or a traitorous idiot who thinks he's smart enough to use your own philosophy against you," he emphasised.

"Oh, right. What'll we do about Gelmar?"

"Remember when I told you to send the deserter's head to the fledgling?"

"To Gherm? Yes, yes I did. That wasn't just a warning, right? Don't you think using Pog like that was a bit... extreme?"

"To answer your first question, no, it *was* a mere warning, but not for the reason you think. It was to rile the fledgling up before testing him."

Os' eyes widened. "You're going to send Gelmar to attack him."

"Yup." Vyrga nonchalantly placed his flute off to the side. "I've heard about how he's training his men, and believe me, he's not training them to play lord of the slums—he's training an army. He's as ambitious as I am."

"And if he fails?"

"Then he'll be proven worthless. Would be a shame, really. Not too many folks in our world who can stand up to corruption."

Os nodded. "If you say so. But again, wasn't punishing Pog like that too extreme?"

"For a deserter? Not really. People like that agree to commit all sorts of crimes and atrocities when it's convenient for them, but when they've reached their limit, they think they can wash their hands of it all just like that. They excuse their actions by saying that they had no other choice, even though I never told them to kill and rape. I actually don't like enabling those kinds of activities."

"Yet... you don't stop them. No offence, boss, but that's hypocrisy."

"It is, but if I had to stop every sadistic idiot who does the first thing on his mind, we'd never have grown this big. Besides, infamy has its uses.

It gets these scum in line. And we won't keep them forever—they'll be purged as fodder when it's time to break our shackles."

"But what about the kids? Since when do we kill kids?"

Vyrga hesitated. "We don't. I left the task of killing the lout to Gelmar and he took it too far," he said with a tinge of regret. "Thankfully, Bolo managed to save the wife and daughter and sneak them out of our territory with some extra merits added to their pockets, which is better than leaving them there. Considering those kids were already dead, well, I did approve the use of their heads."

"That's horrible—"

"It is, but we do what we need to do. We'll have our entire lives to regret our actions." Vyrga sighed again. "Right now it's time to call Gelmar. Tell him to gather his men and prepare to attack."

"Alright, boss." Os turned to leave the room.

"Oh, one more thing."

"Yes?"

"There's a "parcel" that we need to deliver to one of our noble *customers*. Remind the courier that we only accept payment in bronze, not merits."

"Shouldn't all our couriers know this by now? They've all accompanied us on our visits to the pigs above."

"This courier is new, and this will be his first assignment. If he fails, it'll be his last," Vyrga said with a sneer.

"As requested. Anything else?"

"No, on your way."

"Will do," he replied before leaving the room

Vyrga was alone again at last. He gingerly picked his flute back up and raised it to his lips. *Don't disappoint me, Gherm. If that's who you really are,* he thought before playing his sad tune once again.

CHAPTER 10
THE LIBERATOR

Inside an ordinary command tent, guarded by even more ordinary-looking grey bogeys, a plan for Lev's inevitable battle against Gelmar forces was being discussed.

"With Rak's men blocking the other routes, his forces will have to come through the corpse-eater caves close to the southwestern slave quarters, which is exactly where we want them," Lev explained as his fingers traced a map of the cave systems laid out on the table in front of him. It'd taken Lev a lot of effort to convince Kul to give him the tattered piece of parchment along with the tools to sketch on it.

Lev lifted his finger. "Volker, how are the barriers coming?"

"The men say they'll be ready by morning. Even if it kills them," Volker promptly replied. He'd grown a bit more accustomed to Lev, but seeing the serious look on the naturally peaceful and playful-looking Gherm always stresses him out like nothing else.

"It will, if they're not ready when Gelmar's army arrives," Lev declared without a hint of emotion.

Volker gulped at the thought. "Yessir. I'll remind them of that."

Volker hesitated. Something had been on his mind ever since they'd started planning for the battle, but he wasn't quite sure how to bring the topic up in an appropriate manner.

He gathered his courage and spoke up. "Sir? I'm a little worried. The men are pretty scared. We're outnumbered, and most of our men have never fought in a battle before. They're not just worried about their own lives, either. We've all heard what Gelmar does to the families of his enemies."

Families... Lev made a mental note.

"As a result, the morale around camp is quite low. I think there's a way to solve it, but..." Volker added.

"But what? Let's hear it."

* * *

I can't believe I'm doing this, Lev thought as he walked through a tunnel unfamiliar to him.

Its cave walls had various paintings, ornately decorated. They told a tale of reverence for the gods with robed green bogeys bowing before the red eye, Zeja's symbol.

Since ancient days, generals have sought the favour of the gods before battle. It seems some things are universal, Lev concluded.

The painting's tale went on before coming to a sudden end. A giant wooden door stood before Lev. The red eye of Zeja drawn on the door almost seemed to have a life of its own, observing Lev with both curiosity and respect. *Though I can see how superstitious nonsense like this sprouts strong roots in the hearts of bogeys... and men.*

Lev pushed against the door, but it didn't budge. "Hello? Anyone here?"

On cue, the door opened, revealing two robed figures bowing on the smooth cave floor before him.

"There you are. I'm here to see Priestess Kathaga?"

One of the hooded figures looked up at Lev.

"All who wish to see the priestess must be cleansed," the acolyte declared, his face still shrouded in darkness.

The other robed figure now stood up and motioned Lev to enter the small side cavern which had been previously sealed by the giant door.

Upon entering, Lev immediately noticed the countless stalactites hanging from the ceiling. He followed the acolytes until they ordered him to sit down on the cavern's floor and wait for the cleanser.

It didn't take long for the cleanser to arrive. An old green bogey woman in simple worn clothes with tied back hair kneeled in front of Lev on a folded blanket.

She bowed before Lev. "I am here to serve." Her eyes didn't stray from the ground. "Meron water clears the soul. You must drink it two times."

Even though she had all the manners of a servant, she felt too eloquent, too refined. Lev would've thought longer before following her instructions had she not mentioned the accursed Meron water.

Meron water? Oh, great. Let's hope it works about as well as last time.

"Where do I get the water?"

The old woman looked towards the ceiling, Lev followed her gaze. Two stalactites, wrapped with thin vines gracefully dripped droplets towards a cup on the ground.

"The gods provide. Wait until the cup is filled with meron water from each of the two hanging rocks."

Lev turned his back towards the woman and focussed on the cup slowly filling up droplet by droplet.

It only took three minutes for Lev's demeanour to change to that of a cranky old man cursed with boredom.

"You seem impatient," the woman said.

"I'm going to be fighting a battle. I don't want it to start without me."

Even though Lev couldn't see it, the old woman grinned. "Strange. Most men would flee battle."

"I guess I'm not most men."

"Why is this battle so important to you?"

Lev felt her eyes burning through his back. "I doubt you'd understand."

"This is a temple of Zeja, the goddess of war. Who would understand better?"

Another droplet fell into the cup. "You have a point. This battle will decide my future. If I win, then I'll be able to change this world into a better place."

Splash. Another droplet had fallen into the cup.

"If I fail, my men will die, and I'll be killed."

The cup was now almost full. Lev grabbed it and turned towards the woman. Her grin was replaced by a neutral expression, the same she'd worn before.

"Is this enough water?"

The woman gestured to him. "It is. Drink."

Holding back the urge to vomit, Lev gulped the contents of the cup. *Bleah! Still tastes like sewer.*

"You said you will make this world a better place. What do you fight for?" the woman asked after Lev had emptied his cup.

Gherm crouched in front of the second stalactite, filling his cup again.

"Justice. I want the world to be just."

"Young one, there is no just world. The world itself is uneven, and justice for one means injustice for another."

Lev suppressed a frown.

Trust me, I've seen how unjust a world can be last time around.

"Your justice is another's injustice. It is a cycle that never ends, except in blood," the old servant added.

Through gritted teeth, Lev tried to remain calm as he looked over his shoulder. "A strange thing for someone who worships a god of war to say. Doesn't your god desire blood?"

"Zeja desires only to bring out the best in this world. Living things grow stronger through conflict," the woman explained.

"I'm pretty sure the dead don't grow stronger," Lev interjected.

"The victors do."

Lev straightened his back and turned around to face the woman. The cup behind him slowly filled up. "If I say your god is crazy, will your priestess be offended?"

The old bogey laughed, revealing shining white teeth. "HAHAHAHA!!!"

Her previously calm demeanour had changed into that of a superior scolding her servants.

"All the gods are mad. If they weren't, would our world be like this?"

Lev turned his attention back to the cup. Only a few droplets were required to fill it now.

"So what," Lev said, "Do I have a choice? Do I quit? Live the life of a lowly worm?"

The woman chuckled. "Foolish child, your heart is so filled with anger that you can't see you fight the wrong enemy."

Lev grabbed the cup with both hands.

"The gods are not against you."

He drank the water.

"You do their bidding."

"So tell me then," Lev said as he faced the woman again, "Priestess Kathaga…"

"Whom should I fight?"

The old woman smiled, her eyes finally meeting Lev's as equals.

"Not so foolish after all, I see."

"You have fine teeth for an old servant living on roots."

Kathaga grinned. "Well played. But I am no god."

"Gods or men, I will beat them all. And anyone else who stands in my way," Lev stated.

"A world shaped by blood will remain a world of blood and violence. Are you challenging the mad gods? Or merely doing their will?"

Lev frowned. "You're saying I'm nothing but a pawn?"

"Can you be sure that you aren't?" Kathaga enquired.

Lev stood up, dusting himself off. "Okay that's enough of this religious nonsense."

I've seen enough at the orphanage last time around.

Lev felt a strange sensation wash over his back as he turned around to walk away from the priestess. Her eyes seemed to pass straight through him. It'd been the same sensation he'd felt when he'd stood before the giant door sporting Zeja's eye.

"You don't want Zeja's blessing for your army then?"

Gherm waved, still facing the exit. "Let your god decide who to bless. I have a war to win."

After having exited the tunnel, he marched back into his camp. It didn't take long for a weary Volker to join him.

"How did it go, sir?"

"It... went," Lev started before pausing.

Even if I don't have Zeja's blessing, I still need to bolster my men's morale. Volker was right about that part. I'll figure something out. I could try Jorm's temple but everyone knows that since he's Zeja's son, his temple is a subsidiary to hers. I'll likely get rejected.

"The goddess of war has spoken. Gather the men together."

A short while later, Lev stood on a raised platform in front of his assembled men.

"Everyone, I want..." Lev began.

"The priestess has arrived!" an acolyte announced behind the crowd of soldiers. A procession of robed figures came into view as Lev's men made room. Priestess Kathaga walked in front, now fully dressed in her white robes, face covered by a mask, with the crimson eye of Zeja on her chest.

Upon noticing it was the priestess who'd joined Lev's speech, his men backed off to make a path for the priestess and dropped to their knees in reverence.

With slow, purposeful steps, the priestess made her way to the front of the platform. "General. May I bless your army before the coming battle?"

Lev stared into her eyes for a moment before gesturing for her to join him on the platform. "Be my guest."

Once atop the platform, Kathaga turned to face the crowd and stretched her arms wide. "Brave warriors! Zeja, the goddess of war, has sent me to put her blessings upon you and give you the strength to overcome your enemies."

The crowd cheered in unison, glad that Zeja was on their side.

"She has also commanded me to give your general a new name, the name of a great warrior he deserves."

Lev felt an uneasy tension tightening around his neck.

"Henceforth," the priestess continued, "Gherm shall be known as Lev the Liberator!"

Lev's army began to cheer again as they raised their fists in celebration.

"LEV! LEV! LEV! LEV!" they cried out loud.

The priestess leaned in closer to Lev, a satisfied expression graced her visage.

"How did you..." Lev asked. He'd never experienced a feeling like this before. This woman knew far more than your average zealot.

The soft smile on her face didn't ease the tension Lev felt. "Your time in the shadows is finished, Lev."

"Show the gods what you can do."

CHAPTER 11
GREY ANGST

Silence.

Silence enveloped the camp as the gathered bogeys stood at attention. The gathering of these newly-organised vagrants fell under the command of one greyborn, Gelmar.

Few would ever have expected such discipline from this bunch of lowlifes. Composed of some of the vilest of Vyrga's men, it was also one of the largest parties under his banner.

However, all eighty of them now looked as tame and obedient as puppies for one reason alone: to avoid their leader's wrath.

Gelmar was livid. Not only had Vyrga chosen someone else to succeed him, but now he'd also sent him off to put down a runt. Not just any runt, but one commanding enough troops to threaten Gelmar's numbers. True, the enemy's force was only half his own, but it was clear his men wouldn't come out unscathed. It was painfully, maddeningly obvious that Vyrga was culling his numbers to crush even the possibility of a coup.

The area, save for the angry shouts, yelps of pain, and other noises of chaos leaking out of Gelmar's tent, was deathly silent. The tension in the air was palpable.

The soft pitter-patter of footsteps approached from behind. The rearmost men turned to see a hooded figure approaching. They raised their weapons, prepared to drive the intruder away, but they soon lowered their weapons and made a path for the newcomer once they realised who it was.

Two soldiers exited Gelmar's tent. The first seemed dazed, with a bloody forehead. The second had his arm around the first, supporting them so that they could walk.

The newcomer called out to them. "Hey, you there."

The uninjured soldier looked towards the hooded figure and nodded. "Oh, Heimo."

"What's wrong with this man?"

The soldier looked to his side, trying to avoid Heimo's gaze. "Ah, it's nothing. Delk here just slipped and hit his head."

Seeing him trying to avoid the question, Heimo sighed. "I see. Have him looked after," he advised before making his way towards the tent.

"Boss?" The man called out to Heimo. "Be careful. Gelmar's in a bad way."

"Thank you. I'll try not to... slip. Take care."

With one hand on the tent's flap, he uncovered the entrance to find a frustrated Gelmar polishing a copper goblet.

"Come to see the show, Heim?" He grumbled.

"Aren't you being too harsh on your men?" Heimo asked back.

Without raising his head, Gelmar kept polishing the goblet. "Just discipline. It's nothing."

"And the reason you're ignoring me? Am I nothing too?"

Startled, Gelmar turned his sight to his brother. "Heimo. I..."

"Gelm, I didn't ask to be Vyrga's successor. What choice did I have? Tell me."

Gelmar put the goblet away. "You could have refused."

"Do you think Vyrga would have accepted that? Would you if you were him?"

Gelmar was silent. Considering Heimo's past achievements, would he have?

He might still be wet behind the ears when it comes to combat experience, but his growth is nothing to scoff at. It's only his second year as an active member of the gang and he's already managed to pit three rival bosses against each other before wiping them out in one fell swoop.

"Exactly. So please Gelm, can you stop this? All of this?" Heimo pleaded. "I don't want to lose you."

"You want me to ignore Vyrga's order to attack Gherm?"

"Stop playing the fool!" Heimo yelled.

"We both know what I'm talking about. Vyrga knows!"

"Of course he knows!" Gelmar yelled back, "Why do you think he's sent me here!? It's all because he couldn't stand that I want what's rightfully mine! I'm the oldest and stayed with him the longest for the gods' sake!"

After his outburst, Gelmar sat down with a huff. "And yet, he chose you and that bastard Os as his successors. I thought about it, and it was frustrating for me at first, but I'd be okay with you taking control. But Oswald? After all I did for him, Vyrga chose his pet over me!?"

In a fit of rage, Gelmar slammed the table in front of him. "He deserves everything coming to him. You think I don't know what he's doing here?"

"This whole campaign is him cutting me off at the knees. If I win, what remains of my men won't be enough to challenge him, and if I lose…"

"So go to him! Beg for forgiveness! Say you'll be loyal!"

Seeing the honest look in his brother's eyes, Gelmar chuckled. *For all your smarts, that's pretty naive. Once you go this far, it's already too late. I'd never be able to earn our "Father's" trust after this stunt. Too bad for him that the high priest of Ainshard already prophesied my inevitable rise.*

He gently rubbed Heimo's hair. "Heim… Remember what Ainshard said? One emperor leads to glory, but two lead to tragedy. Vyrga must be dealt with, if not by my hand then by another's."

Before Heimo could argue back, one of Gelmar's men burst through the tent's flaps. "Boss! The men are ready!"

"Gelmar, I'll warn you one last time, this fight is a mistake."

Gelmar grinned. "Heim, despite what you and Vyrga might think, I'm not stupid. My scouts tell me everything Gherm does. This will be over by lunchtime."

"Lev," Heimo muttered.

"What?"

"My spies tell me he's calling himself Lev now. He was blessed by the priestess of Zeja last night as *Lev the Liberator.*"

"Huh? Really? The liberator?" Gelmar scoffed. "Pathetic. What are the fools in that decrepit temple thinking?"

"Tell your scouts to be more thorough. That might not be the only surprise he has for you," Heimo advised.

"He can be blessed by a hundred gods for all I care. My victory is inevitable for I follow Ainshard's way."

You still believe it, don't you? Do you still believe what that rat-like scammer of a priest told you? That you'll be the next enlightened one?" Heimo complained.

Gelmar frowned. "Despite all the miraculous situations we've been through, you still refuse to believe. A year ago, if it weren't for Ainshard's light healing our wounds, my men and I would've died in that ditch after fighting off Rak's men."

"That was because of the worm moss. It clots blood and the worms inhabiting it give off a faint, comforting light. The healers confirmed that."

"I'd still call it one of Ainshard's many miracles."

"Gelm, be reasonable. Ainshard the Enlightened One is a myth. A character from stories spread by thieving priests. Do you really believe that there was once a goblin who conquered all the people in the forest and united hundreds of tribes to form a great clan?"

Gelmar shrugged. "It's possible. With enough time, martial prowess, and charisma, I don't see why it couldn't happen."

"Really? And what about the part where Ainshard mysteriously grew stronger and changed his form every few battles? Not just a little muscle, mind you, but he grew in mass with each new conflict."

Gelmar put on his gauntlet. "Nothing is impossible for those chosen by the gods. Especially for one who surpassed them all."

"Then why is there nothing left? If he was so great and united everyone, where did it all go?"

Flabbergasted, Gelmar stopped putting on his gear and stared at Heimo as if he'd just grown another head.

"What?"

"Heimo, I thought you knew your history. After his children poisoned him, they fought against each other until there was almost nothing of his empire left."

"Sadly, the idiocy continues," Gelmar continued. "Nobody was able to recover the ancient secrets because goblinoids are always at war. We need a new enlightened one to reforge the world."

"And that's going to be you?"

Gelmar grabbed his axe and checked its blade for nicks. "Yep. I'll be heading out now. My men are waiting."

"What about Vyrga? Are you going to fight him too?" Heimo yelled as Gelmar lifted one of the tent's flaps.

Gelmar stopped and took a deep breath. "Vyrga had his chance. Even a blind man can see that he'll fail eventually. The world's gotta change, Heim. And it doesn't matter who I have to go through to do it."

To Heimo's chagrin, Gelmar didn't wait another moment before again lifting the flap and exiting the tent.

Dammit, you fool. You're letting your ideals blind you.

As Heimo rushed through the tent flaps, he found Gelmar standing before him with his axe raised high. His men stood at attention.

"Alright, boys. Time to squash some bugs! We only have ten days before the expedition, so let's finish this quick and be home for dinner. Are you ready, men!?"

The men's cheers rose to a clamour.

As he watched his brother bathe in the cheers and glory with sparkling eyes, Heimo's lip tightened.

With a regretful sigh, he put on his hood and turned to leave.

"Stay safe, brother. May Ainshard protect you."

CHAPTER 12
THIS MEANS WAR

Two hours passed before Gelmar could make out Lev's encampment in the distance, at the very edge of Rak's sphere of influence. Rak's turf covered the mining area, and just a small slice of the southwestern slave quarters, which happened to be the area Lev and Ghorza lived in. It also happened to be an area of extreme strategic importance. If Vyrga were able to take over this area, he'd be able to extend his control to the entrance of the mining area.

And that could absolutely not happen.

Even though scant pockets of light trickled down from a handful of sky holes in the giant tunnel's ceiling, most of the tunnel's lighting came from haze crystal lanterns spread at various intervals throughout, mostly concentrated near the living quarters.

Gelmar and his men set up camp. An hour later, his scouts returned with intelligence regarding Lev's forces: they numbered roughly thirty-three men, including Lev himself, and there were no obvious traps in sight.

Lev and his men had erected two barricades consisting of whatever wooden objects they could find, mostly sharpened wooden boards and tables with bags of cave dirt propping up the stakes. One barricade was visible with the naked eye from Gelmar's camp, but the other was some distance away, nestled tightly in a residential area.

The scouts had also snuck peeks inside whatever homes they could, where they found unarmed women, youths, and elders hiding from the conflict, but no evidence of an ambush.

"Looks like they've been expecting us," Gelmar mused.

"Looks like it, boss," cut in a scout, eager to be acknowledged. "They're just a bunch of kivvigs between us now."

"Did I ask? And it's *killigs*, not 'kivvigs.'"

"Um... What are killigs?" The flustered thug asked.

"Really? You've gone your whole life not knowing what a killig is?"

"Sorry, boss."

Gelmar kneaded his forehead in frustration. "The Killigs were an order of great holy warriors who guarded the Enlightened One's throne room. They were all the same height, about twice that of a goblin, so goblinoids eventually started measuring things relative to their height."

"So where are they now and why aren't there more of their race?"

Gelmar frowned. "You were around during the last expedition, right? So you've seen their race."

"I did? There wasn't anyone except us, the upper bastards, the nobles, and the goblins, right?"

"Right. And they were goblins."

His answer turned his followers speechless, but then the scout broke from his stupor and asked, "How?"

Gelmar smiled. "A thorough process of selective breeding and the use of one of Ainshard's greatest miracles, the ability to change lifeforms to make them stronger. Now that we're done wasting our time with trivia, do you have anything actually useful to say?"

"Sorry, boss, I got nothing. But something isn't right about them. Call it a hunch."

"It does smell fishy, boss. Isn't it weird they haven't brought some extra muscle to fight us?"

Gelmar shrugged. "Who'd dare fight for them? It'd be suicide. "

"Boss!" another voice, Gelmar's second-in-command Gotthard, yelled. Gelmar spotted a few troops from the rear guard running towards him.

"B-Boss, it's—"

Gelmar threw a hand up, and instantly the soldier stopped talking. "Don't tell me. Vyrga's on our tail?"

"H-How did you—"

"It's obvious. If we disobey him or fail to kill Lev, he won't hesitate to kill us himself."

"You don't mean—"

Gelmar interrupted him again. "Our coup is an open secret, dumbass! The only thing that Vyrga lacks is proof. He might play the scoundrel, but he still won't kill his own without a reason. If we win, some of us will die, but he won't do a thing. If we lose or run away, he'll take care of us himself."

The soldier tilted his head thoughtfully. "In that case, why not join this Lev?"

"Great idea. If we combine forces, we'll be just about two hundred men and a few hundred sets of weapons and armour short." His voice steadily increased in volume. "Why not die with them, right? We'll be remembered as traitors together!" Gelmar barked, spittle collecting on the cowering underling's face.

The rest of his troops lowered their heads as fear took root in their hearts.

"Why the long faces? Do you really believe that we'll lose to some unknown runt and a measly twenty men!" Gelmar yelled, raising their heads. "Have you forgotten who you are? Who *we* are? We're the bane of all greyborns! We're Ainshard's legacy, monsters that cause men to cry! Whenever our enemies hear my name, they lose all hope! For I am the chosen one, Gelmar, and you are my warriors. Even Vyrga will see Ainshard's embers within me after we've squashed these bugs! Are you all actually worried we'll lose to some newcomer and his band of day-labourers?"

"No!" they yelled with fervour.

"Are we going to take what's theirs? Remind everyone why we are feared?"

"Yes!" his men replied with glee. They loved a good pillage after spilling some blood—what could a bunch of conceited miners possibly do?

Gelmar and his army initiated their march. Ten of Lev's troops were lined up side-by-side in the front, broad, rectangular wooden shields in their left hand, short spears in their right. Another ten followed behind them wielding longer spears with harder points. The remaining twelve formed the back line, slings in hand, ready to fire their projectiles at all invaders who came into their sight, and in the middle of the armed force stood the tiny bogey Lev wearing a wooden helmet and proudly brandishing his spear.

Lev and his army were positioned behind a shoddy wooden barricade and in front of a sturdier barricade a short hundred killigs behind the slingers. Gelmar's men wielded a variety of weapons ranging from stone knives to wooden clubs. Gelmar himself wielded a bronze-headed axe, bestowed upon him by Vyrga as a gift for his contribution in a former battle. Gelmar commanded eighty men in total.

Gelmar surveyed the area for anything that could affect the battle. There were stalagmites covered in cloth spread about every few hundred killigs between his encampment and Lev's front line. As for what those were for, he hadn't a clue. Lizard-like corpse-eaters slinked up the walls and gathered en mass upon the numerous stalactites above them. Their black scales glinted in the faint trickles of sunlight as their emerald eyes anticipated the feast soon to come.

Questions raced rapid-fire through Gelmar's head. *A shield wall? Why attempt such a thing with so few men? And why two layers of fortifications? Once we break through the wooden barrier and the shield wall, there won't be enough time for them to retreat behind the second one.*

The more he observed his opponent's setup, the more confused Gelmar was. *Bogeys have decent night vision—why are his men carrying so many torches?* He focused more intently on the row of shields behind the front row, upon each of which was painted a red eye, the symbol of Zeja, the goddess of war. *Why are almost all the shields covered in that... yellowish stuff?*

The questions echoed in Gelmar's mind as he strode forward to meet Lev before the start of the battle. This was a custom of bogey-kind: before two forces of bogeys began to fight, their leaders would either negotiate for peace or wage a war of words before the war of weapons.

Every bogey, from the highest of nobles to the lowest of thugs, followed this custom. Usually, the two belligerents would have a priest or priestess of Zeja mediate the conflict, but Gelmar was under no illusion that they could possibly find one in this blighted place, and why would he want anything other than to win in combat against this no-name runt?

Gelmar at last came face-to-face with Lev at the centre of the battlefield. Gelmar glared down his nose at his adversary; Lev replied with a smirk.

Gelmar was quick to initiate. "*You're* Lev the Liberator? Hah! I thought you'd be more impressive, but you're just a runt!" he boomed loudly enough for all to hear.

"And you are?" his counterpart returned nonchalantly.

"You don't know who I am? Remember it, for I shall be your death. My name is Gelmar!"

"Pfft... Hahaha! Was that supposed to be threatening? And— oh. Gelmar? Thank goodness. I thought Vyrga would send us one of the good ones."

Gelmar's jaws clenched. Lev resumed his diatribe.

"It's true, you're second-rate— wait, no, make that third-rate material. Your men are undisciplined trash who only obey orders out of fear, and we all know you just want Vyrga to acknowledge you." Lev smugly watched Gelmar foam at the mouth. "Meh, you'll do. My men do need some practice after all."

Gelmar was livid. As much as he wanted to tear this arrogant bastard limb from limb, he had to restrain himself. *He's trying to make me lose my composure,* he thought.

Instead, Gelmar stepped forward, invading Lev's personal space until Lev had to crane his neck to maintain eye contact. "You know what? Once we slaughter your men, I won't kill you. I'll just make your life a living hell. I'm going to take everything and everyone you value and break them slowly. Your neighbours? They'll hate you. Your sister? She'll abandon you. Whatever spawn she'll have from my men? They'll curse you! All those who believed in you, all those who put their trust in you, all those who ever cared about you? They'll wither away hoping that you'll burn forever in damnation for turning their life into hell, for pissing me off."

Lev's smile disappeared. Gelmar thought he had claimed a verbal victory, but when he looked into Lev's eyes, he saw no fear. Instead, he saw an emptiness that threatened to devour him whole.

"You know," said Lev in a voice so cold that Gelmar felt a chill on his nape, "usually I can tolerate pointless drivel from scum like you, but you just had to try too hard, didn't you? It was okay when you threatened me with death. Many others have done the same, but none except one," he chuckled cryptically, "have delivered."

Except one? thought Gelmar.

Lev continued, another dastardly smile creeping up his face. "But you just had to threaten my friends and family, did you? Let me tell you, the things I care about can be counted on one hand, and I'll allow nothing to harm them. Not you. Not Vyrga. Not Rak. Not the nobles, not the goblins, not the gods."

"That's blasphemy!" Gelmar replied, his voice cracking.

With conviction that could have made the ender serpent cower in fear, Lev spoke again. "Blasphemy or not, that is the truth." His eyes narrowed. "Now run along and pray for forgiveness from whatever being you believe in, because trust me, you won't be getting any from me."

Lev turned and returned to his men, seemingly melting into a wall of impassioned cheers. Gelmar heard shuffling and hushed whispers from his own side.

"Are you okay, boss?" asked one of Gelmar's henchmen upon his boss's return.

"I'm fine," he began, colour returning to his face. "As dangerous as he seems, threats are nothing but words until proven otherwise." *And getting shaken before the battle won't help at all,* he reminded himself. He closed his eyes and recalled why he needed to win: Vyrga would put his whole army to death if they lost. And they would definitely win.

Gelmar turned to his men, and the whispers and shuffling came to a halt. "Prepare to attack! Kill them all! Let's bring that bastard's head home on a spike!"

His men erupted in a unified cheer, brandishing their weapons as they awaited his signal.

Raising a fist into the air, Gelmar roared, "Kill them all!" His men sped forward.

* * *

"What did you say to him, sir?" Volker asked Lev immediately as he returned to the barricade. Before Lev had faced Gelmar, Volker had ordered the men to cover the barricade with as much dried moss as they could find and position the barrels in front of the shield bearers. Presently, Lev was inspecting the barricade, his protégé in tow.

"Nothing," Lev replied, "I just riled him up."

"If I may, sir, that didn't look like 'nothing' to me."

Lev shrugged. "It's always good to piss off idiots. It makes it more likely for them to make blunders."

"Oh. That explains the rage, but why the fear?"

Lev hesitated. "To demoralise his men?"

"But wouldn't that make them more cautious? What if they discover our—"

"Sir! They've started the attack!" screamed a shield bearer.

"We'll continue the discussion later, Volker. Everyone, get into formation!" Lev shouted, relieved he did not need to explain himself right then. "Shield bearers, block the path! Spearmen, prepare yourselves! Slingers, load projectiles!"

"Sir, yes, sir!" His shield bearers tightened their formation. Their mighty shields slammed on the ground, ready to block the path of their foes.

Lev had theorised that his three-man formation was viable against single opponents of greater physical strength, as well as small squads of enemies. However, it'd never work against Vyrga's men—not in an organised battle, at least. Accordingly, Lev had refocused the training of his men on discipline, formations, and spear thrusting.

Cognizant of how little time he had, he had trained them how to properly form shield walls, a combat tactic that was both easy to teach them and a sizable morale boost. Even impromptu combatants could summon their inner bravery when standing shoulder-to-shoulder with their comrades.

Lev, likewise, knew that the shield wall formation had many disadvantages. For example, it was susceptible to flanks, and would weaken over time under constant pressure. Once breached, the defensive line would be nigh impossible to re-establish. Despite its flaws, though, Lev was quite sure he could secure victory with the bag of tricks he had at his disposal.

"W-Will we be alright, sir?" Volker asked, his voice barely above a whisper.

Gelmar and his men pressed forward, passing the first stalagmite. Their thundering footsteps and madness-filled laughter echoed within the cavern and clashed with the terrified babbling from Lev's men.

"Is this plan going to work?"

"Why am I even here? What's gotten into me?

"Mother, I'm sorry!"

Unlike Gelmar, Lev's men were simple miners and labourers, most of them youths who had neither gone on an expedition nor ever killed anything larger than a rat or a corpse-eater. They were not warriors accustomed to fighting, let alone killing—they were simple folk who wanted to lead simple lives, and that was what Lev had used to inspire them.

"Are you afraid?" Lev yelled.

His men lowered their heads in shame.

"So am I," he continued at an almost pensive, but still audible, volume. "But I'm more afraid of losing. For if we lose, we won't just lose our lives—those bastards will target our parents, our siblings, our wives, and our children! But I won't allow it. Neither," he said, his voice climbing in volume again, "should *you*! We always get trampled on by their ilk! We always suffer at the hands of such scoundrels and never dare to fight back! No matter how much we beg, they never show mercy. They never stop harming those we love."

Perfect, they're paying attention now, he discerned. *But Gelmar's fast. I should wrap this up.*

"For once we will not leave ourselves at their mercy! We will protect our homes! We will protect our families! We will win!"

"We will win!" his men repeated with vigour. With every chant, their voices came to harmonise in synchronicity. They planted their feet firmly to face the approaching horde head-on.

Just as the enemies reached the second stalagmite, the slingers launched their attack.

More than ten leaden projectiles of varying shapes and sizes flew into the air before slamming into the shields and bodies of Gelmar's men. *Just as I'd planned.* Lev mused. *The short distance and the narrowness of this tunnel make it really hard to miss.*

Six of Gelmar's men had been hit already, two of them fatally. One had sustained a small round bullet to his forehead, killing him instantly, while the other had taken a larger acorn-shaped shot to his stomach, knocking him to the ground seconds before the rest of his oblivious allies trampled him.

Yet neither their fallen ally nor the onslaught of projectiles stopped Gelmar and his men from pressing forward. By the time they finally reached the last stalagmite, they had lost ten soldiers, but only Gelmar seemed hesitant to touch the barrier. A few of his men, meanwhile, had begun to scale the barricade.

Is Gelmar the only one noticing the casualties? Lev wondered. "Shield bearers! Push the barrels!"

As commanded, the shield bearers removed the barrels' lids and knocked the barrels over with their shields. A dark brown, viscous liquid spilled onto and covered both the wooden barricade and the moss beneath it.

"Spearmen! Shield bearers! Retreat to the second line!" The invaders approaching, Lev raised a nearby torch with a flourish, then chucked the still-lit torch onto the barricade, which instantaneously erupted into flames. "Hope you like tar," he muttered.

He turned to the slingers. "Let's leave them a little surprise, shall we?" Lev dashed away from the cracking wall.

Gelmar wrinkled his nose at the slingers abandoning their position to run away with the rest of Lev's troops. *Why now?* he thought.

He soon received his answer. Suddenly, cries of shock and pain from Gelmar's more brazen bogeys filled the air. In their race to scale the barricade, the dark liquid had smeared on their arms and legs. In seconds, this liquid caught fire, burning their limbs. Though they waved their arms and dashed about, screaming in agony, the burning tar continued to eat through their flesh.

Gelmar and the rest of his men halted. The billowing smoke from the barricade blocked their sight, to say nothing of the literal wall of fire between them and their quarry.

"Boss! Vyrga's here!" yelled a man in the back.

Gelmar looked backwards. Where he had delivered his speech before the battle, Vyrga now stood. By his side were Os, Ludger, Heimo, and a hundred loyal men brandishing their weapons. Gelmar cursed under his breath.

Panic swept over his men. They understood what Vyrga's presence meant. If they retreated, Vyrga would put them to death. If they waited for the fire to die out, Lev would escape, and Vyrga would still put them to death. And if they forced their way forward, many of them would burn to death. They were trapped.

Gelmar's eyes darted from floor to ceiling, far to near, shack to house to shack. "Men! Raid the houses! Get as much water as you can!"

Screams erupted from within as Gelmar's men forced their way inside the surrounding residences.

Gelmar's mob lugged barrels of water back to the barricade and flung their contents onto the burning wood, quelling the flames.

Gelmar raised his axe high. "These are miners we're fighting! Kill 'em all!" he roared.

The men roared in reciprocity. To them, this was not a battle; it was a farce, but not in the way they had hoped. They had been injured, tricked, and humiliated by mere weaklings who had never before set foot on a battlefield. Even if they annihilated their targets now, the humiliation afterwards would still be unavoidable. So many of them had died already, and they had yet to score a single kill! Against miners!

Gelmar's men, what was left of them, finally recommenced their advance as they climbed over the still-hot wood and dropped down onto the other side.

There they saw their enemy set up behind the second, sturdier barricade, but in a new formation. The shield wall blocked the path, which had yet again narrowed, effectively allowing no openings in the front line. Spears were extended over the shields, ready to impale all those who approached. Slingers stood in the back with their loaded slings, ready to rain death on their enemies once more. It was the exact formation as before, except there were no barrels beside the barricade.

The expressions on the faces of Gelmar's men collectively transitioned from shock, to confusion, to fear, and finally to glee. Behind Lev's men were Rak's, but rather than serving as backup, Rak's party was the entrance to the mines. Just as their path of retreat was cut off, so was Lev's.

Gelmar cackled gleefully.

"Um... Couldn't this be a trap, boss?" asked one of his more cautious fighters.

"Hah! You don't know Rak as well as I do. Out of everything in this world, he hates spineless weaklings the most," replied Gelmar confidently. Every time the nobles gathered the gang leaders to enforce new edicts or run their errands, Rak always looked upon them with disdain. Many of the nobles looked and acted like war-chiefs but cowered like corpse-eaters when the going got tough. "He's testing Lev to see whether he's worth keeping around," Gelmar continued.

"Lev?" asked the fighter, confused.

"That's what Gherm is calling himself now. More importantly, now that we know the situation," said Gelmar emphatically, "what do you say we do?"

"Tear 'em apart! Kill 'em all!" clamoured his men.

"Good! Kill them all!" Gelmar roared, rushing towards his adversaries.

"Kill! Kill! Kill!" his men chanted as they followed. Some rushed ahead of Gelmar, eager to prove themselves on the field of combat.

Once again, Lev's slingers launched their lead bullets. In response, Gelmar and his band raised their shields above them mid-charge. Projectile after projectile slammed into their shields, but only two bogeys fell. The first lost the upper half of his already-worn shield to a round shot before taking an oblong shot to the throat. The second took an acorn-shaped bullet to his knee, causing him to fall and smash his face on a jagged rock.

Gelmar grinned. The losses were a setback, but his men were making ground.

"Aaaah!"

"Owww!"

"What the— Aaack!"

Gelmar's grin vanished as the air filled with screams of pain, including his own. Something had punctured the sole of his right foot, almost causing him to drop his shield, and jerked his foot upwards with a start.

A defensive device with four spikes arranged tetrahedrally—a caltrop—had embedded itself into his sweating, bleeding foot.

In merciless succession, a lead ball slammed into the base of his shield. Gelmar lost his balance, stepping on another caltrop behind him, and howled in pain again.

The battlefield was filled with the wails of Gelmar's men as they suffered from both the rain of lead and the spikes on the ground. They desperately raised and held their shields above their heads, but another five men promptly fell to the bombardment, and their corpses littered the ground.

Gelmar gritted his teeth as he removed the caltrops from his feet. In a display of resilience, he continued moving forward and called out to his men, "Don't let some petty tricks stop you!" He pointed his axe ahead. "We're halfway there! They can't keep this up forever!" The field of caltrops ended a mere twenty killigs ahead.

Their courage bolstered somewhat, Gelmar's men determinedly continued forward, albeit at a slower pace as they tried to avoid stepping on the damned torture devices. Their bodies were covered in sweat, bruises, and still-bleeding lacerations; their minds were weary from all the losses and setbacks they'd experienced in this sick joke of a battle.

But there remained a single thought in their minds, the sole force driving them forward: revenge. Gone were the expectations of an easy victory; gone were the souls of their companions, whose bodies now littered the corpse-eater tunnel and living quarters from start to end. Gelmar and his men wanted to crush Lev more than anything in the world. They wanted to tear those who now taunted and mocked them limb from limb. They wanted to make Lev's men suffer as they had suffered, and nothing more.

Step by step, they growled and cursed as they navigated through the dreadful terrain.

Step by step, their hatred for Lev and his men increased as more lead bullets managed to claim the lives of their comrades. By the time they had gotten past the field of caltrops, another ten men had been lost.

As the distance between the two sides closed with less than a hundred killigs between them, Gelmar could see the panic on the faces of his enemies. Along with blood, sweat and piss, he could smell their fear, though he could not deduce why until the rain of lead slowed to a trickle and eventually stopped entirely.

"They ran out of lead," an observer whispered.

And he was right. The slingers launched their missiles once more, but this time they launched stones.

Gelmar's mob picked up the pace, hoping to break the shield wall and slaughter the men behind them, hoping to end it all and finally drop the curtains on this accursed, bloody play once and for all.

Voooooh! The ear-splitting sound of a horn pierced the battlefield.

CHAPTER 13

DAWN

"Ambush!" yelled Gotthard in a panic.

A small bullet whistled through the air, slamming into the back of a man's head from one of the nearby houses that they passed through, penetrating his skull and killing him instantly.

"Break into the houses and kill those sons of bitches!" snarled Gelmar. Few of his men heard his command above the shrill sounds of the projectiles; those who did charged towards the houses, only to be met with javelins thrown out the windows. Some managed to back away, some blocked the flying spears with their shields, while some were skewered without knowing what was going on.

Even then, Gelmar's men doggedly tried to push their way into the houses, only to find the entrances blocked with large rectangular shields covered in yellowish-white sap with a red eye drawn in the centres. Gelmar's men tried to bash through, but the shields absorbed the impact from their weapons.

Gelmar caught a whiff of the shields—they smelled unusually pungent. In a moment of clarity he realised the source of the smell. It was that of the bluecatcher mushroom, a giant, blue, carnivorous species found on or below the second floor of the monster cavern. The mushroom used its sticky sap to catch prey before encapsulating it for digestion—the sap also worked well as an adhesive for wood, leather, and cloth. He was loath to admit it worked just as well in sticking his men's weapons to the shields.

The men wavered. Not only had they played into another scheme of their enemies, but their numbers were not that much greater than those of their enemies. The only advantage Gelmar's men had left was that they were more experienced in combat, but that was meaningless if they couldn't reach their targets.

With projectiles assaulting them from all sides, Gelmar's men huddled together, shields raised, and formed a shield wall of their own. Because their shields were smaller, their wall was not as effective as Lev's, but it managed to protect them from most of the shots.

"Huddle closer and charge!" shouted Gelmar, intending to overlap the shields into a tight shell. His men obediently huddled closer, but before they could charge forward, something fell on top of them, tangling them together.

"Nets?" Gelmar exclaimed. He peeked through a gap in the shield shell to find women, children, and a couple of elders glaring down at them with seething hate. He could not place them, but some of them looked familiar.

"Hey... Isn't that Pog's wife?" yelled Gotthard, who was tangled in the net with him.

Pog... That's right. He had a wife and kids, Gelmar realised. *Are they all families of those we've killed?*

"B-Boss! Look!" interrupted another soldier, pointing to their back where bogeys holding spears, shields, and slings were walking out of their houses, grouping into the same formation as the ones before them.

Gelmar sharply inhaled. "Cut the nets!" he screamed.

The first formation left their barricade and began its approach, followed by the second formation. Gelmar's men, ignoring the unceasing onslaught of rocks and bullets, the pain from their wounds, and the unmoving bodies of those who had fallen before them, managed to cut themselves free. They immediately stood up and raised their weapons in defiance.

Now the real battle had begun—Lev and his thirty-odd men, reinforced by the vengeful families against Gelmar and his remaining thirty-five.

Gelmar's forces charged at the first formation with all their remaining strength at once, hoping to break through and finish off Lev to throw their enemy into disarray.

As he and his men charged forward, Gelmar saw Lev flinch before yelling further orders at his men.

The shield walls, along with the rest of Lev's men, moved backwards to put more space between themselves and Gelmar, but Gelmar's mob maintained their pace.

Lev then pulled out his horn and blew on it two times. The slingers stopped firing, moved closer to the shield wall, and threw some bags in the air.

Gelmar watched the bags fall to the ground and burst open, spreading caltrops on the floor.

"Not this again! Spikes!" he yelled. His men halted their advance, much to his chagrin. "Who told you to stop? Just avoid them or push them out of the way!"

Gelmar's men continued forth as fast as they could, avoiding the caltrops. Most, but not all, managed to either avoid them or sweep them out of their way, though Gelmar's men had to move in haste to stay ahead of the enemies behind them.

Once Gelmar's and his men passed through the field of caltrops, Lev's slingers shrank behind their barricade once more, while Gelmar's troops quickened their pace against the perspiring protests of their muscles. Their eyes shined with vigour, and they filled the air with defiant roars as they crashed into the now-shaking shield wall.

Despite their zeal, Gelmar's men weren't able to break through the shield wall. Even with their knees shaking in fear, the slingers grabbed their spears and shields, and enforced the wall. The fight quickly devolved into a sluggish battle of leverage. If not for their fatigue, Gelmar's men wouldn't have let it come to this.

Gelmar sneered. "If you think being a little tired will stop us, you really don't know who we are. I'm coming for you, Lev!"

Lev's formation began to buckle. With gritted teeth and shaking arms and legs, Lev and his men were slowly being pushed back.

You never had a chance. It's been prophesied that I'm the chosen one, Lev. Something I'll make you and my father understand! I'd rather die before I throw away my dreams and bend the knee—

"Ahh!" A scream interrupted Gelmar's thoughts. To his surprise, it had come from one of his men, one from the rear.

It didn't take long before a lead shot slammed into his pauldron.

We forgot about the mob hiding in the houses, he realised. Lead shots, rocks, roughshod javelins made from worn-out furniture, clay bottles and plates and much more assaulted his men. A few spearmen led a loose formation of fighters emerging from the shacks. .

With so much assaulting them from behind, many of his men turned their attention and shields toward the new threat.

Without their strength, it was Gelmar's turn to take a step back. Lev's men pushed forward with what remained of their strength, pushing their opponents toward the approaching mob.

"No, no, no!" Gelmar cried.

Losing both ground and men, he had no choice but to order his men to disengage Lev's men and focus on breaking apart the mob.

Just as they sprinted away from Lev and his men to deal with the new threat, Lev's slingers backed off from the shield wall and resumed their volleys, not allowing Gelmar and his men to commence their onslaught. Gelmar's men had no choice but to huddle together to block attacks from both sides.

Gelmar stood frozen inside the shield formation as he saw his men who couldn't make it inside struggle against their enemies. They cried, cursed, and even begged the gods for a miracle before the spears of both Lev's and the mob's formation closed in on them.

"B-Boss. Are you... crying?"

CHAPTER 14
SPOILS OF WAR

"Had enough?" The worst voice Gelmar had ever heard in his life taunted him.

He glared—through tears, though he would never admit it—at Lev, who smugly held his hands behind his back.

"You monster! You ruined everything!"

"On the contrary. You ruined everything," replied Lev, bemused.

"What did you say!"

"I said, *you* ruined everything. For yourself and your men," remarked Lev, beginning to pace in a circular path around the hapless Gelmar. "Wasn't it you who was overconfident? Wasn't it you who let his emotions get the better of him? Wasn't it you who killed your men by falling into every trap I set? Wasn't it you who made your men helpless by not allowing anyone competent to be your second in command?"

Lev stopped walking. "Unlike you, I did some research on whom I was facing, and I learned that you've always gotten rid of anyone who could challenge your leadership." Lev turned to face Gelmar. "Give up. You never had a chance."

"Give up? So that you can just have an easier time killing us? Like you'd allow us to live! Better take you down with us than die without a fight!" said one of the men.

Lev shrugged. "I'd honestly spare all of you—well, except for your leader, of course—because I would gain nothing from killing you. And even if you killed me, unlike your 'wise' leader, I've been training a substitute. How do you think my men were able to follow my plans to the letter?"

Lev took a deep breath before continuing. "So what do you choose—follow your leader to the afterlife, or leave him and live?"

"You think Vyrga would let them live just like that? He'd want to make an example!" Gelmar boomed.

Lev shrugged. "I'm not certain whether he'll let them live, but it's a matter of certain death and a chance to live. Besides, haven't your men done enough? Your men fought for you, bled for you, died for you. They've done their best. The problem was with the task, not them, so why would Vyrga punish them? Or are you just trying to use them to save your skin?" he accused.

"Gelmar. Let me run through a scenario, here. If your men had killed me, my men would have retaliated. Unable to withdraw with your troops, you would have sent them all to their deaths to clear out a path of escape for yourself. Having escaped, you would still be subject to Vyrga's wrath. But you'd have completed your mission, so your life would have been spared, yes?"

"Is that true, boss?"

Gelmar was almost too shocked to speak. "What! No—"

"He did say that Vyrga would slaughter us if we don't kill this guy, but maybe Vyrga would only kill him! We're just grunts!"

"Why, you dirty—"

"Can we really live?"

"Don't believ— Aaaah!" Gelmar screamed in pain as one of his men stabbed him in the back. Gelmar immediately turned around and swung his bronze axe towards the man's neck, beheading him.

He was surrounded as twelve of his men pointed their weapons at him, while the remainder backed off and stood to the side. They didn't want to participate in this betrayal, yet they had no plans on stopping it either.

"Sorry, boss."

"It's your fault, so don't blame us."

"You wanted to be the next enlightened one, hah!"

"I have kids, boss."

"I never liked you."

Gelmar snickered, then erupted into full-on laughter.

"What's so funny?" asked the biggest among the traitors as he brandished his axe.

"I just realised," Gelmar replied, "that none of you are deserving of Ainshard's light." He swiftly kicked his former lackey in the stomach before snatching his axe and lodging it into the lackey's temple.

"Get him!" yelled another. He thrust his spear towards Gelmar, who dodged to the left.

Gelmar grabbed the incoming spear just below the spearhead, pulled it backwards past his waist, and stabbed the goon behind him. In quick succession, Gelmar bashed the spear-wielder with his shield before grabbing the handle of his axe with both hands to pull it out of the large one's head.

Just then, one of the other men swung his club towards Gelmar's head. Gelmar dodged to the right, taking the hit to his left shoulder instead. He growled in pain before swinging his axe towards the club-wielder, who managed to raise his shield in time for Gelmar to embed his axe in it. With but a single working arm, Gelmar struggled to pull his axe out of the shield, sustaining a stab to his flank and a slash to his back before he was able to swing again.

Axe back in hand, he grit his teeth and braced his core to stay on his feet. This pain and sense of despair reminded him of his past, the past he had wanted to forget but never could. As he hazily pondered how things had come to this, he remembered something he had long forgotten: his gratitude to the one who had given him a purpose, the one he now sought to overthrow for his own petty ambition—Vyrga. Gelmar had betrayed Vyrga for lesser reasons than the thugs had betrayed him for.

How could I do that? he asked himself as he received another stab, coughing up blood.

Impact after impact, wound after wound, his body reached its limit. He dropped his axe and tattered shield, and fell to his knees. He looked towards Vyrga's forces far in the distance, and muttered a single line.

"Forgive me."

Gotthard, seeing the light fading from Gelmar's eyes, picked his former boss's axe from the ground, hoisted it high, and ceremoniously dropped it down on its master's head.

* * *

After witnessing Gelmar's failure, Vyrga seemingly lost his interest and retreated with the remainder of Gelmar's men following closely behind.

His sons, save for one, followed suit. The sole laggard stared at Lev with searing hatred in his gaze, then yelled something across the way, inaudible to Lev given the distance between them.

Lev didn't need to know what had been said—he knew he'd see Heimo again soon enough.

"So how many men did we lose?" Lev asked Volker after meeting him. Even though they had just won their first major battle, Lev paced back and forth, mentally running through the next steps in his plan.

"Five good men, sir," replied Volker, suppressing his tears. He was happy that they had won with minimal losses, but they had still lost five of their comrades in the battle.

"Tell five men to guard their corpses. We'll be returning them to their families." Lev continued pacing.

"Do you think their families will be able to handle the loss?"

Lev stopped pacing. "Those five were heroes. Their families might hate me, but I'll always respect them no matter what."

"You're a great man, Mr. Lev—I mean sir."

"Hah!" Lev smiled sardonically. "Remember this, Volk. Most great men are monsters."

"Don't we all have our demons? Don't be hard on yourself, sir. There must be some good in you, or why would you have spared those thugs?"

I didn't exactly spare them. I threw them to Vyrga, Lev thought to himself. Much to his dismay, a naïve part of him still felt guilt and disgust at his actions.

While muttering excuses to himself, Lev saw Rak and Hem approaching. Hem spoke first, before Rak could even open his mouth.

"Hey, kid! Nice slaughter! I would've called it a battle but we all know that... it... sorry, boss." The large bogey's boisterous voice faded to a whisper once he saw Rak glaring at him.

"Never mind," Rak replied. He turned to Lev. "Though, he was right. Nice job on winning the battle."

"Thanks, but I'm sure you're not here just to compliment me."

Rak chuckled. "Yeah, I came to remind you to give me my part of the loot. We didn't fight, but we did help you out, so this does count as a joint operation. And as we agreed, in joint operations you only get a third of the loot." Rak put his hand on Lev's shoulder. "But your men did all the fighting, so it wouldn't be fair to take so much. I'll just take half instead."

Rak was surprised as Lev heartily chuckled. "Isn't half too much for you? You said it yourself, *we* were the ones who fought. Let's make it eight out of ten for me."

Rak's eyes narrowed, but he kept his smile. "So you want to haggle, huh?" Haggling was an important aspect of bogey culture, with it being a part of their religious and everyday life. Thus, although Rak was a bit miffed at Lev's response, he still accepted the challenge.

Rak pointed at a few of the retrieved lead bullets and caltrops. "You did fight by yourself and win, with minimal losses at that. But where did your men train? I believe it was in my territory. I insist on splitting the spoils in half."

"Gelmar would still be alive if my army had failed. Not only did we get rid of one of your enemy's leaders, but you're gaining loot without having risked any of your own men. Seven to three."

"He was a mere annoyance. Furthermore, I helped you find the families of his victims. Four to six."

"Yes, you did. But I was the one who convinced them to come. Still seven to three, but I'll throw in Gelmar's axe."

Rak thought for a moment, then shrugged. "Deal."

"Glad we could come to an agreement. Now if you'll excuse me, we have to start looting before those damned black lizards try to steal them and ruin their clothes."

"Damned corpse-eaters," Rak growled. "Fine. We also have to go." He turned to his companion. "Hem."

"Sure thing, boss. Bye, kid," said Hem before following Rak. With Volker at his side, Lev watched Rak and Hem leave.

"I really don't like that guy, sir," said Volker.

"We don't have to like him, Volk. We just have to get along when we still have use for one another. For now, let's focus on quickly gathering the loot and paying the smugglers back. If we don't pay those misers for all the tar, caltrops, and whatnot, they'll make our lives a living hell. Better not keep them waiting."

"Sure thing, sir."

CHAPTER 15

SLANDER AND BANTER

Ten days had passed since the slaughter, and though the result had been on everyone's tongue, word finally quieted down as important news arrived. It was time for the expedition.

More than three hundred bogeys were to gather right outside the wall separating the mining area from the cavern's monsters. Guards and warriors periodically cleared the area near the wall of hostiles in order to keep the mining slaves safe and productive, but as always, the expedition was slated to proceed far beyond the safety of the wall.

Plodding towards the gathering from the slave quarters were Lev and Volker, who had met up on the way to the rendezvous point. Each carried a shield, a spear, and a cross-shaped pole with a sack tied to it. Inside the sacks were waterskins, food, spare clothes, food preparation tools, clay serving and eating utensils, and other essentials.

The narrow streets were uncharacteristically quiet, aside from the pitter-patter of their footsteps, the soft sloshing of their waterskins, and the occasional sound leakage from the nearby houses. Aside from the chosen adults and youths, most of whom had already arrived at the rendezvous point, no one was out—those not chosen for the expedition had holed themselves up inside their homes. The goblins tended to be *rowdy* whenever they arrived.

Lev and Volker had just reached the area closest to the entrance of the mines, the dilapidated western quarters. It seemed that because neither of them had participated in the expedition two years prior, both of them had been chosen to participate in this year's.

Volker was unaccustomed to the continued silence. Usually, by this point, Lev would have briefed him on their future plans, discussed strategies, or asked for advice if need be. When Lev was this silent, it could only mean one thing.

"Um... Sir?"

"What?"

"I don't mean to be rude, but is something bothering you today? You look... troubled."

"I'm not troubled," replied Lev calmly.

"You're too calm right now, sir. I know you're on the calmer side, but when you're *too* calm, it usually means you're angry about something," explained Volker.

Lev blinked, then turned to face Volker. "What else have you noticed?" he asked, his curiosity piqued. In his past life, before entering the world of politics, he had continuously practised modulating his body language and facial expressions to prevent others from reading him like a book. It seemed that for this second life, he would need to master his old skills anew.

"Um... You love to smile? Don't look at me like that, sir. You really do. You smile all the time and the only time you don't is when something has inconvenienced you, pissed you off, or made you want to kill it."

"Is that so?"

"Yes, sir, it is so."

"I see," Lev replied as he contemplated what he had just heard. He needed to pay more attention to his actions until he had better control over himself. "Anything else?"

"Nothing else to report, sir," replied Volker before continuing his previous inquiry. "Would you please tell me what happened before we met?"

Lev broke eye contact and consciously cleared his face of any tells. "Let's just say it was something annoying."

"Ah, your sister," blurted out Volker thoughtlessly.

Lev's seething stare shined its white-hot spotlight upon the defenceless Volker again. "Apologies, sir! I didn't mean it like that!" he said in a panic.

As though by magic, Lev's face returned to a neutral expression. "Just think before you speak next time. For future reference, you're not wrong. She kept shrieking about how I shouldn't have done what I did, and how there was no way to avoid a war with Vyrga now."

"With all due respect, that's her personality, sir. As your older sister, she's spent most of her life supporting you both, and she does have your best interest at heart. You've been spending your merits on equipment for us, right? It must be hard for her. Everything's getting more expensive. Speaking of, why *is* everything getting more expensive?"

"Haven't you noticed? According to our informants, fewer supplies are coming from the outside. Many bogeys are stocking up on long-lasting food like grains. It's driving the price of all food up. If we weren't willing to settle for cave moss, all of us greyborn would be dead already."

"Oh, gods," Volker whispered. "You don't think—"

"There's a shortage? I believe so." Lev replied, though he feared it was worse than a mere shortage of supplies. Depending on the situation aboveground, this food shortage could soon evolve into a famine.

"What doesn't help either is the way goods are transported," Lev continued.

"How come?" Volker asked with curious eyes.

"Well, grain comes from the surface and the blue nobility, followed by the commoner green bogeys live closest to the surface. Us greyborn live closest to the underground mushroom farms and mines."

Volker scratched his head. "But we also live close to the market tunnel!"

"That's correct, but most commoners and especially the nobility don't buy their goods in the greyborn market. They buy it locally, close to their quarters. Which means—"

"That they're the first to get their hands on surface goods?" Volker completed as they entered the mines' tunnels, getting closer to the exit gates.

"Correct."

Volker shuddered. "Let's return to our previous topic, sir. As I was saying, your sister has your best interests at heart, though she can be—"

Lev held his hand up to cut Volker off. "Overly dramatic?"

"Yes, that's the word. But is there anything else that's bothering you? You grew up with her antics. They can't be the only thing."

Lev rubbed his forehead uncharacteristically. "I was berated by the lover boy."

"Lover boy?"

"Thorst."

"That easy-going overseer who looks like he'd smile his way through an earthquake?"

"Yup, although I wouldn't say he's easy-going for everyone."

Volker's eyes widened. "He likes her? Why would he?" he blurted out before covering his mouth.

"Volker. You would do well to remember that she's my sister."

"Sorry, sir."

Lev grinned. "Apology accepted. You really should watch what you say, though. I'm glad that you're opening up to me, but there are times when you should think before you speak."

"Sorry..."

Lev smiled gently as he saw the kid lower his head. "No worries. Anyway, back to the previous discussion. Yes, he cares quite a bit about her. And despite his act of trying to be nonchalant and uncaring, he can get quite... emotional whenever he believes my actions would endanger her."

"Really? I heard he didn't seem that different when you talked after the knife fight with the thugs."

"Everyone has a limit, Volk. And the closer you get to it, the more irrational and troublesome people act."

"What did he say?"

Lev frowned before answering. "That I'm a danger to her life, and that I'm an ungrateful scumbag like the rest of the ambitious thugs that give greyborns a bad name. The worst he said was that she'd be better off if I didn't exist since I only leech off of her and give nothing in return."

"He said that? The only overseer who lets us off if he finds us slacking? I can't even imagine him being that angry."

"He was emotional at the moment, as I did kill one of Vyrga's elites. What do you think would happen if, in the future, I lose to Vyrga? What do you think he would do to Ghorza? Thorst would try to protect her, of course, but how long would he be able to do that?"

"I can understand where he's coming from."

"Me too, but the last thing I needed was him shouting in my ears moments after she did. My head can only withstand so many headaches."

"I feel sorry for you, sir."

"I'd feel sorry for myself too if I were in your shoes. Well, it seems we're almost there," Lev said with a smile as they approached the mine's exit gates. They were crowded with bogeys of all colours from greyborn slaves to blue nobles, though there were separate lines to divide the bogeys by status and reduce the chance of any conflicts between them.

Still, no matter a goblinoid's status, everyone had to wait in line. Once it was finally their turn, Lev and Volker were stopped by an old, pale green bogey.

"Hey, kid. I heard you've been busy," he said in a disappointed tone.

"I did what needed to be done, Kul," Lev replied with a blank expression.

"But was it the right thing to do? At first, I didn't mind that you made your own crew, but don't you think you took it too far?"

"Before I answer your questions, let me ask one of my own. Is protecting oneself a crime?"

"Yourself? No, it's not. But forcing others to kill for your ambition? Definitely a crime in my book. I've seen nobles, Gherm, and you've been acting like one lately. Why allow innocents to kill and die for you? Didn't you form a group to protect the oppressed from thugs, not to become like them? Why allow your men to bloody their hands instead of telling us overseers?"

"We did tell the overseers, Mr. Kul," Volker interrupted, grabbing Kul's attention.

"You did? Why didn't anybody tell me about it?" asked Kul dumbfounded.

Lev coughed, shifting Kul's attention back to himself. "You know there are factions among the overseers. Even if you did find out, the others wouldn't have let you interfere, by force if need be. And let's say you managed to stop Gelmar. By relying on you, we'd be saying to Rak, Vyrga, and everyone else that we're too weak to fend for ourselves.

"If we didn't stop them ourselves, they'd trample us once you or the other overseers on your side happen to be looking into other matters. As horrible as it was to waste so many lives, it was a necessity to protect ourselves and our loved ones. Or tell me, Kul, can you say otherwise?" ended Lev while staring straight into Kul's eyes turning it into a contest of wills.

In the end, Kul looked away. "Fine! You're right! It was the only way!"

Lev smiled. "Good thing that we agree on that part. Now if you'll excuse us, we, unfortunately, were conscripted to be part of the expedition. We have to get there before we're accused of desertion."

Kul sighed and moved aside allowing the two to continue on their way.

"Thank you. Now come along, Volk. We're already late as it is."

Just as they were about to pass through the gates, Kul yelled, "Wait!"

"Oh, come on! Get on with it!" yelled a bystander waiting in line, who promptly shut up after a glare from Kul. "Sorry... "

"Alright. What is it?" Lev replied, a little bothered at being stopped again.

"Just one last question. Do you think Gat, if he were still here with us, would accept what you're becoming?" said Kul in a sorrowful tone.

"Father..." muttered Lev as he felt a twinge of pain in his heart as the image of the one who was his father, yet not his father, flashed in his mind. Another part of him missed Gat a great deal.

"I don't know what you'll do in the future, but don't disappoint him by becoming one of those monsters."

Lev composed himself and said with a determined look, "Though I won't yield to them, I won't become like them. I can promise you that my plans involve making life better, not only for me and my men, but also for all those I can save."

"How?" asked Kul.

Lev grinned. "Just wait and see. For now, we have an expedition to go on, but once we're back, there will be a world of change."

Just as he finished his sentence, Lev turned around and left with Volker by his side.

"What a show-off, am I right?" said the earlier bystander, nudging the stunned Kul on the shoulder.

Kul stared at Gherm's back a little longer. That confident grin... it was like that of his old friend.

Kul shook his head, then glared at the bogey. "Do I look like I'm your friend? Touch me again and you're going to the back of the line!" he growled.

"Sorry," the bystander mumbled.

Good luck, kid. You'll need it.

CHAPTER 16
EYE FOR AN EYE

Lev and Volker finally reached the expedition site. Shouts, curses and laughter filled the place as crowds of bogeys from different walks of life awaited the arrival of their goblin overlords. Some commoners were excited for the chance to keep some of the lower quality materials and artefacts found in the lower levels; others, mainly greyborn, dreaded the impending death march.

While Lev kept a stoic expression as he searched for his men and kept an eye out for danger, Volker was baffled by the sights he was seeing. It was his first time seeing so many commoners and nobles beyond the wall. His parents had always kept him away from even seeing the previous expeditions, even when it had come time for his brother to join one two years ago.

They'd feared that he would be targeted and manipulated by the fouler members of society, as, despite his intelligence, he was quite naïve. They were already furious that he had decided to join Lev's band—if he had not been forced to join the expedition this year, they would not have allowed him to be here.

He kept looking at the mishmash of outfits, ranging from the white tunics and shirts of the commoners, to the fancy attires of the richer nobles decorated with slightly uncommon jewels and fine metals.

Lev, on the other hand, found them unimpressive. To his eyes, though the quality of their hemp and leather clothes wasn't bad, it wasn't something that would impress him. He also felt that behind this facade of joy and excitement displayed by the more boisterous of the conscripts, there was a tense air filled with fear and worry. In the end, even dreamers and fortune seekers were just like everybody else—afraid to die.

Instead of gawking at a bunch of strangers, Lev thought it would be a better use of their time if Volker helped in locating both Lev and Rak's men. Both groups decided to join together early on to deter other gangs, especially Vyrga's. Most were not stupid enough to do anything right before the expedition started as it would make a convenient excuse for the goblins to toy with them, but the world was not wanting for fools.

"You really should pay better attention to your surroundings, Volk," Lev advised as they continued along the leftmost wall.

"Um, why is that, sir? It's not like Vyrga or any of the other gang leaders are gonna harm us. They're still licking their wounds."

"Oh, really? Tell that to the people stalking us."

"W-We're being tailed?" asked Volker hesitantly.

"Yes. We're being tailed. Don't look back. Things might take a turn for the worse once they realise that they've been found out. Considering they haven't done anything so far, I'm sure they're waiting for something or someone. It's likely there's more ahead and they're trying to either block our way or surround us. It'll be better to—"

Lev stopped talking as he suddenly felt murderous intent from his right. He immediately ducked, avoiding an arrow before turning and locking eyes with its owner. He found a robed greyborn that looked far too young to have been sent on the expedition glaring at him from behind a red facemask. The assassin knocked another stone-headed arrow to his self-bow.

Guess this is the one they were waiting for. Must be Heimo, Lev thought as the hateful eyes he'd seen from Vyrga's youngest matched those of the boy's murderous glare. One of Vyrga's youngest disciples, Heimo had been close to the late Gelmar.

He was also one of the few greyborns who knew how to use a bow, and due to his talents and contributions, was one of two primary candidates to succeed Vyrga in the future. It was known that though he seemed the kindest of Vyrga's elites, all it took was one order from Vyrga for him to slaughter entire families.

In one such instance, after Vyrga took over a gang leader's territory, Heimo killed all those associated. Not even women and children escaped his blade, even though Vyrga had only requested that the leader and his eldest sons be killed.

When Vyrga asked Heimo to explain his actions, Heimo had merely shrugged and replied that while his actions had been distasteful, they had been necessary. Even if the children wouldn't want revenge when they grew up, the mother, grandmother, grandfather, uncles, aunts, cousins, or nieces could bring harm to them in the future. If fate allowed it, it was better to be a merciless pragmatist than a merciful fool.

Lev was about to tell Volker to get ready, only to see him throw his marching pack on the ground and take a combat stance with both his shield and short spear raised.

Lev smiled. "Looks like you're learning."

"Are you alright, sir?" the young lad nervously asked.

"For now, calm yourself. It's time for battle."

Volker nodded, his expression turning wary and guarded. "I'm ready."

Another masked and robed bogey pushed his way through the nearby crowd and charged at Lev, knife in hand, only to have his face slammed by Lev's marching pack. The figure staggered backwards and felt a sharp pain in his abdomen as it was sliced by Lev's obsidian knife.

The crowd screamed in shock and terror and retreated as they watched Lev slam the thug with his shield. Without care for the bystanders, Lev twisted his knife as he extracted it from the robed bogey's guts, causing his entrails to spill on the ground. After swinging off the blood, Lev resheathed his knife and grabbed his spear from his back.

"Back off!" yelled Volker as another robed bogey staggered backwards. Lev saw the robed bogey grit his teeth as he retreated, bleeding from a wound on his thigh.

"Arrow!" Lev yelled. Volker glanced over and raised his shield just in time to block an incoming arrow.

Lev spotted Heimo pushing his way through a group of three while approaching him from the left side. Lev glared at him and pointed his spear at the figure. "Don't even dare."

Heimo tucked away his bow and grabbed a short bronze glaive from one of his men, then stepped forward to join the fight.

Volker pointed his spear at the attackers and slowly moved until he was right next to Lev. "Sir! How many are there?"

"Who knows—"

Lev was interrupted as Heimo's glaive clashed against his shield.

"Hold your breath, Lev. I'll make sure it's your last," Heimo warned.

Lev smirked. "You can't even guess how many times I've been warned of my impending death."

He blocked and parried Heimo's attacks with ease, and with a single thrust from his spear, pushed him back.

Instead of shock or panic, Lev saw a sinister grin form on Heimo's face. *So he was only testing the waters. He's smarter than he looks.*

With a snap of his fingers, Heimo's assassins lunged at Lev. At the same time, Heimo backed off, back into the crowd.

Seeing the incoming attackers, Lev couldn't help but chuckle. *Hah. You're leaving things to your goons? These odds remind me of my years of service.*

Lev dodged to the side as a knife flew by inches away from his head while two axe-wielding assailants flanked his sides.

In response, he spun his spear around, hitting the right axe-wielder on the side of the head with his spear's shaft.

Unable to turn in time, Lev let go of his shield and used the spear's shaft to block the left axe-wielder's strike. The strike cleaved the spear's shaft, turning it into a makeshift short spear which he shoved into the axe-wielder's eye. After a swift twist of the spear, the attacker fell limply on the ground.

"Ah, my horn!" Lev heard Volker scream before two more attackers rushed towards him from behind.

Without the time to retrieve his spear, Lev kicked the first attacker in the face before dodging the other's spear. He unsheathed his obsidian knife, grabbed the spear, and pulled the attacker towards him before slashing his jugular.

"You'll pay for that!" The first attacker screamed, red-faced, before lunging towards Lev.

Lev grappled and slammed him to the ground. The last thing the attacker saw was Lev pulling his spear out of the nearby axe-wielder's skull before shoving it into his throat.

A gut-wrenching scream filled the expedition's gathering cavern.

He found an assassin clenching his spilling guts, trying to keep them inside his body, whilst his companion, axe in hand, had Volker pinned down on the ground.

Seeing his second in command covered in knife wounds along both his arms and left leg, desperately struggling to keep the butcher's axe away from his face, didn't sit well with Lev.

Volker's arms were shaking as he did his best to push away the assailant, and just as he was about to give in, his opponent shook before slumping over with a spear in his back.

Lev helped a grateful Volker to his feet, receiving a toothy smile in return.

"Thank you, sir. For a moment there, I thought I was a goner."

"You can thank me once we're out of this mess," Lev replied. His steely gaze was locked on three approaching foes.

Volker grabbed the axe of what would have been his killer and turned to Lev. "We'll be out of it soon. Heimo's goons made sure to break my horn but I'm sure it won't be long before our men arrive."

Lev frowned while picking up his shield. "We'll make sure he'll pay for every offence. For now, you take care of the one on the left and I'll deal with the other two."

"Will do, sir."

Lev turned towards Volker. "Also, Volker?"

"Yes, sir?"

"I always have a spare horn. When the time's right, take it from my sack and remember, don't let your guard down."

Two masked robed figures approached from the front. They tried charging Lev at the same time, only for one to be immediately speared through the head. The other was shoved back by Lev's shield, and when he tried to dodge around it, he screamed as he was stabbed in the eye with the still-bloodied obsidian knife.

Once they were dealt with, even more attackers arrived to challenge the duo. Much to Heimo's chagrin, they all swiftly met their end.

There stood Lev and Volker, ragged and bruised, but still standing strong. Lev looked around for Heimo, only to find him glaring down at him from atop a boulder.

Lev smiled. "Don't be so melodramatic, Heimo. What are you waiting for? Come on down. We both know we haven't got all day."

Heimo's silence and the sneer on his face was the only answer Lev needed.

* * *

Out of morbid curiosity and a need for excitement to kill the boredom, a crowd of all sorts of goblinoids gathered around Lev and Heimo as they prepared to duel.

Two female goblins joined the crowd.

"Come on, Rapha! We're missing it," urged the taller one, Ruune, as she pulled her friend, and commander, through the crowd.

Rapha struggled against her friend. She wanted to prepare her troops for the coming expedition, not waste time on the squabblings of some greyborns.

"Ruune, wait. I—" she was about to protest when she tripped over a rock and stumbled into a big wall of red flesh.

It was a deka. One look at his muscular body and the myriad of scars covering it was enough for Rapha to know he was likely ranked high among the warriors.

Seeing the deka turn towards her with an inquisitive look in his eyes, Rapha responded the only way she knew to.

"What are you looking at? Mind your own business!"

The deka chuckled and turned his attention back to the fight.

Ruune grabbed her friend's hand, and with a shake of her head, sighed. "Still making friends wherever we go. C'mon, we're almost there."

The two goblin girls pushed their way through the crowd, towards the front row, and stared wide-eyed at the fight.

Lev and Heimo wielded their weapons with remarkable finesse, showing a mastery that the two goblins wouldn't have thought possible for greyborns to attain.

Ruune looked at her flabbergasted superior and couldn't help but grin. "I'd close my mouth if I were you. Before you swallow a bug."

Rapha grunted in embarrassment before giving a slight nod.

"Don't mind it. From what we've seen from most of the slaves here, I never would have imagined there could be such skilled fighters among them."

Ruune nodded before noticing that Volker, embroiled in his own fight, had managed to beat the red-masked assailants.

"Never underestimate your opponents, Rapha. Even that whelp looks like he has some potential," Ruune remarked.

"I'm coming sir!" Volker yelled, a new spear in hand. His dead opponents wouldn't need it, so he'd chosen to drop the axe and keep the spear, the weapon he was most familiar with.

"Stand down, Volker," Lev commanded. "Deal with your wounds before you catch an infection. You'll find what you need in my sack!"

Lev glared at a corpse-eater slowly crawling towards one of the corpses around them, its curious eyes ready for a feast. "But it looks like we need to deal with this juvenile critter first. You know what to do, Volker."

"And after that," Lev continued, "I'll handle this grey pest over here."

Many in the crowd erupted in laughter at Lev's words.

In a fit of rage, Heimo lunged forward and let loose a flurry of slashes with his glaive, but Lev managed to block all the attacks with his shield.

"Stop hiding, coward!" Heimo roared.

Lev shrugged. 'Sure." He let go of his shield, pushing Heimo with it. Then he threw it towards his foe.

Using the shield as cover, Lev lunged forward with his spear. Heimo, having narrowly caught the shield, was able to use it to divert the attack. For all the flash, Lev's attack had only resulted in a small cut on Heimo's cheek.

Heimo jumped back with a sneer.

"What's wrong, Heimo? You wanted a fight and I'm giving you exactly that. And for what, a nonsensical cause?"

"You call justice a nonsensical cause? Gelmar was like a brother to me!"

Still seething with rage, Heimo rushed to attack again.

As the onslaught of attacks continued on, Ruune cheered. "Yeah! Kick his butt, handsome!"

Rapha looked at her friend.

"Really? Isn't the one with the glaive your type?"

Lev avoided another swing from Heimo, barely dodging it.

"Who did you think I meant? Obviously the one with the glaive."

Seeing Ruune reveal a coy smile, Rapha's face turned a fuming red. Her partner laughed as Rapha averted her eyes and stared at the floor.

"Your enthusiasm is misplaced. The aggressive whelp will lose," a gruff voice said from behind the two.

The two girls turned in surprise, finding the deka from earlier standing directly behind them.

Ruune crossed her arms. "Yeah? What do you know, merc?"

The deka frowned. "Are you really asking that?"

"Well…"

"I absolutely know more than a mere Jiira harem guard. What's the last thing you fought? The chief's underpants?"

Ruune growled. "You want to die, mercenary?"

Rapha took a slight step forwards. "Quiet, Ruune."

The deka turned towards Rapha. "The name's Gozzag. And why do you think Vyrga's bastard will win?"

"Well for one, his opponent is just a poor miner who can barely afford the clothes he's wearing."

Just as Ruune was about to support her commander, her ears twitched in hesitation. She decided it best to observe instead of stepping between the quarrelling goblinoids. While she turned silent, the deka and Rapha continued to argue.

"Hah! That's what happens when you spend too much time around gold and silver—you start judging everything by wealth. Use your eyes girl, and pay attention."

Just as Rapha was about to retort, Ruune finally stepped between them.

"Ruune?"

"What's the matter, girl?" Gozzag asked.

"Rapha, do you hear that?"

The sound of a horn filled the cavern. Moments later, more horns responded to its call.

"What was… Look!" Ruune yelled. The fight was reaching its climax.

Once the horns had let out their thunderous call, Heimo threw his remaining sliver of caution to the wind.

He charged forward, rapidly closing the distance, and thrust his short glaive at Lev's head. To no avail, as Lev had already pivoted his head in anticipation of the blow.

Out of rage and desperation, Heimo kept pressing on, but Lev continued to dodge and parry his attacks with seemingly minimal effort.

"When will he die already? Doesn't he get tired from running around?" Ruune complained.

"I hate to break it to you, Ruune. Seems we were wrong and Gozzag was right," Rapha admitted, much to the deka's glee.

"Now you see it, girl."

Rapha nodded. "Yeah. So that's how it is."

"See what? How what is? What in the name of the gods are you two talking about?"

Rapha sighed and looked towards her partner. "Can't you see it? That miner. He's doing it on purpose."

"No, I can't. He's doing what on purpose?"

Ruune heard the crowd gasp and turned her attention back to the duel before her friend could answer.

She saw Lev jump over Heimo's glaive the moment he tried to swing at Lev's knees.

Using his own spear as a pole, Lev dug it into the ground and flew towards Heimo, delivering a solid kick to his jaw. Heimo was sent sprawling to the ground.

Unable to believe the sight in front of her eyes, Ruune stood there dumbfounded with her mouth open wide.

"I'd close my mouth if I were you," Rapha said, mimicking her friend's earlier tone with a grin.

"What? How did he…?"

Gozzag grinned. "This was never a fight between equals. He was merely studying how his opponent moved. He was in charge all this time."

Lev grabbed Heimo's glaive and pointed it at his throat. "You're beaten. Drop the grudge now, and I'll let you go for today," he declared with a frown.

Heimo tried to spit at Lev, only to receive a kick to his sides. Lev proceeded to remove Heimo's mask and threw it to the side.

"This isn't a joke, Heimo. The only reason I'm even considering letting you go is because this isn't the time or place for Vyrga and I to settle our scores. So, are you done?"

Gritting his teeth from the pain, Heimo tried to glare up at Lev when something caught his eye.

With his sneer turning to a grin, he defiantly leered at Lev. "No, but you are."

More assassins emerged from the crowd from all directions, encircling Lev. Their red masks glimmered maliciously under the light of the cavern ceiling's crystals.

"It's my victory, Lev. I'm going to make sure you pay."

Hearing those words, Lev couldn't help but sigh. *Some people never learn.*

He brought Heimo's short glaive even closer to his neck. "Someone seems to have forgotten that they can be used as a hostage. If you're as smart as they say, I suggest you drop the charade. Otherwise, you'll die with me."

"I'd gladly do that. I'll make sure to drag you to hell with me."

"Then our friends here will lose their employer. Will Vyrga pay them if his successor dies? Does he even know about this?" Lev said aloud.

To Heimo's displeasure, this got the assassins to pause their advance.

"What are you oafs doing!? He's right there, he's—"

Before he could finish his sentence, a javelin pierced one of the assassins.

With a boisterous warcry, armed greyborns rushed to the fray.

More horns could be heard throughout the cavern, many of them from nearby.

"Seems the cavalry has arrived."

The sight of the fleeing assassins and Heimo's despair brought a smile to Lev's face. His captive's rage-filled screams were like music to his ears.

"What are you doing!? Damn you all!" Heimo cried as the red-masked men slipped through the crowd. This wasn't a simple mission anymore but a full-out battle. Professionals or not, they weren't being paid enough to face Lev and his men head-on. This was a far bigger situation than they'd anticipated, one they weren't prepared for.

"Don't worry, Heimo. Those men you hired will probably make up their losses by providing some services to the blues," Lev noted.

Looking at the dispersing crowd and some goblins approaching from a distance, Lev couldn't help but complain, "So much for avoiding attention."

Some distance away, he found Vyrga marching along with his lieutenants. The two stared at each other and seemed to come to an unspoken agreement.

"Seems time's up," Lev told Heimo before pulling the glaive away from his neck.

"Now, scram," He added as he threw the glaive back at Heimo. "Learn to fight with it first. Only then will I be open for a rematch."

Heimo glared at Lev one last time before making his way back to his father.

"Are you okay, sir?" asked one of Lev's men as he muscled through the crowd.

"If you'd arrived a moment later, I wouldn't be! Where were you? I believe I asked you to keep watch over the entire vicinity!" Lev scolded the man with a deep frown plastered on his face.

"Sorry, sir, but we were baited by Vyrga. A few moments ago it looked like there was going to be a fight between Rak and Vyrga farther along in the cavern. As you know Vyrga has about three times the number of men, so we interfered to even the odds—"

"Leaving you unable to cover the whole area, which allowed Heimo to set his trap. Is that right?"

"Yes. Thankfully, Captain Jem decided to leave some of us nearby in case you came," the man replied.

"Jem, huh..." Lev thought back to the cautious middle-aged greyborn he'd assigned as a captain. Back when he had introduced the three-man formation, he had chosen a captain for each formation. Among the captains, Jem was the oldest and most experienced in combat, as he'd once been the second in command for a gang in the western slave quarters ruled by a greyborn named Dagga.

Dagga had been known to be many things—daring, ambitious, wise, just, and loyal. He had been popular among his men, as he had kept everything fair and never targeted those who didn't deserve it. Alas, as with all good, ambitious men, he had been betrayed and killed by the greediest of his followers.

After Dagga's death, his men had dutifully fulfilled their last assignment by hunting down the traitors. But after that, the group slowly fell apart until they had all separated ways.

After the collapse, Jem had continuously switched allegiances, notably serving Rak at one point, but had never stuck around. He hadn't found in any of the leaders the qualities he was looking for. He eventually gave up his search and chose to live as a regular miner, until recently.

It seemed that Gherm had reminded him a lot of Dagga, so he'd chosen to get his hopes up for the last time and joined the band. For the time being, not only did he show great skill and discipline, but also showed strategic prowess. He'd also been one of Lev's advisors when planning the battle against Gelmar.

Looks like I found my third-in-command, Lev mused before focusing on the waiting soldier.

"Can you forgive us, sir?" asked the soldier nervously, breaking Lev out of his thoughts.

"That will depend on how you handle this task. Gather the others. Take six of them with you to check the perimeter for any more surprises! And make sure not to fall to any ploys this time!" Lev ordered.

"Sir, yes, sir!" the man replied before heading off to fulfil the task.

Lev looked at what remained of the crowd and yelled, "Alright folks, the show is over! Better get ready before the goblins arrive!"

This caused the gawkers, most noticeably a red giant and two female goblins, to continue on their way. Lev was right, as there were more important things to do.

"Now that they're gone, may I ask a question, sir?" asked Volker.

"Go ahead."

"Is letting Heimo go really a good idea?"

"Never underestimate a vengeful father, especially someone as dangerous as Vyrga. From what I've deduced of his character, he's not the type to blame us for what happened to Gelmar. After all, he's the one who basically signed his death warrant."

"And Heimo's different?"

"Yes. If we'd killed Heimo, we'd have shot ourselves in the foot. Heimo is a threat, to be sure, but not as much as his father. Vyrga's experience, ruthless nature, and connections to the higher-ups make him a far bigger threat than that whelp of his."

"I see your point but I hope this won't come to bite us in the rump, sir."

"We'll see. It's better to be cautious. And a word to the wise—never underestimate your foes."

"True. In case letting him go backfires, we'll think of a solution on the way, sir. Now, don't you think we should go meet with the others? It's better to join up with them early and think of a way to deal with Vyrga just in case," Volker asked Lev.

Lev nodded. "Let's go then. We also need more info from Rak about the other gangs joining this expedition."

And so they joined with their remaining soldiers and continued towards the gathering spot. The other soldiers joined them once they had finished searching the area.

CHAPTER 17
HAZE O' PLENTY

"Skraaaaaaaaa!" a hiveling screeched. Its broken body lay convulsing on the ground; its bluish-green haemolymph dripped from where its abdominal segment once was.

Lev and two of his men simultaneously pierced their spears into its head, and the yellowish light in its eyes dimmed.

It's dead... those hellish creatures... every last one of them is dead, Lev raggedly breathed.

The hiveling had managed to take down five other bogeys, one of them belonging to his group. Lev offered a silent prayer to his late ally.

Two months had passed since the expedition began, and six of his men had died before the expedition even reached the fourth floor.

He thought back on how it had all begun. The number of men, whether goblin or bogey, was double the usual. Past expedition teams had typically been composed of only goblins and bogeys, but more goblinoid races had joined the fray this time around.

Few bogeys had ever encountered other goblinoid races in the cavern, so few that the bogey consensus was that the goblins prevented contact between the enslaved races out of fear of collusion and mass uprising. Accordingly, this was the first time many commoners and greyborns encountered these different yet similar creatures.

The goblins had brought with them many goblinoids, from the twenty giant, yellow ones, known as bugbears, to the fifty red, single-horned goblinoids called dekas. There were also twenty-five burgas, a species that appeared similar to normal goblins but was slightly larger, with a tail and a larger and stronger jaw. Finally, there were forty dargs, a captivating, purple-skinned species of goblinoids sporting long hair and long ears that, Lev thought, looked quite similar to elves. They were the only professionally-equipped race present. Lev had heard of the deka; goblinoid mercenaries trained in a faraway country. He had never imagined them, even though they had been hired, to fight alongside lowly greyborns.

What was more shocking than the addition of these new goblinoids was that the youngest heir of the chief of the Jiira, Bulgu, was the spearhead of the expedition. First the food shortages, then the increased number and variety of soldiers, and now this? Lev was more than sure that something was going terribly wrong on the surface.

To start, the expedition force had marched after a speech from Bulgu and a recital by the shamans of the hymn of bravery. There was a tale known among bogey-kind that when Jom, the father of all, was slain by "the one from the void," plunging the world into darkness and madness, a drop of his blood had formed a young girl with long dark green hair, pointy ears, and red eyes known as Zeja.

Unlike the children and wife of Jom, she'd braved the dark depths of the underworld to gather the fragments of his soul and bargained with the death god Dorn so that he would re-forge the fragments into one whole and revive Jom.

After reviving Jom, Zeja had gained his blessing and the right to lead the gods in the battle against "the one from the void" and his minions. She had then pushed her enemies back into the abyss of space, ending the chaos and gaining her the title of the goddess of war.

* * *

Excluding the foreign goblinoids, the gathered expedition force had set out with eight hundred bogeys, six hundred and fifty of whom were greyborns, two hundred goblin fighters, along with Bulgu and ten of his goblin nobles.

As the expedition progressed deeper into the cave, the goblin-led army had fought against increasingly larger hiveling hordes and hostile terrain for survival and resources. After clearing the first few floors, about six hundred bogeys still remained, four hundred and forty of whom were greyborns.

"Shall we begin harvesting, sir?" someone asked Lev, breaking him from his stupor. He turned towards the voice to find that it was Jem.

"Yes. You can begin. But do be careful."

Jem smiled. "This isn't my first expedition, sir. I'm sure by now everyone can harvest the crystals from these damn things with closed eyes." Then, as he looked at his surroundings, his smile faded. "I wish we knew how to kill them with our eyes closed too."

Lev could not agree more. This had been the biggest hiveling attack to date, by sixteen worker drones. "Thankfully there weren't any warriors." He shuddered as he thought of the gigantic monstrosity that they had fought three days ago.

A few weeks ago, they'd turned around a corner to collect hiveling corpses to harvest. Instead of the lifeless corpses of drones, they had met a warrior hiveling variant; warriors were three times bigger than drones and as deadly as their size suggested.

The warrior's chitin was so hard that most weapons could not harm it, requiring the expedition force to aim at its eyes and the gaps between its three body segments. Its six feet were equipped with claws so sharp that they could slash through shields, rendering them useless. A sharp biological blade was embedded on top of its head, blood still dripping from its razor-sharp edge.

But the warrior hadn't been alone. It'd been accompanied by three drones and a spitter—a drone specialised in acidifying rock with its spit.

The spitter was slightly smaller and physically weaker than a regular drone, but it was capable of shooting potent acid from its abdomen. Usually, it used its acid to help drones dig through cavern rock faster, but its acid was just as capable of smoothly melting the flesh of its victims. Warriors and spitters rarely appeared before the sixth floor, but as though fate was spiting them, both had attacked in tandem, killing thirty-four bogeys, five dekas, three burgas, four goblins, and a bugbear.

Lev observed his surroundings. Thirty goblinoid corpses, covered by cloth, littered the scene. The wet sound of others harvesting hivelings close by added to the sheer horror of it all. Lev lamented that most, if not all of the injured, would pass away in the next few days if not treated properly. The medical supplies that they were supplied with were insufficient and the medical techniques of the witch doctors and shamans were severely underdeveloped. Thankfully the healers could, to some extent, alleviate the pain.

But that was all

Even though the healers possessed magic capable of mending most wounds, frontline cannon fodder had been deemed unworthy of such life-saving techniques. Capable healers needed to be ready and available to take care of expedition leaders and nobles for the slightest graze. If one of Lev's men was injured, the only first aid he could expect would be from the boss himself.

"Heh, looks like the kid's getting the hang of it too," said Jem as he observed Volker using a long-handled adze to poke a hole in the abdomen of a drone. The drone's digestive acid spilled onto the ground, fizzing and melting through the stone.

Along with the acid, a few yellow stones and metal balls spilled through the wound, which were the biggest reasons for the expedition's deep progress. Hivelings were naturally capable of refining ores, which they mixed into their wax to build their hives. And of course, these refined ores were extremely profitable.

Hivelings were also capable of refining haze crystals, special mana crystals that were great alchemical reagents capable of storing immense amounts of magical energy. Before refinement, though, they were corrosive to beings with low magical resistance.

This was why greyborns were always such a large portion of the expedition force. With their affinity for magic and inherent magic resistance, greyborns were the perfect labour force to mine and collect and handle both refined and raw haze crystals.

In the past, when nobody had known that the hivelings were capable of curing ores and haze crystals, the expeditions had been far shorter and safer, as it had been protocol to avoid the local creatures, who in most cases, also avoided them.

But once the goblins discovered that hivelings were capable of neutralising the haze crystals' corrosiveness, they tried farming them. But since hivelings are part of a hivemind, governed by a queen which until this day has never been seen, that had failed. It had suddenly become necessary to hunt them for what came to be known as "refinement sacs."

Due to the greed of the goblins and their overhunting of the hivelings, the hiveling queen now considered all goblinoids a threat. One that was to be exterminated.

"Come on, you lazy louts! Harvest all the loot! You know it's worth more than your miserable lives!" roared a vile voice.

"Gods, I hate that guy," said a certain large greyborn, accompanied by another one slightly shorter than him.

"Rak and Hem, how're the losses on your end?"

"Ten loyal men, kid. Ten loyal men," muttered Hem.

"It's all those damn goblins' fault," grunted Rak, grinding his teeth in anger. "What are they even after? It's clear from the way they handled the expedition and previous events that this isn't just about some damn rocks and mere trinkets! Why are they in such a rush to kill us all!" he roared.

"Maybe he can explain," said Lev as he pointed at another approaching duo of greyborns.

"Vyrga and one of his pets. And it had to be Oswald." Hem spat on the ground before turning to Lev. "As much as I respect you, kid, do we really need to work with such scum?"

Everyone had realised it during the first month, but this expedition was the wrong time and place for them to undermine each other. The expedition had always been an opportunity for bogeys to settle grievances with each other, as goblins had always displayed a lack of interest in the discipline or quarrels between conscripted slaves.

But this time, things were clearly different. The decapitated head of Veer, a leader of a small gang who had tried to kill his rival, Guru, now served as a decoration on one of the goblin noble's litters. It proved that, at least this time around, such acts were not tolerated.

Instead of just trying to avoid each other, Lev had thought it best to propose a truce, lasting at least until the end of the expedition, to Vyrga. Of course, neither Lev or Rak were foolish enough to believe that, Vyrga and his men would abide by this agreement, at least under normal circumstances.

But with the death of Veer, none of them wanted to risk Bulgu's wrath. The way Lev had explained it to Rak, they could use this opportunity to closely study Vyrga and his inner circle, though Vyrga would have the opportunity to study them in turn.

It was Rak who replied, "As much as I hate to say it, at the moment we do."

"Fuck!" Hem cursed.

"It seems you're happy to see us," mocked Vyrga.

"Yeah, I'm so happy I could kill you from joy," growled Hem.

"This isn't the time for this, Hem. Not now, anyway," said Rak, wielding his axe.

Vyrga sighed. "Seems like you're still mad about my test, Rak."

"Test? *Test?* You turned my best friend against me! I *killed* him because of you! I ought to—"

"Ought to what? Kill me?" Vyrga cut in. "Veit was going to betray you sooner or later. If I hadn't given him the opportunity, someone else would have. Deep down, you know it was inevitable."

"Graaah!" Rak roared as he sought to bring his axe down on the calm and collected Vyrga, only to be stopped by both Lev and Hem.

"Stop, you fool! Do you want to die?" yelled Hem.

"Calm down! He's just trying to get rid of you without dirtying his hands!" Lev added.

"You think you can order me around!?"

"I can't order you around, Rak, but one's actions determine their identity. Do you want everything you built to end because you fell for his ploy? For just another one of his tests?" replied Lev. "Look at your men and tell me."

Rak then realised that his men had gathered around them, and some of them were being beaten by the goblins as they tried to persuade them not to get involved. Rak calmed his wrath and took a deep breath. "I'm fine now. Let me go."

After a brief moment, Lev and Hem released him, and he made his way over to his men to relieve them.

"Where do you think you're going, boss?" asked Hem.

"Going to fix what we started, of course. Lev will handle everything here."

"Lev?" asked Oswald, who had been silent up to that point.

"That's what the kid goes by these days. You better remember it. And Hem, take care of the kid," Rak said, before going to diffuse the situation.

"Of course."

Lev turned to Vyrga. "Now, I don't believe you came here just to piss us off and try to get us killed. Mind telling us your true motive?"

Vyrga sneered. "I was just informed by a few of my acquaintances of the two main reasons for this particular expedition."

"And they are?"

"A mythical weapon once wielded by Ainshard, and a war between siblings to inherit the chiefdom."

CHAPTER 18

MERCENARIES AND BOUNTIES

Another three days passed safely with no further attacks from either hivelings or other local beasts, and the expedition force finally reached the fifth floor. All the floors after the first were enigmas, but the most mystifying were the fifth, sixth, and seventh.

The fifth floor consisted mostly of a field of bluish-green glowing grass with spots of white glowing crystals covering the ceiling, resembling what the elder bogeys called stars. After the untameable forest of the sixth floor and the mind-bendingly bizarre terrain and its inexplicable properties of the seventh, the fifth floor still remained the most fascinating floor currently known to both bogeys and the rest of goblinkind.

Upon arrival at these underground grasslands, Bulgu had formed seven groups consisting of bogeys, burgas, and dekas, and had ordered the dargs and goblins to stay behind for protection. The others were tasked with scouting ahead for valuable resources such as useful metals, unearthed artefacts, magical herbs, water sources, edible plants, and large herds of prey. Alongside those tasks, the groups were to help the expeditionary force to locate and avoid nasty surprises such as traps, ambushes, and hostile fauna.

Among these groups, one was composed of four of Lev's men, two dekas, and a single burga. That squad was just heading back to the rendezvous point to meet with the rest of the scouting groups.

"So when are you gonna tell us what the boss was mad about, captain?" inquired Gul, a known chatterbox among Lev's men.

Volker pursed his lips. This was the thirtieth time Gul had asked today. "As always I'll give you the same answer. He wasn't mad about anything, and even if he was, how would I know? I was harvesting haze crystals. Jem was the one tailing him then."

"Come on, Volker. You're his favourite—you have to know something. The guys and I are just worried about him, you know. Can't you tell us what happened? Maybe we could help."

"You? Worried about Lev? Do you expect me to believe that?"

Gul stayed silent under Volker's scrutiny. "Alright," he sighed, "I'm just curious and a little worried that he'll piss off the wrong goblins and drag all of us into a fight."

"Funny that that's what you're worried about, since from what we've seen, Lev ends fights," interrupted Molg, one of the more silent followers of Lev.

"I was talking to Volker. Though you did remind me of something odd. Why did Gherm change his name permanently? I know that old priestess announced that he's now Lev, but it's not normal to just throw away something you've been called your entire life just to please the gods."

"Don't tell me he's one of those crazed false chosen war fanatics. Will his eyes start glowing red before he goes berserk!?"

"No!" Volker yelled. He shuddered from hearing the idea. "Everyone knows that chosen ones are a myth."

Gul shrugged. "Yeah, they probably are. Why do you think Gherm changed his name to Lev?"

"I honestly don't know. I believe he has a good reason."

"So you don't know why he was mad, and you don't know why he changed his name. Did he tell you anything?"

"He did, but it's mostly classified information."

Gul smiled mischievously. "So he's hiding his secrets from you as well, huh? I'm sure Jem knows. Looks like the boss prefers gruff old men over young boys like you. Never thought he swung that way—*ouch!*" he yelped as Volker bonked his helmet with the blunt end of his spear.

"Shut up, Gul. The last thing we need is you spreading yet another rumour."

"Well, it's not a rumour if it's true. That darg girl Varra has a thing for you. Can't blame her, you must've looked like a hero, saving her from getting squished by that giant cavern centipede," Gul said with a grin. "Must've been weeks ago by now. I bet she's crying as we speak, considering you've never returned her feelings."

"I know, but it's not the time for love. I doubt the goblins would allow a relationship between us anyway."

"They won't, but I think it's more about you being too shy. You keep blushing whenever she talks to you."

"I-I'm not that good with girls, especially not of the purple variety."

"You weren't that good with men either. But look at you now! It hasn't been long since we joined Lev, but little Volk's already growing up. I'm happy I was able to convince you to join," Gul said while snickering.

Volker smiled. "Thanks for that, by the way." He still could not believe that not only had he joined a gang, something that his overprotective parents still could not accept, he had become a part of his leader's close counsel.

Volker had never believed himself to be special, other than being perhaps marginally smarter than the other bogeys. Truthfully, he'd expected to end up making pottery for a living like his father did. Even though he found no joy in it, it was a fair, honest way to make a living.

Now though, with Gul's help, he had found something more to his liking. He wasn't a fan of bloodshed, to be fair, but he enjoyed the excitement, the sense of unity, and the dream for a better future.

Volker's ears twitched when he heard a rustle in the distance. When he turned towards it, he found a small yellow lizard pushing a rock towards a stack, likely to cover its home.

"We really need to pay attention to our surroundings. Wouldn't want to be ambushed, now, would we?" Volker asked as he took a look at his surroundings to see if there was any sign of movement in the seemingly endless field of grass.

"You shouldn't worry about that. Our burga friend Rogga here has some seriously sharp senses. Heck, he smells those insects before any of us even see them," replied the oldest of the two dekas in Gul's stead. Rogga nodded in agreement before turning his attention back to their surroundings.

"That's good to hear, but we still need to pay attention in case they can hide their scent, muffle the sounds of their steps, or lie in wait underground. And sorry if we were bothering you, mister, um…" Volker paused as he looked at the one-horned goblinoid who was now staring down at him.

"The name's Gozzag, kid. And there's nothing wrong with being able to have a good, long conversation. Something that bugbears and goblins still don't seem to get… Isn't that right, Ban?" he asked his companion, who sported a nasty scar under his left eye.

"He's right," replied the companion. "Try talking to one of them and the first thing they'll do is growl or start a fight. A while ago I asked one of those green Jiira bastards for a drink, only for him to grab a knife and try to stab me." Ban sighed.

"Is that how you got that scar?" asked Gul.

"What? No. Got it from a battle with a tribe of short-ears in the east. It was fun while it lasted, but the druids had to interfere and ruin our fun."

"Short-ears? Druids?"

Ban was confused for a second about how a native of these lands was unfamiliar with druids and short-ears, but he realised soon after. "Oh, yeah... Your tribe isn't allowed to leave the caverns. Sorry..."

"It's not a problem."

Ban frowned. "'Not a problem,' you say? It's definitely a problem! How can you even stand to live under dirt for so long? I could never accept a life without the warmth of the sun and the beauty of the star-filled night."

Volker shrugged. "I was born into this life, so I've only seen carvings and paintings of those things along with a few glances through skyholes. And it's not like we bogeys have never tried to reclaim our place outside. There have been many uprisings, but they were all brutally crushed by the goblins. If you want to know how horrifying the last 'war of freedom' was, there's an old green bogey overseer called Kul. You can ask him once we get back."

Ban raised his left eyebrow. "Once we get back? Don't you mean if?"

"I have no intention of dying," Volker replied solemnly.

Ban smiled. "So you do have guts. Don't you have any intention of ever being free?"

"Of course, but I'm biding my time for now. My leader told me that nothing lasts forever and everything can change in an instant. One day we will be free, but until then, we need to become strong enough to be able to retain our freedom."

"Wise words. I'll have to meet your leader then."

"Thanks. So can you explain what you meant by 'short-ears' and 'druids'?"

"Right, right. In simple terms, short-ears are dirty, pink-skinned dimwits, a bit bigger than burgas. Their culture can differ a lot depending on the location of their tribe. The ones we fought, the Pallax, prefer to live near swamps and have no problem fighting naked as long as they have their bodies covered in their war paint." Ban shook his head.

Hearing that, Gul couldn't help but gasp. "They fight naked? Are they insane?"

Ban laughed. "They could be. I asked one about it and he said it's to show both the enemy and their war gods their courage. Don't think too hard about it, it'll give you a headache."

"Something tells me they attacked you before you could even ask them that." Gul remarked, causing Ban to smile viciously.

"As much as I would've liked to fight those lunatics, we only went to their village to pay them a visit for stealing pigs from a neighbouring short-ear tribe. The druids stopped us before we could get into a real fight, They're like a bunch of priests, always looking to stop conflict."

Gul scratched his head. "Pigs?"

Ban, Gozzag, and Rogga, who was now engaged in their discussion, stopped walking and stood there shocked. Gozzag facepalmed as the other two hollered in laughter.

"Hey! There's no reason to laugh!" Gul argued, his face turning a shade of red from both anger and embarrassment.

"Never mind, kid," Ban replied, wiping tears from his eyes.

"I don't want to disturb your storytime, Ban, but how far do we need to go until we reach the meeting spot with the expedition," Volker interjected.

"Let's see," Ban said as he loosened the small wooden box strapped to his hip.

"The counter says it took us 10230 paces to reach the farthest point in the scouting range, and we have taken 3478 paces during our return, so I figure if we follow the stream ahead we have another six thousand steps to go."

Volker paced around Ban, scrutinising the small box. "Your box talks?"

"Ha! It don't talk, kid. It just counts and lets me know how many steps I've taken, is all."

"It's time to move," Rogga announced.

* * *

As the small scouting group moved towards the meeting spot, Volker couldn't help his curiosity.

"Can I ask where you got that box from?"

Ban glanced over his shoulder, his eyes glittering at Volker's inquiry. He slowed his pace to meet Volker's.

"Got it from one of the druids while we were fighting with the pink-skins out east."

Seeing the puzzled look on Volker, Ban continued. "Remember the druids I mentioned? The ones who always try to broker peace? I saw one of them had this box and he said he'd give it to me if I wouldn't fight so I figured why not?"

Ban lifted the box, and Volker read a number: 6542. "Best deal I ever made! You wouldn't think it, but this box has saved my hide lots of times."

"They're okay then, I guess?" Volker replied.

"Oh yeah. They are. Here's a lesson for the future. In case your tribe ever regains their freedom and happens upon a tribe of those peaceful southern short-ears, respect their religions and traditions and they'll respect yours."

"That won't happen," Gozzag remarked, "The Brizilum Republic killed most of them."

Ban sighed. "You're right. Dammit."

Volker curiosity reached a new high. "What? Who're they?"

"They're even further east. An intense bunch. Wear matching outfits and carry banners everywhere they go. The dargs on this expedition were trained there to fight as mercenaries, hence their fancy equipment."

Gozzag visibly cringed. "They're the exception up top. Never try to broker peace with those bastards. They'll only try to backstab you once you're comfortable with their presence."

"Dirty skirt-wearers killed the druids of the Gallas, who were trying to negotiate peaceful resolutions to conflict, in cold blood. Not to mention, they burned down the Gallas' shrines and tore down the statues of their gods. They even replaced them with their own. I'll never work for them ever again even if they offer us a mountain of gold."

"You worked for them?" Volker asked, his curiosity about the outside world surpassing his previous caution.

"Yeah. We're from a clan of mercenaries, though you probably didn't know that. The Brizilum Republic is made of warriors who fight for gold, silver, and other valuables. We fought many battles and won most of them against all odds."

Ban grinned. "We're one of the best!"

"So you're here not as slaves, but as mercenaries?" Volker asked, causing Ban's grin to fade and Gozzag to groan.

Gozzag cleared his throat. "Not quite. We made a blunder during our last assignment. We were supposed to defend Bulgu's second youngest brother during a Kur attack, but they had more men than we'd thought and caught us off guard. It was bad, but not the worst mistake we've made. Anyway, we're paying for our failure by joining Bulgu's expedition. I guess Bulgu's ilk has learnt since now the purple lads are protecting them instead of scouting with us."

Ban rubbed his forehead. "The worst thing we did was participating in the Brizilum Republic's invasion of the Gallas. We only joined a few battles and trained their men a little, and you wanna know what we got in the end?"

"What?" Volker asked.

"Our reputation was ruined in the east, and that's where most of the good fights that pay a lot are. I really wish we'd known they were sacrilegious assholes before accepting their offer."

"The bastards..." muttered Gozzag.

"I don't get it," said Gul.

"They're changing the people's identity to theirs. Give it a few generations and there will be a whole new loyal Brizilum vassal ready to serve the Republic," Gozzag explained.

"But that's not our problem, right? It's not like they'll spread all the way to the west. What resources would they find here? Unless they want to fight the hivelings for it, I don't think they'll find much. Besides, from what I've heard, the south's far warmer and more fertile," Volker stated, wary of a possible future invasion.

"I don't think it's about resources, Volker. Once Ban and I return to the surface, we're going to inform the other goblinoid tribes."

"Do you think they'll listen to some speculation? And even if they do, we're stuck here until we finish our goal—I'm sure Bulgu wouldn't care and we can't fight our way back," Ban said through gritted teeth.

Gozzag sighed. "Dammit, you're right. Well, you greyborn know now. So be a bud and spread the message if we die."

"Alright, time for something else," said Ban, "let's talk about the time we ambushed the Jakkar—"

Rogga interrupted Ban as he growled towards the left.

"What is it?"

"An army of hivelings. They're heading towards the expedition force."

CHAPTER 19
THE BRAVE

Everyone took Rogga's announcement differently.

Gozzag sighed, Ban grinned savagely. Rogga remained still, keeping his attention on the stench of the incoming hiveling swarm. Gul shuddered, Molg prayed, and Jag, the most average looking of Volker's party, gripped his spear tightly. Volker himself took a few deep breaths to steel his nerves before blowing his horn.

"What was that for!" yelled Rogga.

"I was letting the other groups know that we've encountered hivelings, so that they can come and help us deal with them."

"While letting more of the bugs know where we are?" asked Rogga, glaring fiercely at Volker.

"Hivelings have terrible hearing. They may have other ways of communicating with each other, but from what we've observed over the years, we believe they mostly communicate through smells." Volker told the burga.

Rogga sniffed the air. His ears twitched. "The bugs are still just marching towards the expedition, but I can smell their aggression from here. There's something else too.. something..."

After a few short breaths through his sensitive nostrils, Rogga spoke up again. "It seems you're right, Volk."

"He's right? About what?" Ban asked as the distant sound of replying horns entered his ears.

"That they don't hear us. I smell different but distinct patterns around and within the swarm. Seems like they do really communicate by smell," Rogga replied between sniffs.

Hearing that, Volker smiled.

"Rogga." Gozzag started. "You're our best trailsman. Can you get us back in time while avoiding the bugs?"

Rogga snorted. "My big nose will try."

"I'll buy that big nose of yours as much crimson ale as it can handle if it gets us home, friend."

Rogga eyed Gozzag suspiciously. "Crimson ale? You trying to poison me?"

"It's the best a deka like me can offer you right now. It's made of fruits from the surface, something I bet you haven't tasted in a long while. The delicious sweet undertones of wild red amaranth will soon be yours."

Rogga turned around, already marching where his nose led him. "Deal."

* * *

The squad halted its advance as they spotted a few hiveling scouts standing in front of a small cave entrance.

"What? You want us to fight?" asked Gul as he cautiously eyed three nearby hiveling scouts.

Volker looked at his friend. "Yes. Do you have a better idea?"

"I'm sure there's one of those ancient shrines nearby. We could use it to teleport away," Gul answered in a panic.

"Bad idea. Previous expeditions marked all the functional ones and none of them are nearby. Besides, we don't know how to use them. Even if we did, we'd be leaving our comrades to die."

"Damn it all," Gul cursed.

"Why are they just standing there? It's like they're guarding it," Molg added.

Volker observed the scouts. It certainly looked like Molg was right— and that was bad news. The cave led right to the expedition force, and was the only path they could take if they were to make it back to warn the expedition force in time.

Gul noticed that the tips of Volker's ears were constantly twitching. The kid was afraid.

"Who knows," Volker said as his eyes narrowed, "but it's the only way to reach the main expedition force before the hivelings do. We need to get past them."

"Let's run for it," Gul suggested in a worried tone. "I'm sure we can outrun them if we catch them off guard."

Ban laughed. "Run away? Sorry, kid. I'm not into the habit of running away from bugs."

Gozzag sat down with a tired huff, catching everyone's attention. "Here's how I see it. We have two choices. One of us leads the bugs away so the rest of us can go through, or we fight them. Together. Which will it be?"

The tips of Volker's ears twitched once more, faster this time. "I'm the fastest here. I'll lead them away. The rest of you should warn the expedition."

When Volker saw Molg and Gul's reaction to his words, he let out an audible gulp. Their dark grey skin had turned a sickly pale white.

"Volk," Gul hesitated before continuing, "why would you sacrifice yourself for us?"

"I just don't want my friends to die before me."

Having recovered from the shock, Molg too joined Gul's plea. "Volk, hivelings are faster than we, or you, are. There's no way for you to escape them. If anything, the mercenaries should be the ones to distract them."

Ban rubbed his eyes. "He has a point, lad. Gozzag and I can take one on by ourselves."

Volker shook his head. Scared as he might be, he wasn't about to let his friends die. "But not three of them, right? After they beat you, they'll come after us."

The group went silent. All of them now knew it'd be child's play for the hivelings to track them by scent after shaking off the mercenaries.

After a few moments, Volker broke the silence. "It has to be me."

He felt the warmth of a huge hand patting his head. Turning around revealed that its owner was Rogga.

"We know you're brave, greyskin. Don't be foolish."

"But I..."

Volker noticed Gozzag shaking his head. "The big one's right, lad. You have nothing to prove to us. We appreciate your courage, but keep the life your mother gave you a while longer."

"Besides," Rogga announced as he brandished two bronze-tipped javelins, "not a single of my kinsmen would ever back down from an opportunity to fight together to the last man. I'm no different."

Volker was taken aback. For a moment it seemed like he'd swallowed his tongue.

"Thank you. All of you," the words finally escaped his mouth.

Everyone prayed for aid from their respective gods. The two dekas prayed for a valiant battle, the burga for a worthy hunt, and the bogeys for protection against the blighted beasts.

They stood in a loose three-man formation shaped like a reverse arrow consisting of Jag on the left, Volker on the right, and Molg in the centre, with Gul a short distance away to provide support with his sling.

"The left one is mine," Rogga announced with a bloodthirsty grin.

"Then we'll take the middle one," Gozzag said as he equipped both his shield and axe, "you lads keep the one on the right busy."

"You're kidding, right? How?" Gul shivered at the thought of keeping a giant ant *busy*.

"It's easy." Ban beamed as he inspected his axe's handle, hoping it would survive the fight after all the abuse it'd already suffered through the monster cavern floors. "Fight it or feed it, runt. Up to you."

"You know, we could've prepared an ambush," Jag remarked, goosebumps all over his skin.

Volker glanced at Jag. "There are only a few creatures that can conceivably ambush a hiveling, and unfortunately our kind isn't one of them."

"Great. Just great... And do you think these weird wooden spears will actually be able to kill them? Wouldn't our normal spears be better?" Jag asked, his gaze switching between his usual obsidian-headed spear that was lashed against his shield and the oddly-shaped wooden one in his hand.

After the battle against Gelmar, Lev had equipped his men with two different spears: one primary and one sidearm. The main spear was designed to be used mainly against hivelings and other large beasts as a ranged weapon while the shorter sidearm spear was to be used as an entrapment tool. To this point, the sidearm spear had been modified with a barbed, detachable head that was bound to the shaft by rope.

"As long as you make sure to aim at the thing's weak points— anything showing through gaps in its shell." Volker specified.

"Sorry, but I regret to say I didn't pay attention when you and the boss were cutting up those things and poking their insides a floor ago. I prefer to keep my lunch in my stomach."

Volker groaned. "You're saying it like we were playing around with the things. It made me sick, but we needed to see how they—"

"Enough talk, let's get on with this before they notice something's off!" Rogga roared, breaking their conversation.

Volker shuddered but took deep breaths to calm himself. "Everyone, prepare yourselves! Gul, load the sling and wait for my signal!"

"A-Alright!" he yelled before he loaded a lead shot into the sling and began the first rotation.

Volker glanced at the scared bogey next to him. "It's like we practised, okay? We've done this before."

Volker tightly gripped his spear and prayed, even though he was sceptical that the gods existed at all. "O Zeja. If you exist, please guide our weapons," he muttered between deep breaths.

He kept his eyes locked on the three hiveling scouts. They hadn't noticed the group's approach yet. If the plan worked, they could potentially end the fight in a flawless victory, or at least one with minimal setbacks. He felt hope well up in his heart.

Volker gave a quick glance towards Gozzag's party and could see him and Ban ready for battle. Each wielded an iron-headed axe and a round iron-banded shield. He still didn't understand why they'd chosen such a fragile metal like iron instead of bronze, but now wasn't the time to ask.

He turned his gaze towards Rogga, who was a distance away, dual-wielding his javelins.

Volker returned his gaze towards the hivelings one last time. "Now!"

Gul and Rogga launched their own attacks at the same time, each grabbing their foe's attention as the creatures separated and charged towards them.

Just as planned, the formation impeded the nearest scout, preventing it from reaching Gul. Molg braced himself as the creature slammed into his shield, nearly knocking him off his feet. Its mandibles lodged themselves in his shield and the thing flailed its head about, trying to yank the shield out of Molg's grip.

"Please! Take care of this thing already!" he whimpered. The scout began whacking him with its front legs between flails.

"We're trying, but it's not giving us a chance!" Jag yelled as he blocked a kick from the giant insect.

"Hyuguhyuguhyugu!" It let out a shrill chirp from its abdomen before trying to turn and slam Jag. It then tried to lunge at Volker, but the latter immediately slammed his shield into its head, disrupting its attempt before thrusting his spear towards its right eye and striking chitin.

The scout then grabbed the sides of Molg's shield with its front limbs and attempted to climb on top of it to crush him with its weight. Molg quickly let go of the shield and rolled to the left. He then rolled once again as it followed him and tried to bite his torso.

He continued to evade the hiveling's attacks as it locked onto him, perhaps considering him the weakest of the bunch. With a tackle, the hiveling threw Molg towards the ground. Just as it was about to bite his throat, Volker stabbed it in the eye with his spear.

Agitated, the scout suddenly charged at Volker. He failed to evade, and the insect pinned him to the ground. Volker tried to scamper away, but the scout blocked his path with its feet. He stared at it in fear and it gazed back at him with its cold compound eyes. Saliva dripped from its mouth, onto the ground between them.

Volker managed to keep hold of his spear and thrust it forwards towards the monster's right eye, only for the hiveling to block the spear with its mandibles, catching it, and snapping the shaft in half before throwing the broken parts to the side.

Volker shivered as it chirped and brushed him with its antenna. It clicked its mandibles preparing to strike. He closed his eyes. *I shouldn't be here... I shouldn't die like this... I wanna live... Mr. Lev, Gul, guys, someone, anyone, help!*

Suddenly a loud bang rang out, and the beast screeched. Volker opened his eyes and saw that instead of attacking him, the hiveling had turned its head to the left. Past its head, he saw Gul in the distance.

"You like that? How about another one!" shouted Gul. He hurled another lead shot towards the hiveling, hitting it in the thorax and cracking its shell.

Volker quickly got up and ran away. The scout turned back towards him and was about to give chase, but instead shrieked in agonising pain.

"Got ya!" Jag yelled. He yanked the spear shaft out, leaving the detached head in the right side of the scout's abdominal segment, and jumped backwards.

Still shrieking, the hiveling wiggled its abdomen, trying to get the alien object out, but the barbs on the spear-point kept it in place. Molg followed, after a delay, jamming his own spear into the hiveling's thorax.

"Spin around and tie its legs!" shouted Volker, brandishing his spear.

The two bogeys did as asked. The hiveling struggled—it could not reach the ropes even when it curled its body. It charged forward, aiming to drag and tire the two bogeys so they would release the ropes, but it could not maintain its balance as it kept getting pulled from both directions. Once its legs tangled with the ropes, it stumbled and fell to the ground.

As it was trying to untangle its feet and stand up, Volker lunged and stabbed it in the head.

The hiveling let out a terrible cry and thrashed around, but Volker kept hold of his spear. "Stab it now!" he roared.

Molg and Jag approached and stabbed it with their standard spears, one in the bottom of the head and the other in the middle of the thorax, causing it to struggle more violently as a beast in its death throes. They then took out their stone knives and stabbed it once again. The beast thrashed less and less, until it finally stopped entirely.

"It's over..." Molg muttered exhaustedly before sitting down on the ground.

"No, it's not. We have to help Gozzag and the others deal with the other two," Volker said before searching for their companions. In the end, he found a shocking scene.

Molg rubbed his eyes. "It doesn't look like they need our help."

Gozzag's party had chopped the other hivelings into multiple pieces. The head, along with the legs, was lying on the ground in a pool of bluish-green hemolymph. All the dismembered body parts were covered with serious injuries, especially the abdomen, in which Rogga's javelins were still stuck.

Volker turned to their companions. They had suffered only a few minor injuries.

"Nice job!" yelled Ban as he approached with a grin on his face.

"Thanks. Looks like you're alright yourselves."

"Yeah. It was a good exercise." Ban's words caused everyone to flinch. Who would take fighting giant beasts as an exercise?

Gozzag swaggered over. "From the looks on your faces, I can tell what you're all thinking. But remember that these two were smaller compared to the norm and honestly, dumber too. If we'd fought a weaker but smarter and less predictable foe, I can assure you that nobody would be smiling."

Volker nodded. "Alright, now that's settled, can you ask Rogga if any more hivelings are coming?"

"We already did. Having smelt the death cries of their compatriots, three more scouts are coming. However, they won't be here before our reinforcements. They'll be easy pickings."

"Do we know who's coming?"

Ban turned to Rogga's general direction. "Hey, Rogga! Who was it again?" he yelled.

"A few bogeys and a party of goblins! One smells like a female!" Rogga yelled back.

Volker thought about the information. "Goblins that are actually doing something and are led by a female..." He rubbed his forehead. "It's Rapha, isn't it?"

"Yup," Ban said with a grin.

"Wonderful..."

CHAPTER 20
RAPHA

For as long as Rapha could remember, nothing had gone well for her. She was born to the Ajiin, one of the "dim" goblin clans who'd migrated from the south-western lands. Because the Ajiin had not been "enlightened" by Ainshard, the Jiira and other descendants of Ainshard's once-great empire considered the Ajiin "dim."

Once the local tribes discovered that the Ajiin were too powerful to be conquered, that idea lost traction; as it turned out, all Ajiin, no matter their status and gender, were born with a weapon in hand and were trained their entire lives for blood and battle.

Rapha should have been a mother, or better yet, a war-maiden. A beacon of fear for the people of these lands as they looked out of their dwellings. Alas, a long time ago, during a drunken stupor, her father, Hijmald, had chopped off the chief's son's hand. Not without reason, as the dastard had tried to force himself onto her aunt.

This matter had been taken to the high council, the Otum, which had decided that not only did Hijmald have to pay thirty golden Karls, but that he also had to chop off his own left hand.

This obviously hadn't sat well with the fool, so he had opted to issue a duel of storms to the chief instead. And so, he'd fought the chief on a narrow wooden platform above a pit full of spikes, during a heavy storm, under the gaze of the four gods.

Rapha bit her lip as she remembered how her father had fallen to his death, impaled in the sharp wooden spikes. How his eyes searched for salvation, left and right, only to lose their light as his cries for help slowly turned into gurgles of blood, before ending in silence.

Then had come their turn. Per the rules of the duel of storms, the victor could dictate the fate of the loser's family. It usually ended in either death or enslavement for three generations, but thankfully the chief had decided to exile them instead. Despite his grievances with her father, the chief had already settled the score and was not the type to take his anger out on women and children.

His family, and a few of the other houses were of a different mind though, so he had believed that exile would both appease his kin and protect Rapha's family from them. Sadly, fellow clansmen hadn't been the only threat. Rapha, her sister, her mother, and her paternal uncle, who had joined them to pay for his brother's foolishness, had soon encountered a Jiira war band returning from battle. Needless to say, it hadn't ended well...

They had tried to resist, but it had all been in vain. Her uncle was slain after killing three men, while she, her sister, and her mother were captured and separated after they were appraised in the Jiira's hometown. Her sister, who'd been deemed old enough, was sent to "the house of desires" together with her mother, while she, who had trained and aspired to become a war-maiden, was sent to serve as a harem guard.

"Is everything alright? Still thinking about the past?" interrupted Ruune, her second in command. The two had served in the harem guard together and had become close friends since.

"Thinking more about how we got in this situation," replied Rapha before surveying the terrain around them.

They were entering a new part of the fifth floor. A forest made out of mushrooms lay a few killigs in front of them. Good thing, too. She was getting sick of the seemingly endless fields—she felt naked and vulnerable to enemy attacks in such an open environment. Entering a more sheltered section of the floor was more than welcome.

"Well, it's all a certain Jiira bastard's fault," said Ruune in a hushed tone before taking a glance at the nearby hand-carriage carrying Bulgu.

"Sometimes I don't know what's worse, serving in the old chief's harem guards or serving in Bulgu's."

"They're both bad. Both of them are a joke, and you can tell that by what we're wearing." Rapha's armour—if it deserved to be called that—was the same design as the harem guards' armour, but red instead of the usual dull-gold of bronze. It consisted of an artistically crafted ceremonial chest plate attached to two shoulder plates of similar design that foolishly left the abdomen exposed, gaudy boots unsuitable for marching, and a small plate over the hips, covered by a flowy, short skirt.

Ruune sighed. "These outfits just show that we're nothing more than decorations in his eyes. We're not amazingly beautiful decorations either, apparently. Once the fat bastard realised how truly dangerous this place is, he threw us on grunt duty."

Rapha gestured at several goblin girls sitting on and near Bulgu's lap, feeding him grapes. "If you want, you could be up there serving him instead. Just show him your charms."

"No. I'll gladly face cavern monsters over that."

"There you go, Ruune. Problem solved."

"Always finding the light in the darkness, aren't you," Ruune said with a smile.

"Everything will get a lot brighter once we get out here. I heard the next floor has an artificial sun."

Ruune frowned. "I wouldn't count on that. I heard the it's way worse than the current floor. It has a thick forest teeming with creatures, most of whom are probably hostile."

"Of course it is… why wouldn't it be. That's what we need, right? More death and more bugs…"

"At least we found some reliable company." Ruune pointed at the formation which consisted of greyborn bogeys.

Most of them, with a few exceptions, were unruly and shivering as they huddled together, afraid of the unknown. But even within the exceptions, a single squad stood out. They marched confidently in their matching gear, a spear in their right hands and a marching pack slung atop their left shoulders. The red eye of Zeja at the centres of their wooden shields seemed to glow as they hung from the men's right shoulders.

Rapha frowned. "Reliable, yes. Trustworthy, no."

"I don't understand what you've got against them. From what we've seen, they're disciplined and versatile, *and* they've had our backs whenever we've had any trouble. Sure, we saved Volker less than a month ago, but even before that, they were pretty nice to us."

Rapha sighed. "A little too nice, you mean? I just can't seem to trust their leader. I keep feeling like there's something wrong about him. My guts tell me he's a snake."

Ruune looked towards Lev. As always, he was discussing some matters with Volker, Jem, and some other members of his group. "Can't see what you hate about him. There's nothing wrong with a leader who informs his men of his plan and takes their advice seriously."

"I feel he's more of a manipulator than a leader. He has the smell of an elder of the Otum... One who's more of a merchant than a warrior."

"What? Haven't you seen him fight?"

"We both saw. But that's why it makes even less sense. How many warriors have we seen fight with words and spear as well as he does?"

"I don't know. You're the expert in these things. You know I used to guard pigs at night in my village's farm before this—"

"What's wrong?" Rapha asked,

"Something's happening at the front."

The sound of a horn bursted through the air.

"It's coming from the front," another harem guard yelled.

They heard one of the nearby burga growl.

"What is it?" Rapha asked.

"Something smells... wrong," the burga replied.

"Where's the smell coming from?"

The burga sniffed the air, ears twitching. Suddenly his eyes widened. "Above us!" An unidentified scream came from the back.

Rapha looked behind her and saw a green bogey tangled by a yellowish thread before being lifted up in the air.

"What the fuck is that?!" Ruune shouted as she saw a giant brownish-green insect with eight long, thin legs, and eight piercing yellow eyes feasting upon one of the vanguard members. The figure stared at them while dragging the bogey, using the thread hanging from a pouch, closer to its mouth.

"Hivelings!" yelled another warrior.

Lovely! We've got spiders, too? Rapha squeaked to herself.

Hivelings were known to come in various shapes, but the spider form was one of the rarest. Spiderlings were commonly found in the lower floors, especially the sixth. The forest there is quite hospitable to them—spider-form hivelings could use the abundance of thick branches to manoeuvre. To see them here, hiding in the giant mushrooms' gills, was an unwelcome surprise.

The creature grinded its plates and emitted a horrible chirping sound before ten more sets of eyes started to glow. In quick succession, the area was filled with a chorus of chirps, cancelling out most of the natural sounds that Rapha had thought were familiar to this floor.

"Javelins! Kill those things, now!" yelled one of Bulgu's men.

"What a fool," Rapha said as she saw them throw their javelins at targets far too high up in the mushrooms to reach. Rapha brought out her shortsword and took out a red-eyed shield she had borrowed from one of Lev's men after its owner had died a week ago. "Get into formation! Protect our lord!" she yelled. Her squad hoisted their shields above them, forming a barrier, and braced themselves for impact.

Before the other men could grab their weapons, the spiderlings dropped down en masse and began clawing at their goblinoid enemies.

Most of Rapha's guards, nearly empty-handed, defended themselves as best they could from the incoming barrage of swift attacks.

The creature slashed at the wooden wall, trying to break through to the prey beneath. The armour on its limbs was lighter than the average hiveling, so Rapha and the rest baited it by leaving an opening in their shield wall. Once the spiderling extended its limbs through the opening, the spear-wielders pinned them to the ground using their bronze-headed spears.

"Kill it!" Rapha yelled. They dragged the creature down onto the ground before releasing a merciless barrage of attacks on the wailing beast. It tried to fight back, but only managed to injure the exposed abdomen of a single harem guard before Rapha stabbed it in the head, covering her in the creature's haemolymph—which, to her surprise, was yellow instead of the ant-like hiveling's blueish-green.

"Got one. Six more to go," Ruune panted.

"Only six more, huh? Who has the most kills?"

"It's a tie between Lev's group and the dekas— oh, wait, Lev's in the lead with three kills."

Rapha smiled. "Not bad. Let's try our best as well. We have to make sure these fuckers pay for injuring one of us. Another one, incoming!" she belted out. "Prepare fo... for..." Her voice trailed off. She stumbled and fell to the ground.

"Rapha!" Ruune screamed. She saw a few other warriors fall to the ground, all of whom were covered with yellowish blood.

"What's going on?" Thought Rapha as she tried, to no avail, stand up. She glanced at her surroundings before she noticed movement in the nearby bushes that surrounded the giant mushrooms. A few tiny spiderlings emerged and covered her with their threads. They then tried to drag her away while the other guards dealt with the bigger spiderlings.

"I *really* hate this armour..." she cursed before losing consciousness.

CHAPTER 21
YELLOW BLOOD

"Uuugh," groaned Rapha. Her vision was blurry and her head felt like it was going to split in half. She tried to massage her forehead, but to her surprise, her arms were tightly bound to her torso in a cocoon.

"I would stop struggling so much if I were you," said a somewhat familiar, masculine voice from her left.

"I'd agree with the lad. The last thing we need is to anger these foul creatures even further," sighed an older and gruffer voice.

"Who're you? Where are we?" asked Rapha.

"What's the last thing you remember?" asked a younger fellow in kind.

"We were ambushed by spiderlings... And the guards and I took one down. Then I fell on the ground and passed out..."

"Pfff! Only one?" laughed a third voice to her right. She glared at the large blurry figure.

"How many did *you* kill?"

"Well, last I'd checked, Lev over there killed four, I killed three, Rak killed three, and this piece of shit here... also killed three."

"You're such an amiable fellow, Hemgall."

"Shut it, Vyrga," Hemgall growled.

"Charming, aren't you? That's just what I'd expect from one of Rak's pets."

"It's called loyalty, you wretched pig!"

"A meaningless concept meant to tame fools. It's only ever a matter of time until self-interest compels you."

"Well, I'm compelled to rip a hole in your guts!"

"You wish, you dirty mutt."

As they continued throwing insults at each other, Rapha turned towards the only individual she knew among the crowd.

"So even you're here, Lev."

As her vision cleared, she recoiled a bit at his smug expression.

"I would have preferred not."

"That's one thing we can all agree on," Hemgall replied in her stead.

"I concur," Vyrga said with a frown.

Rapha sighed. "Looks like we'll all die here, right?"

"Maybe. But they're doing a lot of work just for a snack.," Lev replied.

"How so?" asked Rapha.

"Guess. Better yet, look. Even if everything's still a bit blurry, isn't there something missing? And isn't there something weird happening around you?"

The place was dark, though a few luminescent shapes here and there emitted soft white light. There was no greenery, but there were weird forms floating about, three of them resembling hivelings.

Vyrga sighed. "If intellectuals like you all haven't guessed yet, then I fear for the future of our races. And before you open your mouth, Hemgall, we're on the seventh floor. Where the rules of nature don't apply."

Vyrga's announcement shocked everyone except Lev.

"It can't be—" Hemgall muttered.

"But it is, Hem," Vyrga reaffirmed. "We're too deep to be rescued. Yes, we're not dead, but we may be soon if we keep bickering. Those bugs must be preparing something—why else would they bring us here?"

Hemgall shook his head. "There's no way they're that smart. They might be able to ambush us from time to time, but any creature with strong instincts can do that."

"Would a creature with merely 'strong instincts' figure out, in its own short lifespan, how to deceive the burgas' senses and strategically target half, if not most, of its enemies' leaders?" Lev rhetorically asked.

"We've been underestimating the hivelings. Vyrga and I believe their last attack was coordinated. Unless you have a better idea as to why we're stuck here,"

"That's because... it's—dammit, you're right," Hemgall admitted.

Vyrga smirked. "He is, isn't he?" He turned towards Lev. "So, Lev, how do we get out of here?"

Lev raised an eyebrow. "You're awfully nice today."

"To avoid death, I can be the nicest man in the world. Make no mistake. I won't surrender my soul until the time is right."

"When would that be?" Lev asked, somewhat intrigued.

Vyrga would have shrugged if he could. "When I fulfil my desires and am satisfied with the way of the world."

"So never."

Vyrga chuckled. "Who knows? My desires don't matter to the world, but I will force my will on it until I'm unable to do so anymore. Now tell us, what's your plan?"

"The paralysis has worn off and your vision has stabilised, right?"

"Yes?"

"Then we at least have time for one last thing," Lev continued as he looked in Vyrga's direction.

"And what is this 'last thing'?" Hemgall pressed.

"Before the spiderlings come for us, you can settle the score."

"Spiderlings? You mean those spider-like hivelings that ambushed us on the fifth floor?"

"Exactly."

"Settle what score?" Vyrga added with a sneer.

"From what I've heard, I thought you'd enjoy bashing Hemgall's head in. You know, for breaking ties with you, joining Rak. All that."

Vyrga's eyes widened. "What do you think you're trying to say, Lev?"

Lev ignored him and turned towards Hemgall instead. "By the way, Hemgall, have you heard the things his goons have been saying about you?"

"What!" Hemgall seethed.

Vyrga shook his head. ""Why would my men sully their tongues by mentioning the ilk of this drooling dog?"

"Because you're that kinda guy, you filthy bastard!" Hemgall shouted. "If you have something to say, say it to my face!"

"I would, but I bet you can't even count the number of the things I dislike about you, you irredeemable cur."

"I'm sure you'd rather go play your sad little flute like always!" Hemgall spat. "If I could use my arms, I'd—"

Using his bodyweight to swing towards Hemgall's cocoon, Vyrga headbutted his adversary.

"Owww!" Hemgall howled.

Though Vyrga's mouth was smiling, his eyes were not. "You went too far, whelp. I'm not going to need arms for what I'm about to do to you."

"Neither am I!" Hemgall growled.

The two began to brawl, drawing the attention of the three nearby hivelings.

"Rapha, keep an eye out in case any other threats appear," Lev requested in a low voice.

"Why?" she rasped.

"Because I'm going to get us out. I have a spare knife on me."

Rapha assented. All three insects were occupied trying to paralyse the brawlers.

She heard a soft sawing noise followed by a snap. After making a hole in his cocoon, Lev cut the rest of himself free and fell to the floor.

The sound of his landing caught the hivelings' attention, but by the time they had turned towards him, he had already freed Rapha.

Lev put his hands on Rapha's shoulders. "Can you still fight?"

"You're not running away?" she asked.

"Where would I?" Lev suddenly grabbed her by the arm and dragged her away. Before she could complain, she heard a loud crash behind her and stone fragments rained in the vicinity. When she looked behind her, she found the largest of the three hivelings staring at them and the other two floating around.

"What's... What's going on?"

"Seventh floor. That's what's going on. You haven't done any research, have you? This place defies the laws of physics."

"'Physics?"

"The laws of this world. On the seventh floor, there are places where the force holding us down to the ground, also known as gravity, is stronger, and in other places it's non-existent. Seems like hivelings are used to this kind of environment."

"So what should we do?"

"Boost our numbers. I'll distract the hivelings and try to free those two blockheads while you release the other captives. I've determined the areas where gravity changes by observing the hivelings' movements. And before you ask, no, I'm not sure I can take on the hivelings myself. But we don't have a choice, so go."

Rapha nodded and quickly moved to perform her task. She brought out a secondary sword that she had strapped to the back of her waist in case of emergencies. It had maddened her that she had been unable to grab it when she was restrained.

She reached the first cocoon on her right and proceeded to slice it open. Out fell a deka, onto his knees. He took a couple of deep breaths before yelling, "What the fuck's going on?"

"A fight! Get up!" Rapha helped him to his feet.

The confused deka looked about and saw Lev, who was armed with a short spear, getting tackled by a hiveling mid-air "Bugs! Again? And since when can they and bogeys fly!"

"Since now! Move it!" Rapha growled as she shoved the man forward.

"Okay, okay!" The deka muttered as he grabbed his sword and charged forward.

Rapha continued freeing captives left and right, until they reached eighteen in total. She then turned and joined the battle herself.

The hivelings had also bolstered their numbers and had now become twelve. Eight drones, three spiderlings—and a warrior.

"Gods, no," she muttered. The behemoth, clicking its mandibles, gazed down at them from the ceiling with its menacing compound eyes. Everyone nervously awaited the warrior hiveling to join the battle, and once the other hivelings had worn out the men by sacrificing five of their own, it made its move.

It floated slowly towards them, but in the blink of an eye, the surrounding air glimmered, and the giant slammed into the ground, sending out a shockwave. Rapha managed to grab a stalagmite to steady herself. Only Hemgall, Vyrga, Lev, the two dekas, the darg, and a few bogeys managed to keep their footing. The others were not so lucky; their screams echoed as they plummeted into the depths below.

The hivelings used this opportunity to charge at the goblinoids. They attacked from both land and air, but the goblinoids refused to back down. Nobody wanted to be devoured by the beasts, and as there was no way out, they fought as hard as they could. Swords, axes, knives, and bare fists if need be, against claws and mandibles. Cries of war from men who wanted to live combined cacophonously with dreadful screeches from beasts who wanted to devour them.

Just as a green bogey wielding a flimsy stone knife was about to suffer a killing blow from a spiderling, Rapha charged and slashed at the creature's eyes, forcing it to back away from its prey.

"Get up! I'm not fighting this thing on my own!" she growled. She kept her eyes on the spiderling while helping him up, but as soon as he returned to his feet, the ungrateful bastard shoved Rapha towards the arachnoid.

"Forgive me, but I have a family!" he said before running away.

"What—coward!" she roared. She tried to roll out of the spiderling's way, only to be knocked back down. She then tried to roll away from the creature, but it stomped on her left arm, crushing it.

"Aaaaargh!" she screamed. The weight of the beast bore down on her arm. When she tried to slash at it with her other arm, the hiveling ripped the sword from her hand by the blade and threw it to the side.

"No. Not like this! Someone help!" Rapha yelled as the spiderling lowered its head towards her neck, clicking nonstop. She thrashed and struggled; its leg pressed harder on her arm. Her screams heightened to a pitch she never knew she could reach.

Her vision spotty, she looked around for salvation. Everyone else was occupied.

"Please... Someone help," she choked through tears as the spiderling scrutinised her with its empty yellow eyes. It clicked its mandibles one last time before everything was covered in blood—yellow blood.

The spiderling screeched as it received a spear to one of its right eyes. Suddenly it released her and started bucking uncontrollably. There was a grey bogey riding on its neck joint and repeatedly stabbing it with an onyx knife.

The spiderling bucked and rolled, threatening to crush Rapha until two grey hands dragged her away to safety.

"Got her, kid!" she heard a voice say before she passed out.

CHAPTER 22
REPRISAL

"Got her, kid!" yelled Hemgall as he dragged Rapha away from the hiveling.

"Done squabbling with Vyrga already?" Lev asked with a slight smirk.

"Settling the score can wait," Hemgall said in between breaths. With all his might, Hemgall popped the head of the spiderling off its body and hurled it to the ground. The head clicked its mandibles a couple of times before its eyes lost their light.

"One more hiveling down. Just a spiderling and a warrior drone to go," Hemgall looked towards the warrior that was fighting the others in close range while two green shaman bogeys, along with a bow-wielding Vyrga, provided ranged support. The remaining three surviving greyborn bogeys gathered around Lev and Hemgall.

"I still can't believe that such ungrateful shits exist," Hemgall growled as he looked towards the previous green bogey's corpse.

"What'd you expect from someone who's never fought for his life before?" Lev asked.

"Something more honourable, at least."

"No offence, but honour won't help much when you're dead."

"Then why didn't you leave her to die?"

"I have my reasons." Lev smiled. "Let's talk later. We have some hivelings to take care of."

"Sure. Can't let that shitbag take all the credit," Hemgall replied with a smile.

"Then let's go. We'll deal with the remaining warrior and spiderling."

Hemgall readied his axe. He was itching to make the hivelings pay.

"You're guarding her, by the way," Lev interrupted.

"Oh, come on!" Hemgall whined. "Why me? And who told you you could order me around!"

"What do you suggest then? Leave her alone?"

"No, you guard her while I take care of the big guy. You know I'm the most battle-hardened bogey here—it would be a waste for me to stay back. Besides, you're the leader-ish type of guy, so it's best for you to maintain order while battle-maniacs like me deal with the bloody part."

Lev shrugged. "If you insist. If you die, don't blame me."

"Don't worry, I won't."

Lev watched Hem leave and join the others as he sat next to the unconscious girl.

He smiled. "That's one way to avoid dying, I guess."

We've got some skilled fighters here, but it's not enough against their numbers, Lev thought as he watched the goblinoids clash against the two remaining hivelings from a distance.

There would be a time to strike, but for now, it was time to wait and observe. Besides, even if Rapha was still wary of him, he wanted to help her. She, along with the mercenaries, would be a vital source of information about the world outside the cave—she was too valuable to die.

With a precise shot from Vyrga, it didn't take long for the spiderling to fall.

Hemgall breathed heavily, his body covered in bleeding lacerations as he glared at the hiveling warrior as it was about to launch its next move.

"Out of the way!" Hemgall yelled as the hiveling warrior charged towards them. He rolled out of the way and evaded being crushed by the giant ant. When he looked back, he saw three more victims added to its kill count. Two greyborns and a shaman bogey had been crushed under the beast's feet. Half of their bodies had been turned to mush while the other half continued to wriggle about.

"Hey, weren't you asses supposed to provide us support? Where's your fancy magic now?"

"We're working on it, greyborn! Magic is neither easy nor fast!" yelled the remaining shaman bogey, pointing her focus, in the form of an amulet, at the hiveling. She tightened her grip and chanted faster and faster. Moments later, an energy bolt shot out of the focus into the hiveling, but did little more than dent its carapace.

"Wow, so powerful," mocked one deka, drawing the shamans' indignation.

Hemgall could not believe his luck. He was stuck battling a giant insectoid monster with a bunch of barely competent fools; in his eyes, the only other individuals here who were worthy of respect were Lev, the darg, and unfortunately Vyrga. Whether it was a miracle or dumb luck, he was thankful that they had somehow managed to deal with all the other beasts, saving this giant for last.

The hiveling warrior was about to charge once again, but it cancelled its attack after receiving a copper arrow to its left eye which caused it to screech and turn towards the attacker, Vyrga. *At least that bastard is doing something right,* Hemgall thought before running and sliding under the hiveling's legs.

He hacked away at the unarmoured portions of its legs with his axe, causing it to switch its attention to him. It tried to crouch to crush him with its weight, but he managed to roll out before it landed.

As the hiveling turned towards Hemgall, he stood up and raised his axe. "Come on! Show me what you've got!"

The hiveling clicked its mandibles and twirled its antenna in response. The embedded blade on its head glittered in the crystal light that illuminated the alien terrain of the seventh floor. It turned just a bit to the left before charging in that direction, towards a wall and chasm leading deeper into the abyss. Hemgall wondered why it was not charging directly at him, but once it touched the wall, everything clicked.

"Get out of the way!" yelled the darg.

Hemgall immediately rolled out of the way. His foe reached the wall, rebounded off of it, shimmered a little and floated before slamming into the ground onto where he was standing.

The hiveling immediately stood up and charged head-on at Hemgall again. He tried to sidestep the attack and avoided its horn but the hiveling suddenly turned and slammed him with its mandibles. Hemgall collided with a stalagmite, ripping it from the ground.

"Uuugh," Hemgall groaned before spitting out some blood along with a tooth. Near the hiveling distracted by shamans and a team of close combatants, he saw his axe, too far away and in too dangerous a location for him to grab. He got up and cracked his neck back into place before grabbing the broken stalagmite like a club.

This isn't enough, Hemgall thought. The stalagmite was too heavy and poorly balanced to be used offensively.

He looked at his surroundings trying to find something better. *Nothing but floating rocks around here— wait, they're floating!* With a savage grin, he jumped towards the hovering rocks and found himself released from the bounds of gravity.

He tied his improvised club to his belt, grabbed a few rocks, and immediately advanced towards the warrior by monkey-swinging, or perhaps pulling, on the nearby stalactites. Every few pulls, he let loose a few rocks and avoided the space where they fell. He kept doing that until he was above the warrior. Good timing too, as it was about to finish off the darg.

He grabbed the stone club and with a great roar, he jumped from the ceiling towards the unsuspecting beast and slammed its head to the ground as gravity took hold.

The hiveling screeched as it bled hemolymph. The top of its head armour cracked and its horn caved into its skull.

As it shook left and right, disoriented, Hemgall kept smashing it on the head till the stalagmite broke. He jumped off and grabbed his axe.

"Now! Kill it while it's dazed!" Hemgall roared before sliding below the hiveling and slicing at its legs once more.

Lev was watching the battle. Rapha lay unconscious next to him on the ground, a wadded-up cloth supporting her head.

"Looks like it'll end soon," he said to unhearing ears as Hemgall and the other fighters lopped off the hiveling's other front leg, causing it to not only lose one of its weapons but also to have a hard time balancing the front end of its body, hurting its movement.

The hiveling warrior grew more erratic as it tried to fend off its foes, but it was continuously pushed back without being able to inflict another major wound on one of its targets. It at last tried to escape towards the chasm.

While the remaining shaman raised the stone in front of it to block its path, Hemgall and the rest attacked its back legs and took out the left one, crippling it and sending it to the ground, unable to move. Seemingly sensing its end, it used its central legs to quickly turn and swipe at its opponents with its head and abdomen.

The goblinoids managed to evade the swipe attack. It opened its mandibles and used its remaining strength to lunge forward, putting extreme stress on its middle legs and snapping the greyborn in front of it in half. Bound by its jaws, the bogey was frozen in shock until he realised that he was cut in half. He screamed in agony, crying and cursing before the hiveling slammed him on the bloody ground, cracking his skull.

While he was watching this scene, Lev noticed Rapha stir on the ground.

"W-What h-h-hah— raaargh!" Rapha screamed in pain.

Lev immediately grabbed a gourd of mushroom mead mixed with crom powder—a known fast-acting sedative Rogg had provided after a few favours—and forced a spoonful into Rapha's mouth. She choked and sputtered from the vile tasting substance. He patted her back as she coughed and cursed before slowly losing consciousness and passing out.

"Well, that's one problem delayed," Lev muttered with a look of pity as he stared at the unconscious girl. "This world isn't kind to the disabled." He contemplated the girl's future. She might be a goblin, but from what he observed, she was neither high in the Jiira social ladder nor indispensable to the expedition. It would be hard to convince her superiors to heal her.

"So Rapha—well, I suppose it's meaningless to tell you this since you're out of it. I'm going to try to squeeze out a favour from an outcast healer. They're hard to find, they only accept payment in haze crystals, and aren't that powerful or they wouldn't have been thrown aside. It'll cost you more than info and it'll take a long time for you to heal. I thoroughly expect your gratitude." He turned his gaze back to the battle to witness its end.

The once-formidable warrior, whose kind had terrorized the expedition, now lay limbless on the ground, wailing pitifully as six of the eight remaining goblinoids hacked at its carapace and dismembered it slowly while making sure to keep it alive out of spite.

If they would only cackle madly and froth at the mouth, Lev thought, *this scene would make a great historical painting of savages.*

As the warrior let out one last wail and its eyes dimmed, Lev got up and carried Rapha in a fireman's carry. "Time to meet up with our companions."

"So the coward's here," grumbled one of the dekas before Hem smacked him in the face, knocking him to the ground. "What was that for!" he yelled once he got up.

"Call him a coward again and our insectoid friend here won't be the only one I rip to pieces," Hem growled. The deka lowered his head.

"Not to mention that he and the goblin lady in his grasp are our benefactors," Vyrga remarked. *Just this once, I'll let you off the hook. For earlier.*

"If it wasn't for them, we would've stayed stuck in those cocoons until we became bug food," said the darg with a look of disgust.

"Who asked you, you purple slave! Shouldn't you be in the eastern lands crawling under a pink's feet, ready to stuff your head in their crotch?" yelled the deka.

On cue, he screamed as the "purple slave" kicked him in the nether regions.

The darg wiped his sandals on the floor as if he were cleaning them from something dirty, then spat near the fallen buffoon, causing him to flinch. "I was a gladiator before this, you red bastard, and a great sailor before that. I don't know what you hear about my kind in your lands, but I'm a proud seaman from the prosperous state of Edoros on the fertile north-eastern isles. I am a master of the white sea."

The deka sneered while standing up. "Former master, you mean. Your people are now vassals to those invading pinks."

"Yours will soon follow if all dekas are like you."

The deka laughed. "I wish all of them were like me! If they were, there wouldn't be cowards afraid of some fancy-dressed pinks like Gozzag and Ban! But don't worry, I'm Drogg Grimmerson! And after I defeat my brothers and inherit my father's position, I'll make sure that there won't be any more weaklings amongst my people!"

Hem, Vyrga, and Lev exchanged glances. They'd each drawn the same conclusion: this Drogg needed to be disposed of, and soon. But not now, while they were still in danger.

"Will she be alright?" asked the darg, ignoring the red deka's ramblings about how all those who wronged him would pay once he rose to glory.

"I was about to splint her arm, though I doubt it would make a difference," Lev admitted. "Without magical interference, it'll be a miracle if she can ever use her left arm again." He gently put her down on the ground and began the operation.

"So she'll be crippled? That'll be the end for her," the darg said.

"Don't worry. I'll take care of it if we get out of here. Well, I'll try."

"I hope you succeed. We owe our lives to you two. I heard what happened earlier, and I have to thank you, Lev."

"No problem. By the way, I haven't gotten your name."

"Shahn Kafar, son of Kafar Ramun, at your service." The darg bowed.

"It's a pleasure." Lev bowed in reciprocity. "By the way, is there a way to shut him up?" Lev asked as he finished setting up the splints.

"It'll be an epic for the ages! The epic of the mighty Drogg, king of kings! I'll have the entire world under my people and we will—" The delusional deka kept spouting off, and Hemgall seemed ready to throw him to the dark abyss just to shut him up.

As Drogg kept spouting his drivel, Hem turned towards Lev and asked, "Most dekas aren't this dense, right?"

"You don't need to worry. My men and I have worked with dekas before. There were some reasonable and respectable members, and then there was a minority of people like... that. At least the other one seems normal."

"These lands will bow to me!" the deka continued, unfazed. "I will engrave my name among the gods' and I will—"

"Fool! More of them are coming!" Vyrga cut in.

"From where?" Lev responded, to Drogg's chagrin.

Suddenly, swarms of hivelings were crawling down the walls. The painfully loud din of hiveling screeches shook the foundations of the stone and forced everyone to cover their ears or risk going deaf.

"What... was that!" yelled Hemgall before the room was engulfed in purple light.

"I believe it was that," Vyrga said as he pointed at the source of the light. It was a winged purple hiveling, larger than a drone but smaller than a warrior, surrounded by an entourage of warriors. The purple hiveling opened its large, magnificent wings and they seemed to shine even brighter as it emitted another screech, forcing everyone to their knees.

"Aaagh! Make it stop!" cried Drogg.

As though on command, the purple hiveling halted its approach. Shortly afterward, the rest of the hivelings recommenced their forward movement.

"Tch," spat Lev. "Too many hivelings, not enough men. Great. Just great."

CHAPTER 23
THE HIVE'S WRATH

In the darkest depths of the abyss, in a place untouched by goblinoids and unclaimed by hivelings, a hiveling corpse lay on the hard ground. Its scarred form was broken and limbless; its cracked shell oozed its bluish-green nectar of life. Other than the corpse, there was no movement in the area until a certain grey bogey, lying in the centre of the beast, twitched.

"Ugh... What happened? And why is it so dark?" Lev mumbled as he touched cold chitin. "Wait. Am I sitting on a dead warrior?"

Lev suddenly remembered that he had smuggled a couple of haze crystals inside his pack. "Where's my marching pack?" he yelled as he frantically felt around for it.

He touched something warm and soft. He immediately pulled back his hand and drew his knife, trying to detect any movement in his surroundings. He picked up on a few feminine groans and the sound of laboured breathing.

"Rapha?" he asked, half-expecting a response. Lev warily pointed his knife in the direction of the sounds. He prepared himself to face some kind of predatory, or at least threatening, creature capable of mimicking sounds. But after a breath, he lowered the knife. *If there were such a creature,* he realised, *it would have targeted me earlier when I was unconscious.*

Judging from the absence of light—which precluded the growth of plants—anything that lived here would be not only a blind scavenger but also not picky enough to ignore a free meal. On the other hand, it could have eaten one of the others...

Nevermind. There would've been some kind of sound if that were the case, Lev deduced. *As far as I know, everyone smuggled a few crystals, so Rapha must've kept some on her. Looks like I'll have to risk it.*

He cautiously approached the source of the noise, knowing full well that he was unlikely to prevail in a fight if it struck back, and prodded it with the back of his knife. He perceived no reaction; he proceeded to touch it.

Seems like it is Rapha. Thankfully she hasn't woken up yet. He moved his hand to the left and grazed the smooth metal of her boots—if she had been conscious, she would most likely have kicked him. *Now, if I were Rapha, where would I store those crystals?*

By the faintest reflection of light from his own eyes, Lev could just barely make out the worn straps of a backpack lying among the leftover rubble. He recognised it the instant he saw the red ribbon sticking out behind the edge of a fallen stalagmite.

He remembered how most of the harem guards had used these reflective ribbons before to quickly find their equipment in low-light conditions. Lev manoeuvred around the rubble to locate the source of the reflection.

He dug his hands deep into the backpack for the crystals. *Dammit! Not here either?* he cursed to himself. He sighed and closed it, but another idea struck him. He grabbed the bag again and ran his fingers up and down the seams—some were looser than they should have been. He quickly tore apart the loosest seam, uncovering a pocket from which he plucked out a small, glowing pouch.

Bingo, he almost whispered. He grabbed the haze crystal from the bag. At the same time, he felt a heavy, familiar presence emanating disgust.

There you are, Gherm, he scoffed in his mind. *You haven't been active lately, so I assumed you were gone.*

Traitor... said the foreign voice in his mind.

Hey, now, I'm just doing everything I can to ensure we survive.

Shameless... fragments... within your soul... can't hide... your past, replied the voice.

Well, shame is only a concern if you live to experience it, and you can rest assured it would be easy for me to handle something as measly as "shame." If you can't bring yourself to appreciate my experience, I can't possibly expect you to understand me or appreciate my decisions.

Broken... all of you... broken...

Lev was now quite peeved. *The sad truth is, we're all broken on the inside, but only few realise it. You have access to my memories, so you should know this about me, or—wait.* His thoughts betrayed his deepening condescension. *Did you skip the important parts because they were too much for you?* he asked.

Gherm said, or rather thought, nothing.

Good. It's easier for you to keep your sense of self that way. Lev exhaled. *Sure, I'm more broken than the average denizen of these caverns, but thankfully, unlike others in my previous line of work, I haven't hit rock bottom yet. At least I still try to do some good.*

Not... by much...

Still, not much is better than nothing.

You're... unstable...

Lev shrugged. *True, but we can talk about my mental instability later, once we're not in danger. We have more important things to do, alright?*

Gherm didn't respond.

I'll take that as a yes. Lev returned to Rapha's backpack and picked his new source of light back up. *Now how did we end up here?*

From what he could see, there was nothing but dirt and stones nearby. No grass, no insects, nor any other kind of fauna or flora were visible. It seemed as if the place was absorbing light—a crystal of this size and radiance should have illuminated everything within a wide radius, but here it could only shed light upon a short few killigs.

He raised the crystal to the ceiling. Light reflected and refracted off of a grey, jellylike substance. *Huh... Guess that's how we weren't reduced to paste.*

Lev lowered his guard, sat down, and thought back on what happened before he woke up. *Hmm... We finished off the hiveling warrior, the dim-witted deka started an argument, and then a swarm of hivelings appeared, led by a winged purple one— ah, that's right!* he recalled.

We realised we couldn't handle the swarm, so before the hivelings could reach us, we dragged the warrior carcass to the edge and held on to it tightly as we threw ourselves into the abyss. He crossed his legs contentedly.

But... it's strange. Nobody said a word about this plan, yet we all cooperated... Why? Lev contemplated. *And how come the others aren't here?*

A feeling of warmth caressed his mind.

"Come..."

"What was th—" Lev tried to protest, but the comforting warmth was becoming hard to ignore.

"Come..."

It must be a trap.

"Come..."

But why does it feel so... nice? he thought. He felt warm and secure as if he were a child in his mother's lap. *Maybe it isn't a... trap...*

Lev looked towards his left. Something told him there was a path there leading to everlasting joy and happiness.

It is! Gherm shrieked, reemerging in Lev's mind.

I know. Even if it feels nice, it's... obviously a trap. Lev took a step towards the path.

It revealed itself... when it tried to show me a path of happiness. There's no... such thing, Gherm explained.

"Come!"

Shut up... Only a fool would fall for this. Lev took another step.

"Come..."

"Come!"

"I said shut up!" Lev roared, halting his forward motion and snapping himself back to his senses.

The whispering stopped.

"Finally. Guess that explains where most of the others went."

Gherm resurfaced. *Most?*

We've worked with Hemgall and... cooperated with Vyrga enough to know those two wouldn't fall for this trick, Lev explained. *You should know neither of them are simple-minded fools. And I'm sure some of the other captives should be able to handle a situation like this.*

So where did they go? Why leave us?

Lev shrugged and looked to his right. *Don't know about the others, but I bet Vyrga and Hemgall went the other direction to get as far away from that thing as possible. Still, it's likely that there's other dangers over there. We need to get down from here to investigate first.*

And... Rapha?

Yeah, I'm bringing her along, Lev replied. He hoisted her up in a fireman's carry. "Let's go, shall we?" he said to both the unconscious girl and his spiritual companion before slowly and carefully climbing down the giant insect's carcass.

Using the light from the crystal, he searched around the hiveling's corpse for any abandoned equipment and any sign of his missing companions.

He kept searching around till he stumbled on some footprints and a broken gourd, pitch leaking from it. Lev examined the label—it was one of his.

Thieves. Gherm whispered.

Really? Who would've guessed? Lev replied. He returned his attention to the footprints. *Don't take it so seriously. Thieves peeve me and I've been having trouble controlling my emotions in this body.*

It's my *body.*

You mean our *body. At least 'til I find a better alternative.*

Thief...

Lev chuckled. *I am one, aren't I? Though I didn't want to live again as a member of a marginalised class, now, did I? How ironic... I tried my best to free myself and those I care about from oppression only to fall right back to the bottom.* He remembered that Gherm was listening to his thoughts. *Don't worry, though. You should be able to guess that I don't plan on staying like this.*

Becoming a leader... isn't enough? Gherm's voice resonated with a rawness Lev had not foreseen from his disembodied host. *You're now... a greyborn! How high do you want to fly... before you... fall!*

Don't be a coward, Gherm. I'm planning something big and you should know it.

Ghorza will be hurt! Gherm yelled.

No, she won't. I'll make sure she stays out of this. That part you should already know.

Why take... things slow... then? Why be... friendly to Rak?

It takes time to train men and gather resources and it takes alliances to fight the status quo in society.

But—

I don't plan to take over the world. I only plan to free it.

Why him?

Look, I know you're angry that you're not in possession of this body anymore, but can't you at least pay attention for once? Rak's more trustworthy than others, his men are reliable, and as long as I don't break our agreement and try to usurp him, I can be sure he'll follow your people's code and not stab me in the back, Lev ranted.

You know, for thugs, you greyborns are quite honourable. An act for an act, and loyalty for loyalty... Though I guess greyborns wouldn't want to kill each other too often. Class solidarity is a wonderful thing.

Fine...

Let's try finding a way out for now. We should at least find some food, water, and a place to rest before she wakes up, yeah?

Gherm paused for a moment before Lev felt him calm down. *Let's...*

Good. Posture relaxed, Lev proceeded to search for a path out of the abyss.

CHAPTER 24
EDGE OF TOMORROW

A few hours had passed since Lev regained consciousness. He'd only found one path out of the room, at least within the boundaries of the area he allowed himself to explore. Only in case he found no other solution would he have explored where the whispers were trying to guide him.

Despite his weariness, he kept his eyes peeled for nasty surprises as he marched forward with Rapha draped over his shoulders. The only times he stopped were when he needed to take a break to replenish his strength and rest his aching feet.

Finally, something to drink! He silently rejoiced as he came upon an underground lake. He gently placed Rapha and the haze crystal on the ground near a pool of water before he removed his helmet and dipped it in the water to use as a bucket.

He shined the light of the crystal into the water to check for anomalies before raising the helmet to his face. He sniffed for odours. *Hmm, nothing out of the ordinary. Does that mean the water's safe? There could be some harmful minerals...*

He stared into the water, resisting the urge to lick his cracked lips. *There aren't any corpses nearby or signs of struggles from suffocation or paralysis. But my allies have my waterskins, so they could have drunk from those instead...*

As Lev contemplated whether he should risk drinking from the lake, he heard a weary cracked voice from behind.

"W-what happened? Where... am I?" Rapha asked. She tried to push herself up with her splinted arm, only to wince in pain.

"My arm... I can't move it! What happened to my—" She erupted into a fit of dry coughs.

Lev dropped the helmet on the ground and rushed to her side. "Easy! Calm down!"

"How do you expect me to calm down! My left arm was shattered by a bloody insect! And why can I barely feel it?"

"I've applied some medicine to save the nerves. We'll get you healed up when we reconvene with the others."

Rapha chuckled ruefully. "Please, Lev. You know they won't heal me. Even if I do survive, I'll be nothing but a liability. I'll either end up a sex slave or be tossed aside to die like the expendable I am." Her chuckles increased in volume before they turned to sobs, tears streaming down her face.

"I'm damned and doomed! It would be better for me to drown myself now..." she cried.

Lev shook his head. "I don't think so."

"Why, though? I'm useless now. There's no way we could convince Bulgu's healers to fix my arm."

"Who said anything about needing help from that bastard and his pawns?"

"Is there anyone else who would heal me?" Rapha asked, a slight tinge of hope in her tone.

Lev lay down on his back next to her and let his own arms flop at his sides, knees pointed at the ceiling. "I have contacts. It will probably take a lot longer, but I assure you, I'll get you fixed up."

"What makes you so sure?"

Lev turned his head to face Rapha. "I'm sure because I know myself and I know my capabilities. Healers in bogey-kind aren't rare—they just don't usually choose to treat greyborns like me. But like I said, I have contacts."

"And if my contacts fail me," Lev pulled out a haze crystal from Rapha's bag. "Everyone has a price."

Rapha sat silently for a while, gazing down at Lev. Without warning, she abruptly looked away, but not before Lev glimpsed a sparkle return to her eyes. "If you manage to do that, I'll do anything. Heck, I'll even marry you."

Lev grimaced. "I wouldn't offer that last thing so lightly if I were you."

"A life for a life. You'd be saving me from a dog's death, you know."

"So you did mean it," he sighed. "It's true that you'll owe me your life, but that doesn't have to mean marriage or slavery."

"How so?"

"I just find it distasteful."

A moment passed between the two. "Then what do you want instead?"

"Loyalty without chains and knowledge will suffice. Once we're out, teach me all you know about the outside world and help me take down those who stand in my way. I want you to be a companion who'll question my actions and guide me when I'm wrong, not a trained war hound who'll commit any atrocities I'd tell them to."

"So you want me to be a part of your council as your war-maiden?" Rapha asked excitedly.

"That's one way to put it. If I heal you, would you agree to that?"

"Definitely!" she yelled, giddily enough to nearly forget the pain in her arm. That was, before she overestimated her ability to stand up and underestimated how parched her throat was.

"Here, let me help," Lev reached out to help Rapha stand.

To Lev's surprise, she unsheathed her sword and stabbed it into the ground, as was custom for a shieldmaiden's vow. Despite the pain, she clasped his hand with her left. Lev acknowledged her gesture and helped her up.

"Thank you," the goblin girl blushed.

"No problem."

"By the way, do you have any water? My supplies were with the carriers…" She watched the corners of Lev's mouth drop.

Lev stood quiet for a while. "Sadly, no. We've been robbed."

"You're kidding me."

"I wish I was. Thankfully they left my equipment alone. My helmet, specifically."

She looked towards the wooden headgear lying on the ground with water trickling out of the ear holes. "You used it as a bucket, right? Though looking at you, it doesn't look like you've drunk from it."

"I'm not sure if the water's safe to drink yet."

"Lev, if we don't drink, we might not find another water source. Where are we by the way? This doesn't look like the seventh floor."

Lev hesitated. "We're in uncharted territory. I presume the eighth floor, if there is such a floor."

"What? Did I hear that right?" Rapha asked, flabbergasted.

"You did."

"Great. Just great. Then what do we do now? How do we get back up with no supplies, no weapons, half our party lost and probably unable to fight, and giant bugs waiting to kill us?"

"By being careful and paying attention to our surroundings. So far we haven't encountered any hivelings." Lev paused as he gathered information from Gherm's memories. "And we have an escape route. On every floor, there are certain shrines that can teleport you to corresponding shrines on the floors above."

"There are? Then why aren't they being used?"

"For two reasons. The first is that the shrines can only teleport small groups, no more than ten at a time. The second is that the shrines above the third floor were destroyed a long time ago. When the Jiira first started exploring the cavern, they foolishly destroyed the portals, thinking they were icons of false gods.

"The only reason the other portals survived is because a scouting group once went ahead of the expeditionary force and accidentally activated a shrine's teleportation while trying to escape with treasure."

"The Jiira must be the foulest, most undisciplined, and most sacrilegious fools I've ever met," Rapha growled.

"Descendants of the Enlightened One or not, it's a wonder they became strong enough to rule others in the first place."

"True. By the way, can you please help me drink? I'm dying of thirst, so just let me test it for the both of us," Rapha asked with a hoarse voice.

"Are you sure?"

"Yes, I'm sure, and even if I wasn't, this isn't the time to be paranoid."

Lev lifted his helmet, which was still full of water, and placed it on the ground near Rapha. "There. Let's see if it's drinkable, shall we?"

"Y-Yeah."

Lev helped Rapha raise his helmet to her lips, and she drank.

Lev stared at her in silence, trying to observe any change in her behaviour. Rapha stared back, shoulders tensed and lips pursed, trying not to fixate on his piercing, golden-yellow pupils.

"Looks like it's safe to drink. Hopefully."

"Hopefully?"

"Never mind." He sipped from the helmet and refilled it again.

"*Hopefully*, we'll find something to eat," retorted Rapha.

"We may. So let's continue looking for our thieves, shall we?"

"We're not looking for food first?"

"Are you proposing that we just give them our equipment? Depending on why they took our gear, a few extra hands might be welcome. And that's a big 'might'—I'm more in the mood to dish out some punishment—but we do need numbers to survive."

"Then let's go already."

Lev nodded. "Lets."

* * *

What felt like a few hours had passed since they had resumed walking. The path was now lit with numerous large, bright haze crystals, revealing pockets of other magical stones and various signs of life.

As they approached a corner, Lev suddenly stopped to inspect the wall.

"What is it?" asked Rapha.

"Nothing. Just thinking we should prepare ourselves beforehand. Who knows what could be hiding on the other side?"

Using her good hand, Rapha shined her haze crystal on the ground and spotted an unusually dark spot further ahead near the left wall of the path, devoid of crystal growth and seemingly absorbing light. She pointed it out to Lev. "What's that?"

"Stay here. It's probably a trap." Lev drew his blade.

"Most likely, but I don't think staying here would be to my advantage. If there's something out there, it would most likely want to separate us."

Lev stuck his left arm out to block Rapha's advance. "Or it could want to kill us both at the same time."

"I still think it's better for me to come with you," Rapha insisted. "I could at least save myself the trouble of being a hostage."

"I might use you as a shield if you come."

"Doesn't matter. If you're killed, I'm next."

Lev lowered his arm. "Suit yourself." Gripping his knife tightly in his right hand, legs tensed to jump backwards in case of any sudden movement, he advanced towards the object while repeatedly scanning his surroundings.

"Seems we've found our first victim," he said.

He crouched next to the freshly-mangled corpse of a young-looking, green bogey. Judging by the way he had held his now haze-coated focus amulet, Lev concluded that the bogey must have been a shaman. His broken legs along with the wear on his clothes made it clear he was one of the unlucky who'd fallen off when the warrior hiveling collided with the large floating rock they'd been fighting on.

His body lay between two stalagmites. His right arm was ripped from the shoulder blade, his freshly concave skull was missing its lower jaw, his tongue lolled out, and his kneecaps were shattered. His abdominal cavity was split open, but his entrails were missing.

"W-What could've done this?" whimpered Rapha.

"We'll know soon enough."

"Wha—"

"On my mark, jump to the side."

Rapha could only come to one conclusion. "It's above us, isn't it?"

"Now!"

They both immediately leapt away from the corpse, just before it was smashed by an abominable figure.

Rapha quickly identified the figure: it was Drogg. Yet it was not exactly Drogg—his formerly red skin was now purplish-grey with cysts sprouting all over, and his form was three times larger. A gigantic plant-like bulb on his back spouted noxious gas. The bulb had dug roots into his body, and was poking out of all his orifices, starting with a beard of tentacles and ending with a tail of vines.

"I told you to come... I would have made you perfect, like how they once made us... But it seems you have chosen death," spoke the abomination in multiple dissonant voices.

"It seems we did," said Lev, stance steady, head tilted, and attention on a particularly enthralling stalactite.

"Good. Let's end this quickly," replied Drogg.

A horrible screech filled the area. Drogg's back had been set ablaze.

Lev side-eyed Drogg without moving his head. "I never said this would be *our* end."

A gourd sailed through the air and shattered against the creature's bulb. Drogg screeched louder.

Hemgall, Shahn, Vyrga, another deka, and a green shaman bogey emerged from the darkness and charged at the monster. Hemgall and the deka dodged a swing of its arm and chopped down at it. Vyrga and Shahn repeatedly stabbed at the burning bulb with spears, setting the pitch-covered heads alight and burning the insides of the bulb.

The shaman threw another pitch gourd, followed by a briskly conjured fireball. The two collided with the beast concurrently. The beast wailed, trying to retaliate with its roots and tendrils, which burned to ash upon emerging from its body.

As the flames spread into the creature's torso, the beast fell to the ground, moaning and writhing, vines charring and skin singing.

"That ends that," said Lev, hardly batting an eyelid.

Rapha choked out a few words. "How did— Where did—"

Lev chuckled. "Hemgall carved my group's sign for ambush on the wall."

"And good thing I did. We managed to take care of the last of these things!"

Rapha's eyes widened. "You've fought them before?"

"We have. Our glorious leader Drogg wasn't the only star-crossed fool. Some of the burgas who fell off along with this poor shaman were corrupted by something, their bodies possessed by an evil I've never seen before. Fortunately, it was easy to take them down once we discovered their weakness to fire. If only the torches hadn't scared them so easily, they could've been a challenge," Vyrga replied with a smirk.

"The unfortunate part is that *that* bastard had to survive," said Hemgall.

Vyrga turned to face the large greyborn. "Not as unfortunate as your sense of humour. Considering your... intelligence, I expected you to join our late shaman here instead of following me ahead."

"I followed you because I knew you were up to no good. You stole some of Lev's stuff after all. Oh, and here you go by the way," Hemgall continued, walking over to Lev and pulling out Lev's marching pack. "I managed to convince the others to leave the rest of your stuff alone."

"Thanks." Lev inspected his belongings. His shield and spear were both still usable, but his pack seemed to be missing some items.

Lev turned to Vyrga. "Now would you kindly return the rest? I seem to be missing a few gourds of pitch and medications."

Vyrga sneered. "Sadly, I can't. As you just saw, we needed them to deal with these aberrations. I assure you, I'll repay you once we return to safe grounds."

"And you expect me to trust you?"

"I expect you to be logical and refrain from doing anything that might compromise our odds of escape."

Lev and Vyrga stared each other in the eyes, but neither backed down. They stayed like that till Rapha coughed, grabbing their attention.

"So what happens next?" she asked while looking at the shimmering corpse.

Vyrga spoke without looking away from Lev. "The remains will disappear soon—don't ask me how. They just turn into balls of light and vanish into the walls. Even our shaman friend—"

"How many times do I need to tell you the name's Orva?" the shaman cut in.

"As many times I need to tell others not to interrupt me when I'm talking, girl," Vyrga replied.

Orva threw her arms up. "Do it right the first time and I won't interrupt you."

Vyrga continued. "Even our friend Orva here doesn't know how or why that happens. Don't think about it too much. It's just another mystery of this place."

"I see. So are we staying here or are we going to eat something and continue ahead?" she asked.

Everyone turned silent.

Hemgall sighed. "Well, you see… we found a giant gate with a golden door, but we can't seem to open it no matter what we do."

"A gate?" replied Rapha.

"It's not far from here. It'd be better if you two saw it. It's also better to eat there since there's also light, edible plants, and water," Shahn interjected.

"There is, huh… Could it be a trap?"

"It's not. We made sure of that. We also checked everywhere else. There's no other path but that one."

"In that case, we'd better go there now. Maybe we can find a way to open it, and even if we don't, we still need a proper place to rest."

Everyone nodded and proceeded towards the door.

As Shahn had said, it didn't take long for them to reach the gate. Both Lev and Rapha felt their jaws drop.

"Magnificent, isn't it?" Hemgall said as he gazed at the glorious marble figure in front of the gate.

The figure was eight killigs tall. Along the gate were engraved, unknown sagas describing forgotten gods and tales, detailing what Lev assumed was the creation of the world, its evolution, and a great cataclysmic war that would've torn the world apart. There were detailed portraits of all kinds of creatures, both magic and mundane, painted on artificially flattened sections of the cavern walls. There were even depictions of bogeys and hivelings preparing to face off in battle against goblins.

"What… is this?" Rapha muttered. "Is everything predicted here?"

Orva scoffed. "I believe it's nonsense. It looks like bogeys and hivelings are fighting together against your goblin kin. Utterly ridiculous."

"It could also just be the Jiira," she countered.

"Could be," replied Hemgall in Orva's place. "But I can't fathom us fighting alongside those bugs."

Lev cut in. "We can think about that later. For now, let's see if we can open it." He approached the golden gate.

Though it was not as magnificent as the portraits, the gate was stunning in its own right, engraved with symbols in an unknown language and adorned with depictions of five masks. Each mask held gems of a different colour for eyes—crimson red, yellow-orange, purple, black, and white. All of the masks were small, but for the white-eyed one positioned in the centre of the gate.

Everyone closed in on Lev to see what he would do.

There doesn't seem to be a lock, he noted. *Let's see if there's some sort of mechanism hidden behind one of these decorations.*

He touched the gate. Blindingly white light burst forth from the central mask and engulfed his surroundings. Lev covered his eyes and screamed in pain.

"I thought you said there were no traps!"

Lev heard no response. He uncovered his eyes and looked back—not only was nobody there but also the scenery had changed. There was nothing but the void. Even the gate was gone. In its place was a giant figure covered with an intricate white robe, glowing white eyes piercing through a white mask.

Leonard Erand Vandersteen, I've been waiting for you, said a voice echoing inside his head.

What— Gherm? No—who are you?

BONUS CHAPTER I
BEAUTIFUL WORLD

WARNING: you have 10% charge left in your MCS.

Huh. How did I end up in this ditch?

The red blinking light on his visor brought Lev back to reality.

He moved his fingers towards the MCS display screen strapped to his right wrist.

The MCS's display had a few tabs and two large digital buttons at the bottom, conveniently labelled "Open" and "Close." He must have forgotten to stop the automatic visor alert notification system, which projected a flickering red light into his retina.

I guess I need *to recharge my batteries before this annoying light turns off.*

Now, where exactly am I? Lev thought as he rolled onto his belly and propped himself up on his arms. *I've got to make contact with the command centre or I'll—*

Lev was rudely interrupted by a deafening explosion a few metres away from him.

Must have been a mortar shell, Lev concluded; mortar shells had to land near their targets to kill, and since his headgear had protected his eardrums while his combat suit had shielded him from shrapnel, he had been spared from any real harm.

Thus was the benefit of having an MCS, short for Military Combat Suit. This was not the official name of the suit, but many cadets simplified it for convenience's sake instead of repeating the long and tedious "Mechanised Military Personal Combat Protection Gear."

"Aargh!" Lev felt a burning pain in his lower torso. He reached down to examine his body for wounds, and found that a bullet had pierced his suit.

Seems like the visor alerted me because of damage, not drained batteries.

When did I get shot? He couldn't remember much—he only knew that staring at empty dirt impact craters would do him no favours.

Right, I need to contact HQ and get the hell out of here.

Lev opened a new tab on his MCS's wrist display and searched for its emergency signal feature. A few taps later, a prompt displayed.

Confirm your ID.

Lev took out his dog tag and tapped it against the display.

ID Confirmed. Executing action: Emergency Signal.

While the device tried to establish a connection with the nearest base, Lev continued to trudge through the battlefield.

Lev crossed a hill, bristling at the countless bodies—no, body parts—and wrecked vehicles scattered everywhere he could see. Empty shells littered the ground; the smell of gunpowder and discharged plasma rounds still wafted in the air.

Lev's world was embroiled in war—in a worldwide war of untold scale unprecedented in the annals of history. This was not a war about ideology, politics, or anything of the abstract sort; this was simply a war over territory. Both the Eurasian Technocracy and American Empire needed command over the neutral zone, a zone with "plenty of resources and fertile land," or so the propaganda claimed.

Lev heard a familiar beep. His wrist device had managed to contact HQ, and a transport vehicle was on its way to his location.

After an hour or so had passed, Lev heard another familiar noise, the din of atmospheric thrust engines, the same engines that had dropped him on the battlefield so many times before.

The transport vehicle landed near Lev on flat terrain, heedlessly crushing corpses and debris beneath it. A man walked out of the transport's cargo hatch.

"Private Vandersteen, are you enjoying the view? Get on—we haven't got all day!"

Lev glanced over the scorched land reeking of acrid smoke. This was the sight of war, a crude painting unfit to be seen. The tone was too dark: the red stained corpses, the black puddles of oil underneath destroyed vehicles, and a far-too-brown underbelly of craters made for a foreboding scene of death and carnage.

* * *

Lev quickly brushed the inner parts of his MCR-17 combat rifle before quickly reassembling it. He then filled his magazines with another round of plasma discharge capsules.

A small crowd of recruits watched as he loaded his rifle. "I wish I could do it as fast as you," one of them said.

"Yeah. You and everyone else," Lev replied without looking up.

The recruit paused for a second. "Is that a type 17 military combat rifle? I thought they'd stopped producing them ten years ago."

"Ten years ago, I had friends who were still alive," Lev muttered without raising his eyes from the rifle he was loading. Once finished with his checks, he stood up and made his way to the armoury exit. "Now I have this."

This was Lev's first day in Military Zone-10, England. He had never been stationed in such a seemingly peaceful place before; all he'd known were the harsh battles he'd endured in the neutral zone and the less-than-comfortable stations at its borders.

The sergeant held up his arms and shouted, "ALRIGHT MAGGOTS, TIME FOR ANOTHER ROUND OF TRAINING!"

Lev knew he would never be promoted to a higher rank in the military; only people with limited citizenship could entertain that idea.

Limited citizenship was the beauty of the levy system—if you failed to complete your ten years but had managed to survive at least five, you would receive limited citizenship.

If you served the remainder of your original ten years plus an additional five-year stretch, the Technocracy would deem you worthy of full citizenship. The fastest way to full citizenship, of course, would be to grit one's teeth and endure ten years in a single stretch.

Many saw the levy system as a trap. Limited citizenship would entice people to enlist and quit after five years, but the moment the poverty and helplessness of life as a "limited" citizen set in, those same people would enlist for another ten years.

"THAT MEANS YOU TOO, VANDERSTEEN!"

Private Leonard Erand Vandersteen, tenth year, Eurasian Army, stood up and followed the others for his next training session. First up was the standard eight-kilometre full-gear run. Lev had prepared himself for this session, his muscles hungry for more.

"Sergeant. This Vandersteen... How long has he been in the levy system?" Mark asked the sergeant. Mark was Lev's platoon's second lieutenant and another victim of the limited citizenship system.

He'd noticed Lev earlier—there was a way that greenhorns floundered about, and there was a way that veterans did their business. From what he saw, Lev could very well be the most experienced soldier in this base, even when compared to the sergeant barking orders at him.

"Well, at least three years longer than you, Lieutenant," answered Eric, the sergeant. Eric, like most NCOs in the Eurasian army, had served five years before he quit. It had been out of necessity, to recuperate from the various physical and mental traumas combat had caused. He had then returned to the battlefield, ready for an additional five years in hell. "This guy's been here for over nine years, according to these records. He always survives battles with his magazines empty and his combat suit a wreck."

"Talk about a killer. At least that explains his stamina." Mark shook his head sorrowfully. "He must've been outmanoeuvring those mortar shells for years."

"Damn those Imperials. If only they'd accepted Higman's proposal, we wouldn't have had this war to begin with," bemoaned Eric. Councillor Arnold Higman had proposed measures to unify all of Earth under one state. In his most famous, penultimate speech, he'd started off with these famous words: "For peace to reign, we must first unite the world."

Arnold Higman had been assassinated exactly ten milliseconds after those famous last words.

"Sergeant. Higman was a delusional old geezer who wanted to have dictatorial power over the entire world." Mark had wanted to believe that a world like that was possible, but his faith had run out a long time ago. Now, he was just a drone carrying out orders from the brass.

"TIME FOR SIT-UPS, MAGGOTS!" boomed Eric.

Lev and the other recruits did what Eric ordered, most with loud complaints, Lev without.

"Hah, these pansies must be fresh from their mamas' gardens," Eric jeered.

Mark almost played along, but Lev was still going, doing yet more sit-ups with unwaveringly perfect form. *That Vandersteen, he's something different. Are all nine-year term recruits like that?* Mark had never seen a recruit serve all ten years in one stretch.

Another week passed, and the new recruits had been deemed ready for their first battle. Every recruit was assigned a combat suit programmed to execute complex battle movements and increase their odds of survival, though durability and features depended on rank. Sadly, only the very basics were explained to the recruits, and it would take at least a month for trash from the slums to be moulded into combat-ready soldiers. Time they didn't have.

Lev heard that familiar sound that had been ever-present throughout the past nine years, and before he knew it, there it stood: the dreaded military transport vehicle, atmospheric engines spouting out huge amounts of compressed air.

"Alright, men! Check your combat suits before entering and hang on tight!" Mark shouted at the cadets, knowing that less than half of them would survive this first battle.

"And don't forget, lads, a fresh pint for the lucky one who gets the most kills!" bellowed Eric. The innocent recruits took Eric's joke seriously, laughing about how they would tell their grandchildren about the "Great War."

Lev did not join in; he was preoccupied with checking all of his equipment one last time. He knew he would just see the battlefield tear their legs off and splatter their brains next to their broken skulls. He saw no reason to socialise.

He stepped into the vehicle, securing himself and his suit to the support rack.

"Remember to release your MCS when the light turns green!"

"Aye-aye, sir!"

Lev inadvertently made eye contact with Mark, snapping himself out of his daze. "Aye-aye, sir!" he replied hastily.

This was it, the transport to hell. Lev had long since lost count of how many battles he had fought, but every single one had had the same outcome—he was always one of the lucky survivors.

What Lev did not know, however, was that this would be his final battle as a grunt. He'd redeemed a one-way ticket straight into Lucifer's cage.

The vehicle's engines blasted another wave of compressed air and it jetted away from Zone-10's airbase, not stopping until it reached the neutral zone to deliver its unholy freight.

Lev steeled his resolve as he prepared to release himself onto yet another battlefield.

BONUS CHAPTER 2
ORIGINS

"Are you alright?"

Lev's shouting voice was barely audible.

"Wh-Who are you? State your Eurasian ID!" Eric screamed, his eyes blinded and ears deafened by a flash grenade that had been thrown at him seconds ago.

"My EU-ID is 2406. Private Vandersteen" Lev responded.

"What?" Eric yelped.

"I said my EU-ID is twenty-four-zero-six. Private Vandersteen," Lev responded louder this time.

"*What?*" Eric repeated.

"I *said*, my EU-ID is— dammit, you, I'm with the Technocracy! Eurasia!"

Eric, squinting, could just make out Lev's general shape. As his vision slowly returned, he recognized the blue motif of the Technocracy on Lev's standard-issue MCS model. "Alright, 2406— I mean, Vandersteen, is there a way to contact the neutral zone's HQ? I think there's something wrong with my MCS."

Lev glanced at the MCS's display on his right wrist, swiftly opened a few sub-tabs, and took out his dog tag to confirm his ID. He waited for the device to establish a connection, only to find that all communication between his squad and HQ had broken down about an hour ago. He'd been too focused on his immediate survival to notice it.

"Sir, the line is dead. We can't make contact."

Eric blinked faster and harder, still trying to regain his vision. "Vandersteen, tell me," he said, "did we lose?"

Lev surveyed the battlefield. Unidentifiable limbs and mangled cadavers could be seen far and wide. Wrecked vehicles, broken MCSs, and twisted guns created yet another gory scene.

Looks like I'm in hell again, Lev concluded. *When will I finally gain my freedom?*

The confused sergeant desperately dug his hands in and out of his pockets, searching for his own display. "Looks like we're out of options, Vandersteen. We might be the only ones left here— wait, what's that sound—"

"Mortar!" Lev yelled. Both of them threw themselves to the ground. The mortar shell exploded near them; debris grazed their bodies.

"Aaaarrghhh!" Eric screamed in agony. One of the fragments had passed through a small gap in his MCS near his left thigh.

Lev examined Eric's wound. *His MCS must've been damaged during our charge at the enemy lines,* Lev concluded.

Eric tried to stand back up, but the pain was too much for him. He propped himself up on his right arm and moved his left hand shakily towards the now-exposed wound.

"Alright, Sarge, listen to me," Lev began. "I've been in this situation countless times. Lie down on one side and let me patch this up." Lev took out his dog tag and tapped it on Eric's MCS to release the reserve first-aid kit from a pod on Eric's back. "Then we'll just have to locate a contact point to re-establish contact with HQ."

"And how are we supposed to reach that point?" Eric retorted, vision still blurred. "Are we supposed to walk straight into the enemy's fire? Can I even walk like thi— Ouch! *Watch it!*" Eric yelped. Lev had used a medical magnet to extract the fragments. Without a word, he also disinfected the wound and wrapped the wound with field dressing.

"There. You're good to go," Lev calmly replied with a tinge of irritation.

The scared sergeant's vision was finally recovering. "God, how did we survive this massacre? We really are the sole survivors— Eeek!" Eric had lifted his left foot and discovered that he had been sitting on a mangled corpse all this time. He frantically made out the words on the corpse's dog tag: *Mark. 2nd lieutenant.*

"Oh, God, I think I'm gonna be sick—"

"You're new to the neutral zone, aren't you? Where did you serve before this?" Lev asked.

"I-I served as a reserve in the fourth regiment of the fifth defence force."

"Ah, the blaue adler. So you're a rear trooper, and a reserve one at that... That's just great—"

"Don't mock me or the blaue adler! We're what's blocking the imperials in the southwest of Eurasia! I might not have experienced as much as you, but my friends and I have faced the imperials too! We served as backup in the neutral zone and scored a victory against those pieces of shit!"

"Then by now you should know the neutral zone isn't neutral at all. Why didn't you strap your MCS's display on your wrist?"

Eric looked down at his dirty, bloodied boots. "I..."

Lev smiled wryly. "At least you do have a spine. I didn't mean anything against your previous regiment, but I just needed to give you a little push."

"A push?" Eric was incredulous.

"Do you still want to puke?"

"Um... Actually, no."

"Good. You'll have to endure the pain a little longer. We need to escape the enemy's sight. It'll take a while to get to our contact point, but we'll at least make it in one piece." Lev gestured a path to safety.

Eric struggled to his feet. "Are there still enemies here? How do we find the contact point?"

"To answer your first question, I don't know how they do it in other places, but in the neutral zone, the imperials always send a final wave of droids to hunt down Eurasian survivors," replied Lev in a low voice. "To answer your second question, the contact points are already saved on my map. The closest one is near an abandoned Eurasian trench further down south. Let's head out while we still can."

Eric nodded, then hobbled towards a nearby tank wreckage. He grabbed onto the tank's surface with his left hand for balance and felt something squishy. He looked to his left and found his hand inside a breach in the tank's shell, his finger caught on what felt like a cord. When he slowly removed his hand from the hole, he heard a soft snap. His palm was covered in blood; a single eyeball dangled from his finger.

Lev heard a scream that was now familiar to him and groaned before turning around.

He stormed towards Eric, his face twisted with fury. "Do you have a death wish sergeant? If they heard you, we'll be nothing but minced meat after the artillery hits."

"Sorry," Eric replied.

A nearby artillery shell hit a crater filled with corpses. Blood splattered like a watery spray in all directions, landing in spatters on the ground, on Eric's helmet, and even on his sleeve.

"They've got ears. Get in the tank. Hurry," Lev barked in a tone reminiscent of the sergeant he once served under.

Once in, Eric turned pale. "Excuse me."

Raindrops began to fall through the wreck's countless holes. Both of them took a deep breath as they waited for the artillery to die down.

"Say Lev," Eric started, vomit still dripping down his chin. "What's your deal?"

"My deal? Just finish cleaning yourself up."

"What, are you trying to avoid something?" Eric asked as he looked at Lev.

Lev sighed. "Alright, I'll give you the quick and dirty."

A raindrop fell on top of Lev's heads-up display. He sighed inwardly.

"Like you, I was taught about the major economic collapse that happened a few decades before the war," Lev continued. "That combined with extreme technological growth eventually led to a complete dependence on it by Eurasia's population."

"Without the necessary resources to fuel their technological progress, they had to search elsewhere."

"You can thank the oligarchs for that." Eric interjected as he continued to clean himself off. "Those dogs were always praying for more land to annex anyways."

Another raindrop landed on Lev's heads-up display and rolled down the side. After an awkward pause, Lev spoke again. "In order to secure the homeland, Eurasia had to become a major military power. Soon after, the war started."

"It's the old game of cat and mouse. The strong take from the weak, with brute force if necessary," Eric said, having finished cleaning up.

Lev paused for a moment. "Eric, do you remember those old military propaganda posters?"

"Sure, I remember them," Eric said. "The ones with the idealistic portraits of teenagers. Citizenship through service or something."

Lev nodded. "Those posters really convinced me as a kid. Back then I felt proud at the prospect of serving my country, hopeful for a brighter future."

Eric sighed. "I have to admit, I joined because it seemed like an easy path to citizenship for me and my wife. But this hell... Even if my wife is accorded full citizenship, will she still recognize the man she married?"

Lev's face glowed with exalted purpose. "Full Citizenship is all I need to make a difference in this ruined world. Ten years and I'm off to the United Council."

Eric shook his head. "You? The united council? Do robots dream of sheep?"

"What else do we have left except the grand dream? Something to live for, at least. Something noble to fight for! Without that, why should we even bother?" Lev shouted through the thunder of artillery.

"So tell me, Eric. Do you want to live in the mud with your head down and your neck out, or face the world for what it is and soar towards greater heights?"

Eric stared at Lev for several moments before turning away. "...Seems like the artillery died down. We should get some sleep. I'll take the first watch."

* * *

Twenty-five Years Ago, Slums of Neue Berlin, Capital of Eurasia
"Schweinhund!" yelled an old baker at a child running away into one of the dark alleys of the slums.

"This kid... He always manages to steal my bread!" growled the baker with hate in his eyes. It was already hard to earn a profit in this hellhole without thieves stealing from him.

"What's worrying you so much, old man?"

"Ah, finally, the police arrived. Better late than never, am I right?" The baker said with a sneer.

The officer revealed a smirk, slightly agitated by the baker's remark. "You know how expensive bread is these days. Let the kid have some food."

After the economic collapse caused by continuous wars and setbacks to the asteroid mining project, prices had inflated drastically, causing most of the population to suffer from poor living conditions. The parliament of Neue Berlin had tried to limit the damage caused by the war by investing most of its budget into various stocks—which in turn had limited its abilities to invest into solutions to help the lower and middle class in Neue Berlin.

"What? How could you let a kid who's defying the law just do whatever he wants? A thousand ruble-euros' worth of bread is what he's stolen from me, officer! A thousand!"

The officer grasped in his pocket and revealed a wallet. "Take this as payment then. A thousand ruble-euros for the bread that the kid stole."

The now baffled baker looked at the officer and took the money. "If you insist, but don't blame me when I refuse to give you a refund."

"I won't."

* * *

"Leonard, how did you manage to get this bread?" Ann, one the youngest and last caretakers at the orphanage, asked Leonard.

"I—"

"You stole it, didn't you?" Ann sadly asked.

Kinder Orphanage Neue Berlin could be read at the entrance of the building. An orphanage for the children in the slums, the lower class—the class that the United Council didn't recognize. They were subhuman scum, only ever addressed by their EU-ID. Spoiled meat, whose only purpose was to be used on the frontlines of wars so that more "qualified" individuals could relax in the back.

The entrance door opened, an officer standing in its opening.

"Miss, is this your kid?"

"Y-Yes, he is one of the kids I oversee," Ann replied nervously. "We'll return the bread if this is why you came."

The officer looked at Leonard, who was hiding behind Ann, visibly shaking. Not that the officer could blame him—his uniform was emblazoned with the logo of the Eurasian Police. The EP were known to take out their frustrations on the lower class in the slums, charging innocent people with meaningless crimes and beating them down if they dared complain.

"Don't worry, I paid for it."

This shocked Ann. Why would an EP pay for bread that one of her kids had stolen?

"Y-You paid? H-How much do we owe you?"

The officer started laughing, reminding Leonard of the middle-class kids he'd received beatings from when he tried to sneak from his home in the lower slums to the upper parts of Neue Berlin. They always laughed like that after having their fun with him.

"Don't worry, the bread's on me."

Lev, noticing that the officer was focused on Ann, took the opportunity to run towards the dining area. The cheers of children could be heard when they saw what Leonard had brought with him.

The officer turned back towards the entrance and said one last sentence before leaving.

"You know, that kid Lev could be a great leader one day."

"Why'd you say that?" Ann asked.

"He seems like the type that always finds a reason to go against the law, yet does some good by it."

The officer walked away, into the rain, leaving the confused but grateful Ann behind. This encounter, although rare, didn't change Ann's hate for the Technocracy. Rather, it showed a way out, a way to start something new from nothing. A path the children here could perhaps one day walk.

* * *

Neutral Zone—Eurasian Frontline

"Wake up, Sarge. We've got visitors—explosive ones!" yelled Lev, bringing out his MCR-17.

Eric awoke with a start, disoriented by his surroundings. He wailed in fear as the rain of bullets began.

"First wave! Attack!"

"Aye-aye, sir!"

A flute could be heard coming from one of the occupied trenches.

"What's happening, Lev?!"

"Seems like the 117th Eurasian Shock Infantry Division's finally reached this frontline." Lev explained as he tapped on his MCS's display. Once Eric took a closer look, he saw a rectangle half a klick away from their location. The number 117 was written on top of it. Eric then directed his attention through a hole in the tank's armour, towards the scores of Eurasian soldiers peeking from their trenches, watching their comrades in the first wave being slaughtered.

"Does that mean that we don't have to contact HQ?"

Lev regarded the fresh soldiers pouring into the battlefield, dying one by one under the enemies' fire. "No, we still have to contact HQ."

"What do you mean? They're right there! They can save us!"

"Just wait, Sarge. You'll see what I mean."

A deafening blast could be heard from miles away.

"It's coming. Grab something, Sarge—you'll need something to hold onto when it hits."

"When *what* hits?" squealed the sergeant, hastily grabbing the tank's inner hatch and holding tight.

A railgun-class artillery shell headed straight towards the trenches.

"Here it comes." Lev knew that most of the soldiers would be incinerated when the blast hit the ground.

One by one the soldiers evaporated, leaving dust behind. Lev and Eric heard the soldiers who were partly incinerated screaming in pain. They could do little more than look at their mangled allies, immobilised by the horror unfolding before them.

"Oh, God," Eric muttered.

Lev squeezed his eyes shut. "There are neither gods nor demons here, Sarge. Only death and the dying."

AFTERWORD

Thanks for reading the first volume of Lord of Goblins! This first definitive edition took us longer than expected to finish so we want to thank all of our readers for their patience! However, this story is far from over. Will Lev become the Lord of Goblins? We hope you'll continue to support us throughout our journey as we work on future releases of the series.

We'd also like to give a big 'hooray' to MoonQuill and their publishing/editing! We're grateful for the services they've provided us with.

About Michiel Werbrouck

Michiel Werbrouck was born in Oxford, UK but grew up in the Belgian city of Leuven. He is currently studying Applied Computer Science while working as a freelance Graphic Designer and Marketing Assistant.

Aside from his studies, Michiel is an up-and-coming author, having started out writing short Sci-Fi stories on various online platforms before finally taking the next step. Since then he has improved his craft, honing his writing skills.

In his free time, Michiel enjoys playing grand strategy games, hanging out with friends and reading fantasy novels. As a tech fan, he spends lots of time developing apps and games of his own.

In the future Michiel sees himself developing games about his books, working on software/web IT solutions, writing more books and travelling the world.

About Hadi Y. Bendakji

Hadi Bendakji has always been a fan of fantasy and science fiction, whether they be games or books. Since childhood, these interests spurred a desire to create his own works.

Hadi was born and raised in Beirut, Lebanon and graduated in Bir Hassan's Technical College, graduating as an IT-Software Developer.

Due to his studies and family life, he'd been unable to spend time on creative pursuits until after his graduation.

He now pushes himself to constantly improve his skills in order to achieve his dreams.

On top of his passion for creative writing and gaming, Hadi likes listening to metal, reading books, and watching historical documentaries.

Please consider leaving a review on the book's Amazon page.

Thank you very much for enjoying our work.

Thank you for reading a MoonQuill original novel. To experience more exciting stories, visit us at moonquill.com

To know when we release new books, join our mailing list from our site and receive three books for free!

We will never spam you!

To talk with other members of the MoonQuill community, check out our community Discord.

Finally, we would really appreciate it if you could take a moment to review the book. Every review greatly helps the author and supports their ability to continue writing fantastic books for us to enjoy.